Easy Magic

Book Five in the Boudreaux Series

Kristen Proby

EASY MAGIC
Book Five in The Boudreaux Series
Kristen Proby

Cover Art:
Photography by: Sara Eirew Photographer
Cover Design: Okay Creations

ISBN: 978-1-63350-024-2

For Christine.
I love you to the moon and back.

Other Books by Kristen Proby

The Boudreaux Series:
Easy Love and on audio
Easy Charm and on audio
Easy Melody and on audio
Easy Kisses
Easy For Keeps

The With Me In Seattle Series:
Come Away With Me and on audio
Under the Mistletoe With Me and on audio
Fight With Me and on audio
Play With Me and on audio
Rock With Me and on audio
Safe With Me and on audio
Tied With Me and on audio
Breathe With Me and on audio
Forever With Me and on audio
Easy With You and on audio

The Fusion Series, available through William Morrow:
Listen To Me and on audio
Close To You
Blush For Me

The Love Under the Big Sky Series, available through Pocket Books:
Loving Cara and on audio

Seducing Lauren and on audio
Falling for Jillian and on audio

Baby, It's Cold Outside and on audio
An Anthology with Jennifer Probst, Emma Chase, Kristen Proby, Melody Anne and Kate Meader

PROLOGUE

-Mallory-

No one should have to say goodbye to their grandmother at sixteen years old. Especially when it's a forever goodbye.

And definitely not when that grandmother is the only parent this sixteen-year-old has ever known.

"Stop being so sad, child," she says, her voice coming as a whisper. She's lying in her big, soft bed, her long salt and pepper hair fanned out around her in a pretty halo. I used to love to brush her hair and braid it, over and over again. I get my thick hair from her.

Along with the ability to see dead people and read minds.

"How can you say that?" I ask and wipe a tear from my cheek. "I know what's happening. I'm not a baby."

"No," she says with a weak smile and cups my cheek in her frail hand. Why is she so frail? My grandmamma is the strongest woman I know! "You're not a baby, even though I sometimes wonder where the time has gone."

"I can't do this," I whisper and lay my head on her chest. "You can't leave me."

"Oh, sugar." She sighs and gently pushes her fingers through my hair, brushing it off of my face. "I won't be far, you know. I'll be here, to talk with you, to guide you."

"I can't do magic," I insist.

"Opening yourself up to me is not magic, *cher.*"

"I don't want any part of this," I reply and burrow my face deeper in the covers, feeling her weak heartbeat. "It's taking you from me."

"And I'm sorry for that. I truly am. You've had more loss in your young life than anyone should have to bear." She pauses to catch her breath. I hate that she's so weak. "I'm not leaving you here alone. You have Lena and her grandmother, and they love you like family."

"I know," I reply and let a tear fall into the blankets. "But it's not the same."

"No." She continues to gently push her fingers through my hair. "It's not the same. Not enough. But they *are* here for you, always."

Lena has been my best friend for as long as I can remember. Her grandmother, Sophia, and mine have been best friends since they were small girls as well. The four of us have been close, the only family the other has.

"How am I supposed to do this without *you*?" I whisper. "You're the one who understands how different I am. No one loves me like you do."

"And no one ever will, sugar. Not exactly like me. But someone *will* love you. Understand you. You just have to wait a while for him."

I roll my eyes. My grandmother may be a powerful psychic and witch, but she's also an incurable romantic.

God, I'm going to miss her.

"I just need you," I insist.

"I'll be here," she says again, but I shake my head. "I

know you're afraid of what you can do."

"I'm not afraid. I *hate* it."

"You won't always, love. Look at me."

I raise my head to look into her deep brown eyes. She looks so tired.

"People are always afraid of what they don't understand. You'll learn. You have such a gift, Mallory. You can help people."

"You helped people and it's killing you."

"And that was my choice," she replies and smiles again. "And the outcome was worth it. That little girl was returned to her family."

"And the killer—" I can't even finish the sentence.

"Will get what's coming to him," she insists, but the fear is there at the edge of her voice. He found his way into her head, and did so much damage, she's dying.

I will never do this.

"I love you, sweet girl. You have brought more to my life than I can ever say." She cups my cheek again. "You are wonderful. And I know you don't want it, but your gift is there all the same. Sophia will teach you, and if you'll just open yourself up, you'll see me. I'll be here."

I can't do it!

"I love you, too," I reply and watch as she finally closes her eyes and sighs deeply. I'm so selfish. She's tired, and she's hanging on because I can't let go.

Oh, how I don't want to let go.

I can't take my eyes off of her. I don't want to miss even one breath, one flutter of her eyelashes. Her eyes open one last time and focus on me. She smiles.

"I'll see you soon."

Chapter One

-Mallory-

"I'm sorry I'm late!" I rush into Miss Sophia's house, toss my handbag on the new couch that Lena and I talked her into buying, and hurry to the kitchen. I was supposed to be here a half hour ago for dinner with them both. "I got caught up at the shop."

"It's just jambalaya," Miss Sophia replies with a smile. I swear, she hasn't changed a bit since I was a child. Her light blonde hair has no hint of grey in it. Her face is free of lines, except for the few around her eyes from smiling, and she has more energy than Lena and I put together. "It'll keep on the stove until we're ready for it."

"Were you busy today?" Lena asks and takes a bite of cornbread. She's leaning against the kitchen counter, still dressed in her work uniform of a tight black pencil skirt and red silk top tucked in, showing off her waistline. She's fair-haired, just like her grandmamma, with bright blue eyes and the prettiest heart-shaped lips I've ever seen.

"There better be some of that left for me." I tug the red napkin covering the bowl of cornbread aside and sigh in delight at the sight of the deliciousness. "Oh, thank

God."

"This is my first piece," she says and takes another bite.

"I got delayed at the shop with Charly Boudreaux," I say, finally answering Lena's question. "She ordered some essential oils and stopped by after she closed *her* shop to pick them up."

"The Boudreauxes are good people," Miss Sophia says as she ladles our bowls of jambalaya.

"You know them?" I ask, surprised. "You've never said anything."

I haven't known Charly and her sister-in-law Kate long, but I like what I know. I met them at Charly's shoe shop, Head Over Heels, a few months ago. Since then, we've had a couple lunches and one fun happy hour outing with Savannah, Charly's sister. There are a lot of the Boudreauxes.

"Their family has been here as long as yours and mine," Miss Sophia says and passes the steaming bowls to us. "Rich as Midas, but not showy with it."

"Well, that we know," Lena says. "Everyone in Louisiana knows that."

"I went to school with Mrs. Boudreaux's oldest sister. Sweet woman. Lost touch over the years, and she moved to Florida, I believe. All I'm saying is they seem like good, hard working people."

"Well, that seems to be true," I reply with a nod. "Charly puts in long hours at her shop."

"It's good to see you make a friend," Miss Sophia says, but Lena just watches me, speculation in her eyes.

"We're two businesswomen trying to make a go of it in the Quarter," I reply with a shrug. Lena isn't a jealous woman, but she's a very protective one when it comes to me. And it works both ways. You're not raised by known psychics and witches and *not* get bullied growing up. "You'll have to join us for lunch next time."

"I'd like that," Lena says. "Speaking of lunches, the principal asked me out on a date today."

Miss Sophia and I look at each other, then at Lena. "What did you say?" I ask.

"No, of course," she says and frowns. "I'm a teacher at his school. Of course I'm not going to date him."

"Was he inappropriate with you?" Miss Sophia asks.

"No, he just asked, and I declined."

"I know someone you might want to date," I say, Charly's brother Beau immediately coming to mind. "He's a Boudreaux."

"I'm not interested in dating."

"You went on a date on Saturday," I remind her in exasperation. Lena dates more than anyone else I know.

"Yes, and that one date made me realize that I'm done with it." She takes a sip of sweet tea and shrugs her petite shoulders again. Lena's thin, just like her grandmother.

"He's not ready for you," Sophia says to Lena, who just rolls her eyes and looks at me with desperate eyes. *Help.*

"You don't have to date if you don't want to," I say reasonably. "What was it about Mr. Saturday Night that turned you off of the male species as a whole?"

"Nothing in particular. He was nice enough, but I'm tired of meeting men who are just *nice enough.* Nothing ever comes of it, and frankly, it's beginning to feel like a waste of good lipstick and shaved legs."

"Well, if you change your mind, Beau Boudreaux seems like a nice guy." I keep my eyes trained on my dinner.

"You touched him?" Miss Sophia asks casually.

"I shook his hand."

There's a moment of silence, but I stay quiet, eating my dinner.

"Oh, come on, Mal." Lena drops her spoon in her bowl. "And?"

"And what?"

"You're so damn stubborn. You feel things, even when you don't want to."

Which is why I avoid touching people.

"Wishing you didn't have your gifts doesn't make them go away," Miss Sophia reminds me gently.

"I know, and I stopped avoiding them long ago." I purse my lips. "I see the dead. Not all the time, but enough. It doesn't scare me. And yes, I'm an empath, so I get feelings about people when I touch them."

"And what feeling did you get about Beau?" Lena asks, leaning in like I'm about to tell her state secrets.

"Not much," I admit, still perplexed at the lack of emotion I was able to pick up from him. "But I know he's smart. Not a lot of grey area with him, so similar to you in that respect. And I didn't have to touch him to know that he's a bit uptight and has a stick up his ass a lot of the time."

"Oh, yes, please let me date him," Lena says dryly.

"But I didn't feel anything when I touched him." My voice is soft, as it still takes me by surprise when I think of it.

"Nothing?" Lena demands, her eyes wide, as she raises her spoon to take a bite.

I do the same, thinking back on it. "There was no wave of emotion or memories. It was just...*calm.*"

"Interesting," Lena says, a frown between her

eyebrows. "That's unusual."

You have no idea.

"Beau isn't for Lena," Miss Sophia says confidently and sits back in her chair, finished with her dinner.

"If you're so sure about who *is* for me, why don't you clue me in?" Lena demands.

"Because neither of you is ready," Miss Sophia replies. "You'll figure it out eventually."

Lena sighs deeply. "Maybe Beau is going to be important in your life because he's meant for *you*."

I stare at Lena, blinking slowly, then tuck my hair behind my ear and shake my head. "No. He's not for me."

Miss Sophia doesn't say anything at all. She just sips her sweet tea and watches me with that knowing gaze that's always driven me nuts. Because behind those shrewd eyes is a woman who sees more than anyone I know. Too much, sometimes.

"He's not."

"Okay." She smiles and Lena lets out a loud laugh.

"I have to meet him."

"You want me to set you up after all?"

"No." She shakes her head. "So I can see the man who's going to give you a run for your money."

"How did we get here?" I stare at the two women I love more than anything, completely frustrated. "I already said he's not for me."

"If you say so," Lena says, but Miss Sophia is still silent, just watching me with those knowing blue eyes, smiling softly.

"Do you have any idea how frustrating it is to have a witch in the family?" I demand, staring at Miss Sophia, who just smiles wider, still sipping her tea.

"I know many things," she replies, then breaks out

into a belly laugh when Lena and I just glare at her. "I'm turning it off now, girls."

Miss Sophia's psychic abilities are strong, much stronger than mine, but her gift is in magic. She and Lena make it look like an art form.

The three of us are members of a very exclusive club. One that most people don't understand. Instead, when they learn what we are, they come at us with two things.

Fear.

Hate.

So we're quiet, keep to ourselves, and live our lives.

***

I get home around nine from dinner with Miss Sophia and Lena. It's been a long day. The shop was busy today, and I'm thankful. I'm making a good living at selling essential oils, herbs, lotions, and soaps. My style is whimsical and fun, perfect for tourists wandering through the French Quarter and locals alike. For so long I was just treading water, barely able to make enough to pay the bills, and have enough left over to pay myself as well.

But this past year has been fruitful, and not only can I do all those things, but I've hired a part-time helper as well so I can take a day or two off here and there.

I have dinner with Lena and Miss Sophia as often as our schedules allow, and one weekend a month we go to my grandmother's house in the Bayou to relax and craft. I wasn't able to join them for a while, but now that Shelly is working for me, I've been going again, and I love it.

I enjoy feeling close to Grandmamma. I don't see her. Ever. Sometimes, as I'm waking from a dream, I can just barely hear her voice, but I haven't seen her since the day she died.

And it frustrates me. Makes me sad.

I miss her.

I shake my head and shrug off the blue mood, shuffling through my mail. Nothing catches my interest so I toss the envelopes on the kitchen table and kick out of my boots, my jeans, and wander to the fridge to pour a glass of white wine.

I opened it last night.

It'll be gone by tomorrow night.

The wine is crisp and dry and perfect. I carry the glass into the living room and sit on the couch, pulling my legs up under me.

I feel restless. Should I watch TV? I take a sip and wrinkle my nose. Nah.

Read a book?

Maybe.

But rather than reach for my iPad, I wake my phone up to look over the shop's social media pages and respond to questions and comment on posts and photos of my products. Suddenly a text comes in from Charly.

I love this lavender and frankincense combo! Very relaxing.

I grin and take a sip of wine and reply: *add a glass of wine and you'll sleep like a baby.*

The stillness of my house is a welcome change from the creaks and groans of the old building that houses my shop. It's as haunted as any building I've ever been in, which is to be expected in a city as old and full of history as New Orleans. It's not known as one of the most haunted cities for nothing.

But there are no spirits here in my home. I knew the minute I walked in that I was alone here, and bought it on the spot. This is the one place that my mind can be at peace.

I settle back against the cushions of my soft couch and yawn. My eyes close, and before long, I've drifted off to sleep.

***

I'm dreaming. I always know that I'm dreaming, but I can't change the course of the dream. It's like I'm living it and watching it like a movie at the same time.

There's so much water! I'm in my grandmamma's house, and the water is pouring in through windows, doors, the seams of the walls.

Everywhere.

The rooms are filling up, and her things are floating around me, even things that I either gave away or threw out long ago and it looks like it did when I was a child.

Is she here? Will I finally get to see her?

"Grandmamma?" I call out, but there's no answer. Just so much water. It's up to my waist now, and I can't move. It's heavy against me, pinning me in place. I'm not even floating.

"Help!" My head is thrashing back and forth, looking for someone to help me, but I'm alone.

And the water is rising.

There's a beeping coming from somewhere. Maybe outside of the dream? It's a dream! I'm not going to drown. It's only a dream.

But the water is cold. My feet are numb now, it's so cold. Where is everyone? Why aren't they helping me?

"Grandmamma!" I call again. She never comes, but I hope that she'll appear this time to help me. "You promised you'd be here!"

I'm crying now, and the water is up to my shoulders.

"Help me!"

"Wake up, Mallory."

It's her voice!

"Grandmamma!"

"Get to the shop. Wake up."

I jolt out of sleep and sit up, blinking, looking around wildly. There is no one here, but I'm so cold.

"I heard you," I say to the room. "Why can't I see you?"

I sigh and reach for my pants. It's four in the morning. I slept seven hours? I stare at my phone, sure that it must be wrong. It felt like I'd only been asleep for minutes.

"Weird dreams," I mutter and shake my head. I do not want to go to the shop at four in the morning. I'll end up staying all day.

But she said to go. And she rarely speaks to me.

Or, it could have just been a part of the dream.

I bite my lip, and decide to go check, just to be on the safe side. I live on the other side of town from the Quarter. There's just too much history in that part of the city for me to be able to live there without going insane from all of the spiritual interference.

But at this time of the morning, it only takes me about twenty minutes to get there.

And when I walk in, it's my dream all over again.

Or, my worst nightmare.

The shop is flooded with at least three inches of water on the floor. I can hear it rushing, but can't see where it's coming from until I open the small bathroom and see water pouring out of the ceiling fan.

"I don't think that's supposed to happen." I sigh and prop my hands on my hips. "Thanks, Grandmamma."

I pull my phone out of my pocket to call Beau Boudreaux, who also happens to be my landlord.

Of course, there is no answer.

The man lives upstairs, directly above this shop. Can't he hear the water? Does he sleep like the dead?

Or maybe he's not home.

I frown and open my mind, searching the building.

He's home. I can feel his presence.

And he might be naked.

I immediately slam the psychic door shut and walk outside, up the wrought iron steps to his loft, and bang on the door.

"Wake up," I mutter. "And put some pants on."

I raise my hand to bang again, but the door is flung open and there's Beau, rubbing sleep from his eyes, a frown on his handsome face.

He's pulled some sweatpants on.

Thank God.

"What's going on?" he demands.

"I have a leak," I reply and swallow hard, willing myself to keep my eyes on his face, and not the sculpted muscles of his torso. I've met the man exactly twice, including right now, but what he does to my libido is ridiculous.

I'd forgotten that I have a libido.

Which is a sad statement all on its own.

"You had to wake me up at four-thirty for a leak?"

"I have three inches of water on my floor," I reply and turn to stomp down the stairs. "Come look!"

I don't look back as I wade back into my store. A few moments later, I hear Beau come clomping down the steps and look back as he fills the doorway with his wide shoulders. He's tall, pushing six-and-a-half feet. His hair is dark, and his eyes are like old whiskey.

Those whiskey eyes survey the space, frowning when he sees the amount of water on the floor.

"Do you know where it's coming from?"

"The bathroom," I reply and lead him to it.

"The fucking ceiling fan?" He exclaims and shakes his head. "I was expecting the toilet to be overflowing. Old plumbing is unpredictable."

"I was expecting the same, but here we are," I say and cross my arms over my chest. He glances back at me, and his eyes drop to my cleavage for just an instant before he looks me in the eye.

I don't uncross my arms.

"I'm going to shut off the water to the building."

"Good idea."

He rushes back outside and a few moments later, the water slows to a small trickle, and then fast drops.

He comes back inside and looks up. "Must be a broken pipe."

"Are you a plumber as well as a billionaire mogul?" I ask, unable to resist.

His lips twitch. "I'm good at a lot of things."

Oh, I just bet you are.

I clear my throat. "Thanks for coming down to help me."

"It's my building." He shrugs. "I'm sorry I didn't wake up earlier to catch it."

He brushes past me, just barely grazing my shoulder before I can move out of the way, and just like before, I don't feel *anything.*

Just cool calm.

But when I glance up at him, his eyes are full of emotion, and when he looks back at me, bright lust is front and center.

I can *see* it, but I can't feel it.

"Are you okay?"

"Great."

He runs outside, then comes back with a frown. He's grabbed my broom and is sweeping water out the front door to the street.

This man is...I don't even know.

"He's not for me," I whisper as I pull another broom out of a closet and join him, pushing as much water as we can out the front door.

"I don't think you'll be able to open today," he says. "And I'm going to need help getting the water shut off. The valve is rusted."

"I can't afford to close," I reply. "I have a sale that I've advertised for two weeks, and this is the busiest weekend before the end of tourist season." My shoulders drop. "I'm sure I can clean this up enough to open."

He watches me and shakes his head.

"It's dangerous. Customers can slip and fall."

"Oh." I glance about and blink tears away. *What the hell? What's up with the tears?*

"Are you okay?"

"Fine." I nod and quickly brush the tears away. "Just tired, and this was unexpected."

He's quiet for a moment as he watches me closely, and then he pulls his phone out of his pocket and makes a call.

"Eli? Sorry to wake you, but I need some help."

CHAPTER TWO

-Beau-

"This is a fucking mess," Eli says as he and I survey the damage. "The water must have been running all night."

"I can see," I remind him, my voice calm, as I glance to the other side of the room where Mallory and Eli's wife Kate are gathering products into baskets and talking a mile a minute. Kate smiles and nods at something Mallory says, and then they move on to another set of shelves.

"Are you awake?" Eli asks, waving his hand in front of my face.

"What did you say?"

"I said that I'll have my assistant call in a crew to come clean this up today. She'll have to close up for a few days."

"Impossible," I reply, shaking my head. "She can't afford to do that."

Eli stops and turns to me. "How do you know that?"

"She told me."

He blinks. "Are you sweet on her?"

"Are you sixty? Who says that anymore?"

He rocks back on his heels, a slow smile sliding over his smug face.

"You are."

"Fuck off. I'll have a crew come take care of this today. But thanks for coming to help me get the water shut off. The building should have new plumbing."

"Don't change the subject. You have it bad for the little shop girl."

"I barely know her," I reply honestly and walk away from him, stepping outside to call the owner of the construction company that works for Bayou Enterprises.

"It's barely six in the morning," Eli says just as Larry answers.

"Good morning."

"You're awake," I say, shrugging at Eli. "Good. I have a priority job this morning."

"I can't fit you in until next week," Larry replies, and I cock a brow.

"I need you this morning."

"I'm sorry, Beau, but I'm not exactly at your beck and call."

Larry recently took over for his father, and doesn't quite understand how this works.

But he's about to.

"I pay you between three and five million dollars a year to be at my goddamn beck and call, and that doesn't include the work I have you doing on my house, which is currently three fucking months behind schedule. So I'm going to lay it out for you, Larry. You're either available for me *this morning*, or you can be permanently unavailable for me."

Eli's lips twitch and I narrow my eyes.

"Fuck," Larry whispers. "What do you need?"

I explain the situation in Mallory's shop.

"Okay, I'll take the plumber off of your house and send them over this morning."

"What time can we expect them?"

"By eight."

"Good."

I end the call and shove my phone in my pocket.

"You almost fired our contractor."

I nod and shove my other hand in my pocket, touching a coin my father gave me long ago.

"We pay him too well for him to try to get out of a job."

"Agreed," Eli replies, mirroring my stance.

"They'll be here by eight. That gives us time to help clean up some more and see what she wants to do for business today."

"You usually hire people to do this for you," Eli replies, true surprise in his voice.

"I'm not above manual labor," I remind him.

"Okay." He shrugs.

"She's our tenant, and she's the girls' friend."

"True." That smug smile is back.

"Fuck off," I mutter, rolling my eyes, and march back inside. "The guys will be here in a couple of hours."

"We have a plan," Kate says with a smile. "We're going to set up some tables on the sidewalk, with most of the sale items on them. She can take cash and credit on her phone, and as the stock sells, we can replace it from inside."

"Does this work for you?" I ask Mallory, who's biting her lip and setting my teeth on edge with pure lust. Jesus, she's the sexiest little thing I've seen in, well… maybe ever. She intrigues me, and she turns me on with just a look. Since when is lip biting my thing? Apparently, since now that I know Mallory.

"I think it's against city code for me to have

merchandise set up outside," she says with a shake of her head.

"I'll take care of that," Eli replies.

"Do you have the city in your pocket?" Mallory asks, propping her hands on her hips.

"No, but I can call in a favor to two," Eli replies. "It's just for one day, Mallory. I doubt anyone would say anything."

"Okay," she replies and sighs. Kate reaches out to rub her arm, and Mallory flinches and relaxes, in the span of a millisecond.

But it's there.

"We will help," Kate says. "I'll call Declan too."

"He's probably just going to bed," Eli says. "Wake his ass up."

"Don't do that—"

"Yes, do that," I interrupt Mallory and wink at her. "He won't mind."

"He really won't," Kate says. "Declan is the most easygoing brother."

"Careful," Eli says, but pulls Kate in his arms and kisses her soundly.

"I love you," Kate tells him, "but easygoing is not how I would describe you."

"Let's get to work."

Mallory raises a brow at me.

"I think I'm the boss here," she says, and all of the blood immediately moves to one area of my body. Her independence and bossiness is damn hot. "I need to pull the rest of the product from the shelves, make sure everything is dry, and then I need to go up to your place so I can change my clothes."

"Why?" My eyes travel up and down her petite body,

not finding one thing wrong with the way her clothes hug her body.

"Because I wore this yesterday," she replies. "I have a change of clothes here."

She can get naked in my loft all she wants. I'll never say no to that.

I'd rather also be there when that happens, but I'll take what I can get.

"And one more thing," she says, holding up her hand. "Thank you. All of you. I can't tell you how much I really appreciate all of your help."

"We're happy to do it," Kate says with a smile. "Shit happens, and then you clean it up."

***

It's noon, and the plumber still has his head stuck in the ceiling of the bathroom, swearing at old plumbing and his lot in life in general. The good news is, it's a one-day job.

The bad news is, a lot of Mallory's stock is not salvageable.

But I have insurance, and even if I didn't, I'll be paying to replace whatever she lost.

Eli went to work hours ago. Kate decided to take the day off from the office so she could stay and help Mallory. Declan came for a while this morning, and just left as well.

Mallory's part time help, a young woman named Shelly, came in to work this afternoon.

The set up on the sidewalk is a bit chaotic. Hundreds of tourists walk by each hour, so we have to keep a keen eye out for thieves, but I think she's also selling much more than she normally would.

Mallory is loading a woman's merchandise in a bag and lifts it to pass to her, and I notice, like I have all morning, that Mallory is careful not to touch anyone. However, when the lady takes her bag, she reaches over and pats Mallory's hand.

Her body language doesn't change, but her face goes absolutely still, and then her eyes just look sad as she gazes back at the customer.

"Thank you so much," the customer says. "I hope this helps me sleep. Ever since my husband died, I can't manage to get more than a few hours at a time."

Mallory nods, as if she already knows and smiles softly. "This should work great. Don't forget to put the Vetiver on the soles of your feet."

"I won't." She waves and sets off down the street.

"I'm going to go grab some more of the lavender hand lotion," Shelly says. "It's selling like hotcakes."

"The lavender always does" Mallory says with a nod. "And would you please also bring out a couple of the sage candles?"

"Sure thing!"

"This is fun," Kate says with a smile. "It's a nice change of pace from office work."

"You really don't have to stay," Mallory says and glances up at me. "Both of you. Shelly and I can handle this."

Just then a man picks up a bottle of shampoo and starts to slip it in his pocket.

"You'll be paying for that," I say, glaring at the man, who sets it down and walks away, whistling and smiling like he didn't do anything wrong.

Asshole.

"I'll be staying," I reply. "Between jerks like that and

the plumber inside, I'd like to keep an eye on things."

"And I really want to stay," Kate says. "Please don't kick me out."

"Okay," Mal replies, shaking her head with a smile. "I'm not kicking anyone out."

***

It's been a long fucking day. It's just past eight in the evening, and I'm on my way back to Mallory's shop with food. We've all been on the go since I woke up to her banging on my door. Business was busy today, much to Mallory's delight. The plumber fixed the problem in the ceiling, and with fans blowing all night, she should be back to business as usual tomorrow.

But she hasn't eaten all day, so I'm bringing us both dinner. She just closed the shop. I'm assuming Kate left just after me to go home to Eli.

I frown as I walk through the door. She hasn't locked it yet.

And then I frown again when I find Kate and Mallory sitting across from each other at Mallory's desk, eating Chinese takeout.

"You didn't lock the door," I say, feeling foolish with the bag of Italian in my hand.

"Eli's picking me up," Kate says, her eyes wide when she sees the bag of food. Her phone beeps. "There he is! I'm out of here." She offers me an apologetic smile as she grabs her white carton of food and rushes outside.

Mallory and I are quiet as the door closes behind Kate. Finally, I walk to the door and lock it, then return to her desk. "I should have asked if you have dinner plans. I did bring dessert, so at least that won't go to waste."

"Are you kidding?" she asks, eyeing my bag. "I'm starving. I'll eat all the food." She holds her hands out. "Gimme."

"It's not just for you, you know," I reply, handing her the bag. I can't help but grin at her as she unpacks the bag with the enthusiasm of a child on Christmas morning. "I'm hungry too."

"I can share," she says and sends me a wink.

"They're violet," I say, surprised.

"Excuse me?" She stands up straight, a box of chicken Alfredo gripped in her hand.

"Your eyes. I thought they were blue, but I was wrong. They're violet."

She looks down and nods, concentrating on the food again. "They are."

There's an uncomfortable silence as she sits and dives back into her Chinese. I sit in the chair across from her and open the Styrofoam box she placed in front of me. "This is a fantastic restaurant."

"Oh, I know," she says with a smile. "One of my favorites."

"I like a woman who enjoys food." I take a bite of my lasagna and feel my stomach sigh in relief. I am also starving.

"Did you get crème brulee for dessert?" she asks, those violet eyes shining.

"I did."

"Excellent." She sets her half-eaten Chinese aside and digs into her pasta. "Any other day, I would say this isn't a great combination, but everything tastes good right now. I don't think any of us ate today."

"We were a little busy," I reply.

"Thank you again," she says. "You went above and

beyond the call of landlord duty."

"It wasn't a problem at all." I wipe my mouth on a small napkin. Truth be told, it was kind of fun to spend the day in her shop rather than in my office. And the more time I spent with her today, the more I want to know about her. "So, tell me about you."

"What about me?" The way she's shoveling that pasta in her mouth is awe-inspiring. "There's not much to say."

"Let's start with this shop. What made you decide to open it?"

She shrugs, not looking up from her meal. It's interesting how she doesn't like to look me in the eyes when she talks about things that make her vulnerable.

"It was just a hobby that became my work."

I sit back and watch her for a moment, then shake my head. "I don't think that's it."

Her head jerks up now, and she frowns. "Are you calling me a liar?"

"No, I'm saying there's much more to that story."

She sighs and pushes the food around "Isn't there always more to the story?"

"I'd like to hear yours." Which surprises the fuck out of me. I rarely take the time to chat with anyone outside of business and family.

"I've always had a knack for knowing what people need," she says softly, as if she's choosing her words very carefully. I don't know why that bothers me. I want her to speak her mind, to not have to censor what she says.

But this is a good start.

"In what way?"

"Maybe someone has headaches, or their feet hurt. I have essential oils and herbs that can help with those things."

I nod.

"My grandmother taught me all about alternative medicine from the time I was a child. She wasn't crazy with it," she says quickly, "she still believed in western medicine as well, but why take a pain reliever full of chemicals if you can just put a drop of oil on the back of your neck to get the same result?"

She shrugs and reaches for the dessert, smiles when she opens the box, and digs in with enthusiasm.

"I thought it would be fun to open a store full of those things," she continues. "I wanted the bottles to be pretty, and everything to be tied with a bow. I wanted a place where people enjoyed coming in, even if only to browse. It smells good, the energy is calming."

And I realize that that's exactly how I feel whenever I've been in her store.

"I'd say you've accomplished those things."

"Thank you." Her smile is huge and genuine. "That's really the best compliment I could ever get."

"Really?" I cock a brow and watch her lashes flutter. "I'd also say you're stunning. I want to bury my fingers in that amazing curly hair of yours."

There must be something in the food that's making me speak so freely. But Mallory seems to bring out my flirty side.

I'd forgotten that I had a flirty side.

Her smile slips just a bit, and her cheeks flush, and I know she'd look just like that when I'm buried balls deep inside her.

"That's very nice of you."

"But not what you want to hear."

"Well, don't get me wrong, every woman wants to be told she's pretty."

"I didn't say pretty," I reply and lean in, resting my elbows on her desk. "'Pretty' is too dull of a word to describe you."

"You're an interesting man," she says, tilting her head to the side and studying my face with narrowed violet eyes. "You just say whatever you're feeling."

"Not always." I reach out to tuck her hair behind her ear and she stiffens. I pause, keeping my eyes pinned to hers before I slowly brush just the pads of my fingertips over the outline of her ear, tucking that soft curly hair, then lowering my hand back to the desk. "But I see no reason to not be honest with you."

"I opened this shop because I love it," she says, her voice still soft but firm. She's not weak in any way, and that pulls at me like a siren's song. "I want to help people if I can, even if it's just to moisturize their hands. And I like this building."

"There are other streets with more foot traffic."

"And I like where I am," she says again. "I do well here."

"I'm glad you do." I nod and without giving it much thought, reach out to pull my fingertips over her hand. My eyes are watching hers as I do, and I can see the hesitation just before I touch her, and then the relief when my skin rests on hers.

She doesn't like to be touched.

"Tell me more," I say softly.

"That's all there is about the store."

"Tell me about *you.*"

She pulls her hand out from under mine and sits back in her chair. "I think you'd better go, before I tell you more than I want to."

I cock a brow. "I'm a fan of honesty."

"Good." She nods once and begins loading the empty boxes in the trash. "I'm in favor of being honest, and in that same spirit, I'm exhausted, Beau."

"I know. I am, too."

But I'm not ready to say goodbye to her yet. I'm afraid that we'll go our separate ways, and I won't see her again.

"What are you thinking?" she asks.

"That I want to see you again."

"You live upstairs from my shop," she reminds me. "I don't see how we could avoid it."

"We avoided it for a damn long time," I say and stand, shoving my hands in my pockets. "But I won't make that mistake again."

She smiles as she also stands and walks around the desk. "You are something else."

"True. At least, that's what my mother always says, and I don't think she means it in an endearing way."

"I'm sure she loves you very much."

"She does." I shrug. "And I'd rather not talk about my mama when all I can think about is this." I take her hand and tug her against me, wrapping my arms around her shoulders. She fits. Her face is pressed to my chest, her arms wrapped around my torso, hands pressed to my back.

This is the sexiest hug in the history of the universe.

After a moment, Mallory sinks into me, letting out a long breath. I want to boost her up onto the desk and fuck her until we're both a sweaty mess, and I plan to do exactly that in the not too distant future.

But for right now, I'm content holding her against me, rocking gently, until she finally pulls back and smiles up at me.

"Thank you. I needed that."

I kiss her forehead before letting her go. "Me too."

Chapter Three

~Mallory~

It's almost two in the morning, after the longest day of my life, and do you think I can sleep?

Of course not. I've been up for nearly twenty-four hours, and my brain won't shut off.

I should be thinking about the shop, what I need to order to replace the damaged products, pray that the floor isn't ruined, and if it is, how in the hell am I going to pay for it?

Instead, all I can think of is a certain sexy man named Beau.

Because he's different.

And *different* makes me feel…nervous. I don't like surprises. They don't happen often, and when they do, they're not usually *good* surprises.

I can't read him. At all. He touches me, and there's just calm, like I'm standing in calm, blue warm water. But when I look in his eyes, there are too many emotions to count.

So, why can't I *feel* them? That's what I do. It's who I am. It's why relationships don't work out for me. Not just with men, but friendships too. Because it's too creepy for most people when I respond to words they haven't said out loud.

I've gotten better at keeping my mouth shut and recognizing what they've said aloud and what they're thinking, but it still happens sometimes.

And I learned long ago to not volunteer the psychic information to anyone new. I'm suddenly either a freak show, or their entertainment.

But I can't turn it off. I tried for many years, especially after I lost my grandmother. It's no use. It is what it is, and I have learned to live with it quite well. I have my small circle of loved ones, and that's all I need.

At least, that's what I always thought.

But now, I'm yearning for a man's touch, and that hasn't happened in…*ever.*

I'm no virgin. But sex takes an emotional toll on me and I haven't found anyone that's worth it.

But Beau might be.

Because I can't read him, but the emotions he's pulled out of me after spending such a short amount of time with him is new.

And nice.

Very nice.

I smirk and turn on my side, throw one leg out of the covers, and sigh. My phone lights up with a text from Lena. I grab it and smile.

Why are you awake?

I roll my eyes and reply: *Because my brain won't shut up.*

But my eyes are starting to get heavy.

I'm coming into the shop tomorrow to help you out. Lena's the best friend a girl can have. Rather than text, I just call her back.

"Hi," she whispers.

"Why are you whispering?"

"No reason."

I narrow my eyes. "Is there someone there with you?"

"If I say no, will you believe me?"

"Lena! Who is it?"

"You don't know him," she says and I can hear her walking now, presumably out of her bedroom so she doesn't wake up the dude she's banging.

"Well, now I know why you're not asleep." My voice is dry.

"I could feel *you* awake," she says. "And just because you don't like sex, doesn't mean the rest of us don't."

"I *like* it," I reply and wrinkle my nose. "If they'd stop thinking while we're doing it I'd like it better."

"I know," she says softly. Lena isn't as psychically strong as I am, but she can block emotions and thoughts from others.

I can if I'm not physically touching them. But once there is contact, I can't block thoughts or feelings.

Which is why Beau intrigues me so.

"Did you get all the water out of the store?" She asks, crunching on something in my ear.

"Yeah, and I have fans going tonight to try to dry it all. What a mess."

"What time do you want me there tomorrow?"

"You don't have to come at all," I reply honestly.

"I want to hang out with you. I feel like I don't see you enough."

I smile. "Well, that sounds like a good plan."

"Great. So what time?"

"Ten? I open late on Sundays."

"Works for me. I will want to hear all about Beau."

I roll my eyes again and sigh, regretting immediately that I told her via text earlier today that he had helped me.

"There's nothing to tell."

"Now, I know that's not true." I can hear the smile in her voice. "Be ready to spill it. I'm bringing my tarot cards too."

"No."

"Yes. Love you. Goodnight."

"Use protection," I reply and hang up to the sound of her laugh.

***

I yawn and scratch the side of my head as I unlock the shop and step inside, relieved to see that the floor is, indeed, mostly dry. I can open up later and work inside today.

I'm here an hour before Lena so I can do some paperwork and pay some bills, all tasks that I save for Sunday mornings. It's quiet here, and I just like to be home.

After the bills are paid, and my spreadsheets are caught up, I stretch and change from my lounge wear—yoga pants and a T-shirt—into a flowy, purple skirt and black peasant blouse. My hair gets a good brushing, and I twist it up in a simple knot.

Lena walks in, using her key, just as I'm finishing my makeup.

"Good morning," she says and passes me one of the two coffees she's carrying.

"Bless you," I say and take a drink, then notice the white paper sack she's tucked under her arm. "Are those what I think they are?"

"If you think they're beignets, yes."

I reach for them, but she slaps my hand.

"Hey!"

"You're so grabby," she says with a scowl.

"You better plan to share those."

"I do, but only if you spill the beans about Mr. Boudreaux." She smirks, her blue eyes shining.

"Fine. Gimme." She hands the bag over, and each of us retrieves a hot, powdered sugar covered piece of heaven.

"Jesus, they're always better than I remember them being," she says with a sigh.

"I know." I sit at my desk and Lena sits across from me, where Beau sat last night. Her eyes widen.

"What?"

"He sat here," she says and narrows her eyes like she's listening to something. "He likes you."

"You can read him?" I ask, shocked.

"His energy is strong," she says with a nod. "I may not be as strong as you, but even I can sense that much."

I take another bite, completely confused.

"Mal?"

"Yeah?"

"Look at me."

I comply and she slowly shakes her head from side to side. "You can't read him, can you?"

"No, and I don't know why!" I sit back in frustration and chew my food. "I can see the emotion in his eyes, but when he touches me? Nothing."

"At all?"

"Nada. Zip. It's like he's emotionless."

"Well, he's not that," she says and takes a sip of her coffee. "There's enough residual energy here to light the place up."

"No way." I shake my head.

"So you feel *nothing* when he touches you?"

"I didn't say that," I reply and bite my lip. "I can't read his emotions. I just feel *calm*."

"But you're attracted to him."

It's not a question.

"I mean, he's attractive. And I'm female. So, it makes sense that I would be attracted to him."

"Most stubborn person I know," she mutters and tosses her empty coffee cup into the wastebasket. "Do you want to rip his clothes off and let him fuck you on this desk?"

"That's pretty specific," I say, not at all turned off at the prospect. "Wait. Was he thinking that last night?"

She simply smiles. "He's into you."

"I don't know why," I reply.

"I don't have to read minds to tell you *why*," Lena says. "Because you're beautiful and smart and funny."

"Oh, yes. That's why." I laugh. "Beau is in a completely different league."

"What league would that be?" the man himself says from the doorway, startling us both.

I didn't feel him come in.

My God, what's wrong with me?

"How did you get in?" I ask and then I can't speak at all. He's shirtless, again, and he's panting; sweat is streaked down his face and chest.

Fucking hell, I want to devour him. On this desk.

"I didn't lock the door behind me," Lena says with a smile and stands to face Beau. "Good morning. I'm Lena, Mal's BFF."

"Pleasure," he says and shakes her hand. "I'm—"

"I know," she replies with a grin. "You're Beau. I'm going to go take a look at that water damage."

And with that, she's gone, and I'm left holding a cold beignet, staring at the sexiest man alive.

Half naked.

With sweat.

My eyes are pinned to his chest because I *can't* look away. His abs are just stupid, they're so hot. I didn't think abs like that really existed. Certainly not with the V at the hips. But it's no myth. I'm staring right at him.

"Mallory?"

My eyes find his, and he's smiling, his whiskey eyes pinned to my face.

"Yeah?"

"I'm up here."

I roll my eyes and set the beignet down. "I wasn't staring at your chest."

"Sure."

"I wasn't," I insist.

"You know, I've never been on this end of this conversation before."

I can't help but laugh and shake my head, brushing sugar from my fingers.

"How can I help you?" I ask.

"I wanted to stop in to see how things are today."

"The floor is pretty much dry now. There was some product damage, but—"

"No," he interrupts, "that's not what I meant. How are *you*?"

I blink at him for a moment. "I'm fine."

He steps to me, searching my face. "Did you sleep?"

"I slept fine."

"Liar," he whispers and drags his knuckles down my

cheek, making me tingle in a purely feminine way. And I'm still not bombarded by his emotions and thoughts.

It's just his warm touch, and my femininity responding to it.

Fascinating.

"I didn't sleep at all," I reply with a whisper.

"Why?"

I cock a brow and pull myself together before I embarrass us both and climb him like a tree. "I might have a few things on my mind."

"Not sleeping won't solve it," he replies and tucks my hair behind my ear. "I'll put in a claim with the insurance company tomorrow, but in the meantime, I'll pay for anything that was ruined."

"Thank you."

His lips twitch with humor, and I lick mine in response.

"Let me take you out to dinner tonight."

"Oh, well—"

"Yes," Lena calls from the other room, "she'll be there!"

Beau chuckles and I smile, shaking my head.

"You won't be there?" he asks.

"Yes, she will!" Lena yells again.

"Shut it," I say, not taking my eyes off of Beau. "Not you, her."

He nods and smiles, and my knees turn to Jell-O. What am I, sixteen?

"I'll be working until about six."

"Well, that's convenient because I live very close by."

He's flirting with me. Beau Boudreaux is fucking *flirting* with me.

"Really?" My eyes widen, playing along. "That *is*

convenient."

"So, I can pick you up at 6:30?"

I bite my lip and nod. "Sure."

"Great." The smile hasn't left his face. Beau's smile should be illegal. "I'll see you this evening."

He leans in and kisses my cheek, then turns and waves at Lena as he leaves the shop.

"Holy. Shit." Lena says and props her hands on her hips. "If you don't go out with that man, I will put a hex on you."

"No, you won't," I reply with a laugh.

"Okay, I won't, but I will not speak to you for at least a month."

"You won't do that either." I flip the sign on the door to OPEN and walk behind the sales counter. "Besides, I just told him I'd go."

"Don't bail," she says seriously. "He's not just attractive. *Attractive* might be the understatement of the century."

Well, she has me there.

"What are you going to wear tonight?"

I frown. "What I'm wearing right now. I won't have time to go home."

"I'll go to your place to get you something sexier." She taps her forefinger to her lips, looking me over. "That's a great work outfit, but it doesn't really scream *push me against the wall and do me.*"

"Well, that's a relief." I laugh and rub the back of my neck. "It's the first date. The chances of him making it to home base are slim to none."

"If a man who looked like that wanted to take me out, it would be my mission in life to get his pants off of him."

"Speaking of, who were you with last night?"

She frowns. "I told you, you don't know him. And no, he didn't look like Beau at all."

"Nobody looks like Beau."

"I really feel like it's your duty for your fellow women to have sex with Beau and then write an ode to it."

"You're stupid," I reply, giggling. "I can't write."

"Oh, I think he'd inspire a limerick or two," she says with a sigh. "I know! Let's read your cards!"

"No." I shake my head and begin checking stock, making a list of what I need to pull from back stock.

Ignoring me completely, Lena retrieves her tarot cards from her handbag and sets them on the counter.

"Cut them."

"No."

"It won't be as accurate if I cut them," she says with a huff.

"We're not doing this," I reply. "You know I don't like tarot."

"Fine." She sighs and begins turning the cards over anyway. "Hmm."

I don't want to know the future. That's one thing I can't read, and I don't want to. I'm happy to live in the present, and let life happen.

I haven't had my cards read since I was a teenager.

"This is interesting."

"Shut it," I reply. "I don't want to know."

"It's not bad."

"No means no, Lena."

"Fine," she says again and gathers the cards back into a stack and stashes them in her handbag. "I want you to have fun tonight, Mal. You deserve it."

"Well, I guess we'll see how it goes."

She smiles and wraps her arm around my shoulders,

and the familiar love and affection wraps around me like it always does when Lena touches me. "Bang him."

"No," I giggle. "But if I do, you'll be the first to know."

"Hey. Go big or go home, that's what I say," she says.

"Why do people say that? What's wrong with going home? I like it at home."

"Well, if you go home, take Beau with you."

***

"She brought me *this*?"

I stare at myself in the mirror and frown. I know for a fact this didn't come from my closet. She was sneaky and cut the tags off, but this is not my dress.

I would never pick it out for myself.

It's a simple black wrap dress, with a deep V neckline that shows off the girls and makes me want to reach for a scarf, but I don't have one, and Lena didn't include one on purpose.

She did bring my favorite red heels to go with it, and while I'll admit the dress makes me look curvy and pretty, I'm showing way more skin than I'm comfortable with.

Which was exactly her intention.

If I didn't love her so much, I'd strangle her.

I sigh and smooth my favorite raspberry lipstick on and stare at myself in the mirror.

I clean up nicely.

Suddenly, there's a soft knock on the door, and there's Beau, peering in at me with a smile and a fist full of bright blue forget me nots.

Not roses. Forget me nots.

"Hi," I say when I open the door. "I just have to grab

my bag."

"You're stunning," he says before I can turn away. His eyes move from the crown of my head to my red shoes and back up again. "These are for you."

"Thank you." I fuss over the flowers for a moment and smile up at him. "How did you know these are my favorite?"

He blinks rapidly. "I didn't. They're *my* favorite, and more personal than roses."

After putting the flowers in a vase, I grab my bag and Beau leads us out of the shop, and waits for me to lock the door.

He takes my arm to guide me to his car, and I stiffen, like I always do when being touched, but it passes quickly.

"You're getting better," he murmurs as he opens my door.

"At what?"

"Letting me touch you," he replies, then slams the door and walks around the car to join me. He doesn't ask any questions, or even mention it again, as he drives out of the Quarter. Once on the freeway, he reaches over and takes my hand in his, kisses my knuckles, and smiles over at me. "It's not far."

I nod, but all I can think is, it could be in Florida for all I care, as long as we sit here in the dark, my hand in his. God, it feels good to be touched! I've lived without it for so long, I've forgotten how soothing it is.

But soon he exits the freeway and pulls up to a hole in the wall BBQ place.

"I hope you eat meat."

"I do." I smile and my stomach growls loudly. "I just realized that I haven't eaten much today."

"Well, let's fix that," he says as he exits the car and

walks around to my door, ever the gentleman.

I'm sure manners were ingrained in him from day one. Or, they're just genetically there, given how wealthy he is and who his family is.

Bringing me to the BBQ place is a happy surprise, but I'm grossly over dressed for it.

"Why are you frowning?" He asks and takes my hand again, lacing our fingers, as we walk to the door.

"I think I'm overdressed for BBQ."

"You could wear that dress to the supermarket and it would be appropriate," he says, smiling down at me.

"Right." I laugh. "I hope they have bibs."

"Covering you up would be a shame," he says as the hostess greets us and shows us to our table. I'm careful not to touch her hand as she passes me a menu.

"Molly will be your server," she says with a smile and walks away.

"So who hurt you?" Beau asks, as casually as if he's asking about the weather.

"Excuse me?" He's staring at his menu, and he sets his jaw as he raises his gaze to mine.

"Who hurt you?"

"Why do you assume I've been hurt?"

"I know the signs," he replies softly, sets his menu aside, and takes my hand in his. "I know someone else who was hurt, and has issues with being touched."

"Oh." I sigh and glance down at the lit candle on the table, at a loss for what to say. For how much to say.

"You don't have to talk about it if you don't want to," he says and squeezes my fingers. I glance up, and rather than distain or distrust in his eyes, I see genuine concern, and it only makes me like him more.

"I wasn't hurt," I reply honestly. "And I'd like to leave

it at that for right now."

"That's fair," he says with a nod. "We'll talk about deeper things another time."

I cock a brow. "Another time? That implies that this won't be the only date."

"Oh, this is definitely not the only date," he says with a wink. "Not by a long shot."

Chapter Four

-Mallory-

Dinner has been…fascinating. Beau is ever the gentleman, with those inbred manners showing through all evening, and when he looks at me, those hazel eyes burn in a way I don't think I've ever seen before.

In the best way possible.

Like he'd rather be devouring *me*, rather than the ribs on his plate.

He's asked me dozens of questions about the shop, my family—which I avoid—and my taste in movies and music.

"I feel like I've talked your ears off," I say as the waitress takes our empty plates away. I can't help but be a bit disappointed that dinner is coming to an end already. "What about you?"

"What about me?" he asks and slips his credit card in the folder holding our check. The waitress takes it from him with a smile.

He's damn hot.

I blink at the thought, realizing that it's not mine, it's *hers.*

She's not wrong. He is hot.

And he's with me.

I'm not a jealous woman, but that might have colored me a bit green.

"Mal?" Beau says with a smile.

"Yes?"

"What would you like to know?" He reaches across the table and takes my hand, and I'm suddenly calm, just like all the other times he's touched me. I take a deep breath and look into his eyes, which are pinned to mine, *not* the waitress.

Just remember that. He's here with me.

"What's new and exciting in your life?"

"Besides the gorgeous woman I talked into going to dinner with me?" His smile is smug, and he makes me chuckle.

"Are you meeting up with her later?" Yes, I'm totally flirting with him. It's damn fun.

He just shakes his head and smiles, that crazy hot grin that makes my nipples perk right up and the rest of me tighten.

I'm so not used to all of this sexual chemistry.

"Well, work certainly isn't new and exciting," he begins and signs his name to the check, then sets it aside and takes my hand again. I can feel myself relaxing with him, trusting his touch.

It's the first time in my life that I've been able to trust physical touch, and I'm soaking it in like a sponge.

"Do you enjoy what you do?" I ask him and brace my chin in the hand he isn't holding.

"Very much," he says with a nod. "It was always expected that I'd take over the company with my siblings, but it wasn't something I dreaded. My father made sure that we all spent time in the offices in the summer, working part time. I always knew that I wanted to be a part of Bayou Enterprises. It's several generations old, and it's something to be proud of."

"Absolutely," I agree with a nod. "That's a wonderful legacy. Are you a workaholic?"

He tilts his head and purses those full lips, as though he's genuinely pondering the answer.

"I can be," he finally says. "There's a lot of responsibility that Eli, Van, and I all carry, but it's not a burden."

"That's great. What do you enjoy doing besides working and jogging?"

"I don't really enjoy the jogging," he says with a laugh. "But I do enjoy southern food, so the jogging is a must."

"It seems to be working," I say, then feel my eyes widen in horror as I realize that I've said it out loud.

"Why do you look mortified?" he asks.

"Because I didn't mean to say that out loud."

"Mal, we're attracted to each other. It's okay to admit it."

"I'll be honest," I reply and pull my hand out of his, not wanting to touch him while being completely vulnerable with him. "I don't date a lot."

"Okay."

My gaze whips up to his. "Okay?"

"As long as you date *me* a lot, I don't care who else you've dated."

"What I'm trying to say," I reply, trying to ignore the enormous butterflies that just started doing the rhumba in my stomach, "that I don't have a lot of experience with dating. I'm not entirely innocent." I shake my head, disgusted with myself, and the way my tongue is all tangled and not explaining this the way I want.

Suddenly, he takes my hand again and smiles widely.

"Take a deep breath."

I comply.

"Now, start over."

"You're very patient."

"No. Not typically. But you seem to bring out some good qualities in me. Please, go on."

How in the bloody hell am I supposed to remember what I was trying to say when he goes and says sweet things like that?

"You were saying something about not being innocent," he prompts, listening avidly.

"Right," I say and nod. "I'm not. Innocent, that is. But I also don't date often, and I don't know the rules of this game. I don't know what I'm supposed to say, or when to say it."

"This isn't a game," he says simply. "I didn't invite you here tonight on a whim, Mallory. We're here because I wanted to be here with you. I'm attracted to you, both physically and intellectually, and I want to spend time with you. I don't want you to censor yourself. If you have something to say, say it."

"Well, that's easy."

"Is it?" He cocks a brow. "Being honest isn't easy for everyone."

"I'm not a liar," I reply without any anger. It's a simple statement. "But there are some things that I'm just not ready to talk about."

"As there should be," he says. "You hardly know me."

"Exactly." I smile and glance down at my watch. "We've been here for three hours!"

"Time flies when you're with a beautiful woman,"

Beau replies and stands, holding his hand out for mine. "Shall we?"

"I suppose we shall."

We walk out to his car silently, both of us lost in our own thoughts as he heads back toward the city.

But rather than take the exit to the French Quarter, he keeps going.

"Where are we going?" I ask.

"I want to show you something, if you don't mind."

I glance over at him, his face cast in shadows, then in the full glow of the lights of the freeway. He's simply stunning, and I don't say that easily. His dark hair is a bit long, brushed back off of his face in a clean style. He's also clean shaven, with a strong, angular jawline and the kind of lips that were made to be kissed.

"You're awful quiet," he murmurs. "I can take you back to the shop if you'd rather. But I'm not quite ready to say goodnight yet."

Be honest. This isn't a game.

"I'd like to see whatever you want to show me," I reply softly and sit back, enjoying the sparkle of the city as we drive through it.

Finally, he exits the freeway, driving through a beautiful, older neighborhood with grand homes. "Is this near Audubon Park?"

"It is," he says with a smile, and I turn my head to look out the window, suddenly very nervous. This is an old neighborhood in New Orleans, which means there will be many energies here.

I take a deep breath and pull all of my defenses around me, mentally preparing for what is surely going to be an onslaught of energy.

Beau glances my way, frowning, but doesn't say

anything as he pulls into a driveway, punches a code into the gate, and drives through.

"What is this place?" I ask.

"My house," he says with a smile. "It's currently under construction, but I wanted to show it to you."

"You're renovating?"

Fuck. Renovating old places makes them more active paranormally, which means I don't want to go in there. Not tonight.

"No, I'm building it from scratch." He parks in front of a beautiful home with scaffolding around it. "I bought the property with an old house on it, but it was in such disrepair it made more sense to tear it down and start over."

Okay, this might not be so bad. Ridding the area of the old building and starting new is different than renovating. It's usually like starting with a clean slate.

I can do this. I take a deep breath in relief.

"Are you okay?" he asks.

"Great," I reply with what I hope is a sincere smile.

"We're going to have to talk about those more personal things sooner rather than later," he says, reminding me of our conversation in the restaurant. "Come on. There's electricity in there, so we won't be fumbling around in the dark."

"Well, that's a relief because I'm not terribly fond of fumbling," I reply, making him laugh as he leads me to the front door. "When will it be finished?"

"It was supposed to be done three months ago," he replies. "So, your guess is as good as mine. But I'm okay at the flat in the Quarter until it's done. I want it to be just right."

I walk inside, still prepared to protect myself from

anything, or anyone, who might still be here, as I reach out with my mind, probing the darkness, but I'm pleasantly surprised to feel…*nothing.* Just cool calm, just like when Beau touches me.

I'm safe here.

Beau turns on the lights in each room as we wander through. The walls have drywall already, so it has the shape of a house. There's no paint or flooring, but the kitchen cabinets are in.

"There are four bedroom suites," he says as he leads me further into the kitchen, still turning on all the lights. "The master bedroom suite is on the main floor, and all of the other bedrooms are upstairs. Compared to the rest of the neighborhood, it's not very big at only four thousand square feet."

"That's a lot of square feet for one person," I comment and rub my hand over the smooth quartz countertop. My tiny fifteen hundred square feet would feel microscopic to him. "This feels nice."

He's studying me.

"What?"

He shakes his head. "Nothing. What I love about this room is that it's open to the living space and the dining room."

"It's going to be lovely," I reply, glancing about.

"Just through here is an office, so I can work from home on occasion."

"Is this a wine cellar?" I ask, stunned as we walk out of the kitchen and past a glass door, with floor to ceiling shelves for wine bottles.

"It is," he says with a grin. He's almost boyish in his excitement for this house, and for the first time, I *wish* I could read him, just for a moment.

"You love it here," I say instead, and watch his face as he seems to look a bit embarrassed. He simply nods.

"I do." He takes my hand and squeezes it tightly. "I've always lived in homes that have been owned by my family for generations, or that our company has bought. But this one is *mine*. Not a Boudreaux palace. Not owned by the company. Mine."

"Good for you," I say with a big smile. "That's wonderful."

We pass by a smaller room on our way to the grand staircase, and I pause.

"What's in there?"

"Nothing right now," he says and obliges me as I wander inside, turning on the light for me. It's an oddly shaped room, like a triangle, with a small window.

And the energy in it is *amazing*.

"Oh, this is great." I turn to him. "What are you going to use this for?"

"Well, it's such an odd shape, I was just going to use it for storage."

"That's a shame," I reply, and let his hand fall as I pace the room. "The energy in here is just wonderful."

He cocks a brow, and I continue.

"It's a happy place. It should be a small library or just a reading nook. Or maybe a place to paint."

"Are you an artist?" he asks.

"Not in the least. But this room is truly special. Please don't just use it for storage."

I turn to look at him and he's leaning against the door jamb, watching me with lust written all over his face.

I don't have to be psychic to see it.

He wants me.

He slowly pushes away from the door and moves

toward me, his shoulders broad in the white button down shirt, his arms hard where the shirt is rolled to his elbows. His jaw tightens as he gets closer, towering over me because he's so damn tall, but I'm not afraid of him in the least.

He doesn't say a word as he lifts his hand to cup my cheek, his thumb brushing under my eye. I wrap my hand around his wrist and lean into his touch, soaking up his warmth. God, I've missed being touched.

Being touched by Beau is like being touched for the first time in my life, and I never want him to stop.

He lowers his lips to mine, brushes them lightly, nibbles the corner, and then sinks in for the kiss of my life. He gently urges my mouth open, and licks my lips, and devours me His hand dives into my hair, and the wall is suddenly at my back as he continues to explore me in ways I didn't even know existed.

He braces his free hand on the wall above my head, and I fist my hands in his shirt at his sides, holding on for dear life.

Finally, he pulls back, breathing hard, his eyes bright and dilated.

And in this moment, I know. His touch is safe. I can trust it. Him. I'm not bombarded with someone else's emotions, and I am free to simply feel my own while being intimate with him.

"So that's what all the hoopla's about."

He smirks, and I realize I spoke aloud again, but I'm not embarrassed. Not in the least.

He takes a deep breath and drags his knuckles down my cheek.

"I want to keep you here all night," he murmurs before kissing my forehead. "So I'd better take you home."

I smile. He could talk me into staying. But he's not. And I'll be damned if that doesn't make me like him even more.

***

After the busy summer season is over, I close the shop on Mondays. Today is my first Monday off for the off-season, and I'm already bored out of my mind.

Not that I don't have a shit ton to do. There's laundry and dishes and toilets to scrub, which I hate. Garbage to take out. Basically, all of the things that get overlooked during the work week need to be caught up on.

So, of course I'm sitting on my ass, watching the shows on my DVR.

My phone rings, and without looking at it I know it's Lena.

"Did you watch Sister Wives last week?" I ask as a greeting.

"Do witches dance naked under the harvest moon? Of course I did." She chuckles. "I'm on my lunch break. Tell me about last night."

"No."

"Did you like his house?"

I frown and pull my phone away from my ear so I can glare at it before replying. "How did you know he took me to his house?"

"Hi, my name is Lena, and I'm psychic."

"Well, get your psychic ass out of my head."

"I didn't tell you yesterday when I saw it in the cards," she replies, as if that makes it all okay. "Did you like it?"

"It's a great house," I say. "And he's a great guy. And he kissed me, and holy fuck, Lena, I'm pretty sure there were actual fireworks going off, right there in the room with us."

"It was only a kiss?" she asks, disappointment heavy in her voice.

"It was a pretty hot kiss."

"Okay, well, that's good. When are you going to see him again?"

"He didn't ask me out again," I reply. "It was late. I'm sure I'll hear from him soon."

"But you don't know because he didn't say and you can't read him."

"I *like* not being able to read him. I don't have to keep my shields up with him. I can just be a normal woman."

"I'm glad, Mal. Really. I'm so happy for you. It's about time something like this happened for you."

I nod, even though she can't see me. "Are you having a good day?"

"It's Monday," she says with a sigh. "But I'll muddle my way through it. Dinner Wednesday night?"

"Just like every Wednesday night," I agree. "Text me later."

"Okay. Bye."

"Bye."

Just as I hang up, my phone dings with an incoming email. I open it and frown when I don't recognize the sender.

Ms. Adams,

I need your help. My name is Lieutenant Williams, and I'm with the New York Police Department.. I used to work with your grandmother—

I stop reading immediately, delete the email, and stand, turning off the TV. Hell no. I don't do that, and I *won't* do that. Ever.

I need some air, so I grab my keys and handbag and leave the house, driving toward the Quarter. I don't need or want to go to the shop; I don't want to seem like I'm trying to get a glimpse of Beau. I agree with him; this isn't a game, and I'm no teenager. No stalking tendencies here.

But I'd really like to talk to a friend. Preferably one who knows Beau.

So I go to Head Over Heels, Beau's sister Charly's shoe shop.

Because it's a Monday, the shop is quiet when I walk in. I'm not even sure if she'll be here today. But Charly herself rushes out from the back with a smile on her pretty face.

"Hey, darlin'," she says. "What brings you in?"

"You," I reply honestly. "I was hoping we could chat."

"That would be fantastic. You're saving me from dealing with inventory." She wrinkles her nose. "I hate that shit."

"Me too."

"It's Monday, so it's slow. What's on your mind?"

I bite my lip, not sure how much, or how little, to tell her.

About all of it.

"You can trust me, you know."

And as I look into eyes the same color and shape as her eldest brother's, I know that I can trust her.

"I really like your brother."

"I have three of them, sugar," she says with a smile.

"Beau."

"Ah." She nods and leans on the counter. "Keep going."

And so I spill it all, the broken pipe in my shop, Beau helping me with the mess, and then asking me out.

Dinner. His house.

The amazing kiss.

"And I am freaked out because *I can't read him.*"

"What do you mean?"

I sigh. Might as well spill it all. "I'm psychic, Charly. I can see the deceased, I can feel other people's emotions when they touch me. I can read minds. But that's all gone with Beau."

"Wait." Charly holds up her hand, stopping me. "You see dead people?"

I close my eyes, hoping I don't regret this conversation. "Yes."

"And read minds."

"Yes."

"But not Beau's."

"No. All I feel is this beautiful stillness. I'm at ease with him."

"Well, I think that's quite lovely," she says.

"It is." I nod. "But what about when he finds out what I am?"

"What about it?"

"I'm afraid that he'll run for the hills. They always do."

And yet, I just spilled my guts to Charly, and she doesn't look freaked out in the least. Of course, that doesn't mean that she's *not* freaked out.

Charly is quiet for a moment, and then she walks around the counter and stuns me when she wraps me up in a big hug. It's full of affection and friendship. Happiness. She's happy for both me and her brother.

He needs you in his life.

I immediately mentally pull back, not wanting to intrude on her thoughts. When she pulls away, she keeps my hand in hers.

"First of all, you should give Beau some credit. He's not rash, and he's not stupid."

"Certainly not."

"And second of all, you've been out on one date. There's no need to tell him this right now, especially since you can't use your abilities on him. You're just a woman when you're with Beau, so I say you enjoy that, and tell him in your own time, in your own way."

"He'll think it's bullshit."

"Well, I will admit that Beau is a practical man. You need to be prepared for him to not believe in the paranormal."

"As long as he doesn't think I'm nuts, we'll be fine."

"I think you should get to know each other better. If it doesn't go anywhere, there's no need to tell him. But if you think there's a future with him, then you should talk with him."

"You're a smart woman," I say with a smile. "I'm so glad I came."

"Me too. Just don't tell Gabby that you're psychic. She'll ask you to come do a séance at her inn."

I cringe. Yep, I'm just a parlor trick.

"There's a ghost there," Charly continues. "We all have bets on who it is."

I tilt my head to the side. "So, *you* do believe in it?"

"Scares the holy hell out of me," she says with a shiver. "But yes, there's something out there. Too many unexplained things happen to think otherwise."

Interesting.

"I haven't done a séance since I was a kid." I tap my finger over my lips, considering it.

Charly grins. "But you *have* done them?"

"Honey, I don't need a séance to talk to the dead. But yes, I've done them. And you know what? It might be fun."

Who in the hell am I right now? I haven't voluntarily offered to use my gifts for anyone in over a decade.

But I like Charly and her family. She doesn't think I'm nuts.

And it really could be fun.

"Let's do it."

CHAPTER FIVE

~Beau~

"I sent her flowers," I tell Charly over lunch. It's been several days since I last saw Mallory.

I don't like it a bit.

"What kind?" she asks.

"Ranunculus."

My sister looks quite surprised as she takes a sip of her sweet tea and wipes the corner of her mouth with a napkin. "Aren't you just the botanist?"

"I like flowers," I reply with a shrug. It's true, I do. I plan to have a garden at the new house.

"Do the guys know?"

Charly always has been the smart ass of the family.

"I'm trusting that you won't tell them," I reply. "I know some things about you that you'd rather didn't get announced to the family."

She just smirks. She's not afraid of me in the least.

"How's Simon?" Simon is Charly's fiancé.

"He's great." She shifts in her chair. "He's doing some seminars in London this week."

"It's not easy to be with someone who travels so

much."

"No." She shrugs and tucks her hair behind her hair. "It's not easy, but it's worth it. I have to go to Miami late next week myself to check on the shop there."

"I trust that's going well?"

"It's fantastic, and my team does a great job there."

Charly opened a Miami branch of Head Over Heels earlier this year.

"I hope you don't plan to move there."

"No. I just like to drop in once in a while, to make sure things are running smoothly."

"Will Simon go with you?"

"I'm meeting him there."

I sit back and watch my sister for a moment. I like Simon well enough, but this is my little sister we're talking about. She seems happy, and she says all the right things.

"Stop that," she says and glares at me.

"What?"

"Stop overthinking my life. I'm great, and that isn't a lie."

"You look tired," I say quietly.

"I don't sleep well when he's not here," she admits and takes another sip of her tea. "It's crazy how you can sleep alone for the better part of three decades, and then you're with someone for less than a year, and that's all shot to hell."

"Melatonin is good for insomnia."

She cocks a brow. "Are you a naturopath now as well as a botanist?"

"You're a pain in my ass," I reply with a smile. "It's amazing we've kept you around all these years."

"I'm the most charming Boudreaux there is, sugar. What would y'all do without me?"

"It would be a boring life, indeed. I'm glad that you've found someone who makes you happy."

"I am too," she says and studies me for a moment, as though she's trying to decide what to say next.

Which is so *not* Charly.

"Say it."

"Say what?"

"You don't have a poker face, darlin'." I wink at her and laugh when she narrows her eyes at me. "What do you want to know?"

"Well, I talked with Mallory the other day," she says, surprising me. I know that they're friends, and I don't know why it surprises me and even makes me a little uncomfortable. I've never had this response to a woman before.

"Oh?"

"Yeah. She likes you."

I grin. "Oh, good. I was afraid that she'd tell you during study hall that she was going to pass me a note and break up with me."

"You're a smart ass."

"Seems to run in the family."

She examines her perfect manicure for a moment, long enough for me to want to fidget in my chair. I've been in meetings with people far more formidable than my little sister, but just the mention of Mallory's name has me on edge.

I'm not sure I'm okay with that.

"I like her too," Charly says softly. "She's my friend. She's Kate and Van's friend, too."

"Okay. I'm not sure where you're going with this."

"I'm going to spell it out for you."

"Great."

She sighs and leans in, her elbows braced on the table. "She *likes* you, Beau. And she has baggage that she hasn't told you about yet."

"She's told *you*?"

"Some of it. Not all of it. Confiding in the person you're attracted to is hard. There's always the chance of rejection, and it's hard to be vulnerable with someone."

"Charly—"

"No, let me finish. Mal is special. There are things about her that she'll have to tell you, when she's ready."

"I can already see that," I reply. "I've been with her, and there are times that she seems afraid of being touched. I asked her if she was hurt in the same way that Van was, and she said no."

"Few people are hurt the way Van was," she replies. Our sister, Savannah, was brutally abused by her ex-husband.

"So what is it?"

"I'm not telling you," she says, shaking her head. "This is hers to tell, and she will."

"Why are you even bringing this up?"

"Because I love you. And I really like her. I like her for *you.*"

"Charly, we've only been on one date."

"But the chemistry is there," she says, speaking it aloud before I can. "All I'm trying to say is, if you don't see things with Mallory going long-term, if you're just trying to get into her pants, let her down now rather than later."

"We've been on *one date*," I remind her again. "I'm not ready to pop the question."

"No, but you're a smart man, Beau. You know already if this is someone you actually have an affection for, or if you just want to fuck her seven ways to Sunday."

"Such a lady," I mutter, not entirely comfortable having this conversation with my own sister.

"Have you talked to her?"

"No. It's been a busy week at the office."

"But you sent her flowers," she says with a smile.

"Yes."

"What did the card say?"

I narrow my eyes at my sister and consider ignoring this question altogether, but she'll just keep bugging the shit out of me until I tell.

"Do you like me, check yes or no."

She blinks rapidly, then dissolves into a fit of giggles.

"Oh my God, Beau. Are you seven?"

"I think it's funny."

"You're the COO of a billion dollar corporation and you sent her *that* card?"

"I'm a human being," I reply. "And she'll think it's funny."

"Well, I bet she hasn't received a note like that since grade school." She shakes her head, tossing me a smile full of humor. "You'll have to let me know how she replies."

"No way."

"Why not?"

"Because you're nosy." I reach across the table and tap her nose. "And it's none of your business."

"You're no fun."

***

I want to see her. Right now.

On my way home from the office, I step into her shop rather than go upstairs. It's only a few minutes before closing, and the store is empty of patrons.

In fact, I don't see anyone here at all when I first walk in.

Her shop is small, but cute. Not cramped. She's made it feel homey with burning candles and a plate of cookies out for her customers. I take one of the peanut butter and pop the whole thing in my mouth.

Delicious.

"I thought I heard someone come in," Mallory says and I spin around and almost choke on the cookie at the sight of her.

Her red hair is twisted up again, and I want nothing more than to shake it loose and brush my fingers through it.

"Your cookies are delicious." I brush the crumbs off my fingers. "Did you make them?"

"No, Lena's grandmother made them," she says with a smile. "They're supposed to bring you luck."

"Really?"

She just folds her hands at her waist, as if she's not sure what to do with them, and continues to smile at me. Then she jumps and holds her finger up.

"Oh! Hold on, I have something for you." She disappears into her office for a moment, then comes back holding a little white card out for me.

"You checked *yes*," I murmur, suddenly embarrassed for sending this to her.

"I did. And I'm going to need that back, please."

"Why?"

"Because I'm keeping it forever," she says, as if I should have just known that. "I waited almost thirty years for a boy to send me this note."

"Well, then, here you go." I pass it back to her and she tucks it in the back pocket of her black jeans. "Do you have plans tonight?"

"I have a date with a tub of ice cream and my television."

"Well, I don't know if I can compete with that, but I'd like to take you somewhere."

Her eyebrows climb into her hairline. "Back to your house?"

I smile, remembering how great it was to see her in my place. She looked at home there, and I wanted to boost her up against the wall and make her scream my name.

"Unfortunately, not tonight. Somewhere else."

"I suppose the ice cream can wait." She grins. "Shall we go now? I was about to close anyway."

"Perfect."

She gathers her things, locks the door, and turns to me. "Now what?"

"We're going to walk," I reply and take her hand in mine, satisfied that the stiffness that usually comes with physical contact is brief. She squeezes my fingers. "Have you been to The Odyssey?"

"Several times." She nods happily. "Charly, Van, Kate, and I go there for happy hour sometimes."

"Well, Declan is playing there tonight. I thought we could listen to him for a bit."

"I've never heard him," Mallory says. "I'd love to listen. I hear he's great."

"That he is."

"Do you have musical talent too?" She smiles up at me as I open the door to The Odyssey for her.

"No, ma'am. Declan got all of that talent in the family."

We weave our way through the tall tables and chairs. It's busy, but not packed, at least not yet.

When we reach the bar, Callie, the owner of the bar and Declan's wife, runs out to greet us.

"This is a sweet surprise," she says and hugs Mallory tightly.

Mallory doesn't stiffen, or give any indication that she's uncomfortable at all. Which makes me think again that she must have been hurt at some point by a man. It's the only thing that makes sense.

"What are y'all doing in here?" Callie asks.

"Beau suggested we come in to listen to Declan," Mallory says.

"I'm so glad you did," Callie replies and waves at Declan, who is on the stage checking the sound. He climbs down and walks over to us. "Declan, this is my friend Mallory."

"We've met," he says and offers his hand to Mallory who pauses for just a moment before shaking it. "How is the flood?"

"Gone, thank goodness," Mallory says. "We caught it fast enough that it didn't do too much damage."

"Good." Declan smiles and wraps his arm around Callie's shoulders. "Are you sticking around for the set?"

"We are," I reply.

"So, I'm sorry to be so blunt, but that's just me," Callie says with a smile. "Are y'all on a date?"

Mallory glances up at me and cocks a brow, and I can't help but laugh.

"If it needs a label, then I guess so," I reply.

"Oh, that's so great!" Callie smiles widely and hugs Mallory again. "Oh, and I can't wait for our girls' night!"

Mallory quickly glances up at me, and then says, "Which is for girls only, and the guys don't get to know what we're doing."

"Is it a state secret?" I ask and tuck her soft hair behind her ear. My god, I can't stop touching her. I want to explore every inch of her.

"It's girls' night," Callie replies, as if that explains it all.

"We could tell you, but then we'd have to kill you," Mal adds.

"You won't even give me just a hint?"

"No." Mal shakes her head, but the smile on her beautiful lips says she's enjoying this very much.

"What if I demand that you tell me?"

The girls glance at each other and then bust up laughing.

"You're not the boss of me," Mal says, but takes my hand in hers and gives it a squeeze. "Sorry. But not sorry."

***

"He's amazing," Mallory says as we walk back to her shop. Her hand is firmly in mine, and we're enjoying the warm evening. With fall approaching, the weather is milder, making for comfortable evenings. "He has an incredible gift."

"He does."

"Has he always been interested in music?"

"Definitely. We knew early on that Declan would never want to be a part of the family business. He needs to make music."

"How did your parents feel about that?"

"They encouraged him. My father was adamant that we all do what we love."

"That's great. Is he still with us?"

"No." I shove my free hand in my pocket to touch the

coin I carry. "He died a few years ago."

"I'm sorry," she says, frowning. We've made it to her store, but I'm not ready to say goodnight yet.

"Come up with me for a while."

Her gaze whips up to mine.

"I'm not ready to call it a night," I add, hoping that she'll agree. She bites her lip, but makes her decision quickly.

"Okay."

She follows me up the stairs and into the flat. I turn on some music and unbutton the top button of my shirt, roll my sleeves, and kick out of my shoes.

"Make yourself comfortable. Would you like some wine?"

She smiles and drags her hand over the granite countertop, the same way she did at my house. "Sure."

Once the wine is poured, we sit on the couch turned toward each other, sipping our drinks. The silence is comfortable.

I can't help but reach out and drag my finger down her soft cheek.

"You're beautiful, Mallory," I whisper.

"Thank you." She leans into my touch, her eyes closed, and sighs.

"I like touching you."

"And I like it when you touch me." Her eyes open now, and she gazes up at me. "I'm not used to that."

"You're not used to being touched, or enjoying it?"

"Both." She takes a sip, and I suddenly want to tear whomever made her feel like this apart. "I'm an…*odd* woman, Beau."

"Well, we're all a little odd, Mal." I brush a stray piece of hair off her cheek.

"That's true, I guess." She takes another sip and then puts her glass on the coffee table. "Beau?"

"Yes, sugar."

"Are you ever going to kiss me again?"

And just like that my cock is at full attention. But I just set my glass next to hers and turn to her, my elbow resting on the back of the couch.

"I'd like to just settle this right now."

"You don't have to—"

I touch her lips with my fingertip, shushing her.

"I plan to kiss you often, Mallory. I plan to do much more than that. I am quite taken with you."

"Oh." She licks her lips and her violet eyes widen and dilate.

"But I'm afraid that once I start I won't be able to stop. I had to tear myself away from you in the weird room at my house."

"I like the weird room," she whispers, still watching my lips.

"I seem to be rather fond of it lately too."

She smiles and tentatively reaches out to touch my arm. I don't say anything; I just wait, offering her a silent invitation to touch me. To feel *safe* to touch me.

"I'm quite taken with you, too," she says, lightly gliding her hand up to my shoulder. "Not just with how you look, although it's something to write home about, but also with *you.*"

God, she's so fucking sweet.

And I can't wait any longer. I cup her cheek and lean in, nuzzle her nose with mine, and then kiss her. Lightly at first, just giving us each little tastes. She surprises me by burying her fingers in the hair on the back of my head and holding on for dear life as she takes the kiss from soft and sweet to a fucking inferno.

Jesus, I want her.

She's pulling my hair as I guide her onto her back and cover her sweet, petite body with mine, resting between her legs, pressing my dick against her core, wishing our clothes would magically vanish.

"So beautiful," I murmur as I kiss down her jawline to her ear and then down her neck. She arches into me, her hand tightening.

She likes having her neck kissed. So noted.

She drags her foot up the back of my calf and plants it there. Everywhere she's touching me is on fire.

I need her.

"Beau."

"Yes, sweetheart." I kiss my way back to her lips and sink in for some quality time exploring her mouth. She's sweet, seducing me to the very core with her touch, her warmth.

"We're wearing too many clothes."

I pull back and stare down at her. Her lips are a bit swollen, and her eyes are wide and shining with lust. Her chest is heaving as she breathes heavily, and she has a death grip on my ass.

"I can rectify that."

I grin and push my hands under her silk blouse. Her skin is smooth and warm and the best thing I've ever touched in my life.

I'm a mess, and I haven't even seen her naked yet.

"You're moving awfully slowly," she grumbles.

"I'm savoring this," I whisper and kiss her collarbone. "I'll only ever get to see you naked for the first time once. I don't want to rush it."

"You say the nicest things," she says. "Do you always

mean them?"

I pause. "Of course I do. I told you before, this is not a game."

"I know. Forget I said anything. I'm just dumb with lust. All of my blood left my brain, and now I can't stop talking—"

I cover her mouth with mine, effectively shutting her up as I guide her blouse up, pull back to tug it over her head, and then resume kissing her as I brush my knuckles over her puckered nipple.

"You're so responsive."

"You're sexy," she says and tugs my shirt out of my pants.

Suddenly, there's a loud crash across the room, as a huge mirror falls and shatters.

"Shit," Mallory says, staring at the glass. "She didn't like us kissing."

Chapter Six

-Mallory-

"Who?" he demands, staring down at me, his breath coming quickly and eyes slowly losing the lust that just shone in them.

"Miss Louisa," I reply and sit up when he pulls away.

Fuck me. For the first time ever, I was engrossed in a man and my own carnal feelings about him without being bombarded with his own thoughts. I didn't even notice that Miss Louisa was in the room until the mirror broke.

Which was her way of getting my attention.

She's glaring at me, and talking fast, but I'm not responding to her, and that only makes her angrier.

I guess she doesn't like to be ignored.

"What are you talking about?" Beau says and pushes his fingers through his hair as he stands and retrieves a broom.

"Could you wait to do that?" I ask and work on gathering my own thoughts. I'm still not acknowledging Miss Louisa, who's finally fed up with being ignored and disappears altogether. I can't feel her presence at all now, and I take a deep, cleansing breath.

"That mirror has been on that wall as long as I can remember," he murmurs and sits next to me again. "The nail must have given out."

"No." I tuck my hair behind my ear and offer him a smile. "That's not what happened."

"Your hands are shaking," he says and takes them in his, kisses my knuckles, and pins me in his gaze. "Are you okay?"

"Yes."

"We agreed not to lie," he says firmly.

"You're right." I pull out of his touch and cross my arms over my chest, already distancing myself from him.

He's not going to like this. That's not a guess, and I still can't read him, but I know how most people in my life has reacted, and I don't expect him to be any different.

"Mal?"

"I can see things," I reply immediately. "That mirror didn't fall because of a bad nail."

His eyes narrow, and he sits back, unconsciously distancing himself, and a little piece of my heart breaks. I'm not ready for this to be over. I'm not ready to say goodbye to him.

I feel like I've finally started to live a normal life since he came into it.

"Why did it fall, Mal?"

I love the way he says my name.

"Because a ghost named Miss Louisa made it fall."

"I see."

"No, you don't," I reply, suddenly frustrated. "You don't see at all."

"Okay, tell me." He leans toward me again, and I can't stand the thought of him touching me right now so I stand, wrap my blouse around me, and begin to pace his living room. How did we suddenly go from about to make love to me explaining all about my crazy psychic abilities?

"I'm not sure how much to say," I reply honestly.

"Tell me everything."

I stop and turn to look at him, memorizing every line of his face, the way his shirt fits over his amazingly sculpted body, and how he still has a bit of fondness for me in his whiskey eyes.

"I'm the latest in a long line of women with paranormal abilities." If I keep it sounding scientific, business-like, maybe it'll come out easier. "As far back as we know, and we have records going back about eight hundred years, the women in my father's lineage have been psychic, empathic, and/or mediums."

"Do they always have all of those abilities?" he asks, rubbing his fingertips along his chin, like he's thinking about what I'm telling him.

"Not always. Sometimes they've had one, or a combination of them. Sometimes they've had more, like being able to see the future, clairvoyance, and more scary things like being able to climb inside another person's consciousness, and kill them."

He's staring at me, his jaw tight, and I wish more than ever that I knew what he was thinking.

"How many of those do you have?"

"I'm an empath, I am clairvoyant, and I'm a medium."

"You see the dead."

I nod and fold my hands at my waist. "Hence, Miss Louisa throwing her little tantrum here tonight."

"Do you practice witchcraft?" he asks, which makes me smile. People who know little about psychic abilities often assume that witchcraft is linked to it.

"I don't," I reply. "They don't really go together. I do, however, have friends who do. Lena and her grandmother are two of them. And Lena has some psychic ability as well."

"Why was that funny?"

"None of this is funny," I reply soberly. "It's just that many people link witchcraft with being psychic, but they really don't always have anything to do with each other."

He stands and paces to the window that looks out over Jackson Square and takes a deep breath.

"Look, if you're done here, I get it." I cross to him and touch his shoulder. He doesn't pull away from my touch, which I take as a good sign. "It's weird, and for some people it's scary."

"I'm not afraid of you," he replies and turns to me, drawing me in for a long, tight hug. Tears come now, but I don't want him to see them, so I keep my face buried in his chest and cling to him. "I don't want to be done here, Mal."

"I distance myself from people for a reason," I murmur. "I haven't done that with you, and it's felt so good."

We've agreed to be honest, and I really don't have anything to lose at this point.

Except him.

But I might lose him anyway, so I might as well be frank.

"Why haven't you done that with me?"

I swallow, not sure how to answer him.

"Part of what I do is, I can read what others feel and think when they touch me, or if I accidentally touch them."

"That's why you don't like to be touched."

I nod. "It's an emotional rollercoaster to say the least. Happiness, fear, sadness, anger, and every other emotion there is will hit me like a sledgehammer. I can hear thoughts. Worries. Sometimes it's as clear as if they'd voiced it aloud."

"What am I thinking right now?" he asks.

I DON'T KNOW!

"That you'd like me to leave and take my crazy with me?"

He tips my chin up so he can look me in the eyes. "You know that's not what I'm thinking."

"No, I don't."

"I don't get it."

"That's the thing, Beau. I *can't* read you. At all. When you touch me, a cool calmness settles over me that makes me feel…well, *safe* for lack of a better word."

"So you can't tell when I'm so hot for you I can't stand it? Or when I think you're funny, or beautiful?"

"I can tell that you're hot for me because of the way you look at me, but not because I can read your mind." He smiles down at me like he just won the lottery. "I've never experienced this before, Beau. Sometimes it unnerves me when I *want* to know what you're thinking, but mostly it's just such a relief. I am just a woman with you."

"You're not *just* anything, sweetheart, but I would be lying if I didn't say that it's a relief for me as well. You'd have me at quite the disadvantage if you knew what I was thinking all the time and I was clueless. How's a man supposed to surprise you?"

"I'm not wild about surprises. They aren't usually a good thing."

"We'll see if we can change your mind about that," he says and leans in to kiss my forehead. "And Miss Louisa will just have to get used to me kissing you. In fact, she can go mind her own business."

I smirk. "It doesn't creep you out?"

"Having a ghost watch me make love to a beautiful woman?" He tips his head as if he's giving it real thought. "Well, I've never been an exhibitionist in the past, but..." He shrugs. "Do you typically have an audience?"

"No." I giggle and shake my head. "This was actually a first. I hope we don't repeat it."

"Me too." He sobers and drags his knuckles down my cheek. "How do you feel?"

"Better." I sigh, realizing it's the truth. "Much better, actually."

"That was quite the secret to keep."

"It's not that I was trying to keep it a secret. I'd planned to tell you, but in my own time. This is still new, and I'm enjoying you. I didn't want it to end yet."

"You've told Charly," he says with a half smile.

"I think she suspected because I've said things in the past here and there, but I needed to really confide in someone who knows us both. She gives good advice." I tentatively reach up to cup his cheek, and he leans into my touch, closing his eyes. "How do *you* feel?"

"Concerned about you," he says and kisses my forehead again. "Relieved that you told me the truth. A bit frustrated that the mood is gone because I'm so fucking attracted to you my teeth ache with it."

Damn.

"That might be the sexiest thing anyone has ever said to me."

"Just wait until I'm inside you. There ought to be some interesting thoughts coming out of me then."

I smile and hug him tightly one more time before

backing away.

"I should go home."

"I'll follow you."

"Oh, you don't have to."

"I know, but it's late, and this *is* the French Quarter. If you don't want to stay here, let me follow you home."

I shrug as I gather my things. "Thank you."

The drive home is fast, given the time of night. I pull into my driveway and turn to wave him off, but he cuts his engine and joins me.

"Let me stay."

I blink, completely surprised.

"Not because I want to have sex with you. That isn't even part of the equation tonight. But because I want to just be with you."

He takes my hand, linking our fingers, and I just smile, wanting nothing more than to spend more time in Beau's arms. "Come on in."

"Will we have an audience here too? Do I need to censor our conversation?"

"No." I unlock the door and invite him in. "There are no spirits here. It's why I bought it."

"Nothing here to fuck with your head," he murmurs and drops his keys and wallet on the table next to my handbag. "Would you please show me where your bathroom is?"

"There's a guest bathroom right over there."

"No, *your* bathroom."

I tilt my head. "The master suite is upstairs."

"Perfect." He takes my hand and leads me up the stairs and finds my bedroom on his first try. "You need a hot shower."

"Do I smell?" I prop my hands on my hips, watching

him as he gathers a towel and washrag.

"You smell amazing," he says, starting the water. "But it'll help relax you."

I shake my head, not fully understanding. "Okay."

"I'm taking care of you," he says and takes my shoulders in his hands, holding me in front of him. "You may not recognize it, but that's what I'm trying to do. Help you feel happy and safe."

"I do feel those things."

"Good. Now, get in the shower before I strip you naked myself."

"Um, that wouldn't be a bad thing," I reply and pull my shirt over my head and stand before him in my jeans and bra.

"I'm not going to make love to you tonight," he says as he slips his fingers under my bra strap and yanks me against him so he can kiss the hell out of me. "Get in the shower."

"Yes, sir." I give him a mock salute and laugh when he peeks around the door as he closes it behind him.

A shower is a good idea. It'll give me a few moments to think about everything that happened tonight. Did we really leave my shop to go listen to Declan just five hours ago? It feels like a week's worth of activities and emotions just happened.

And I'm so damn tired all of a sudden. Beau was right, the hot shower feels good. I didn't realize I was holding my shoulders up around my ears so tightly. Careful to keep my hair out of the water, I let it beat over my shoulders and neck. I keep a few essential oils in my shower, so I reach for the lavender and let it drop into the water, filling the air with its scent.

It's lovely.

If this is what it means to let someone take care of you, I could get used to it.

Beau knocks on the door and opens it a crack, but doesn't poke his head inside.

"Did you drown?"

"Not yet," I call back.

"Just checking."

And then the door is closed again. The man was touching me intimately not long ago, and now he's acting like he's never seen a naked woman before.

And let's be honest, I'm sure he's seen his fair share of naked women.

The thought doesn't make me jealous, or even feel threatened. I told him some of my deepest secrets, and here we are. He didn't run away. He didn't recoil in fear or disgust.

He put me in a hot shower.

I'm pretty sure that's a good sign.

I cut off the water and dry off, humming to myself. I don't have any pajamas in here, so I wrap the towel around me and walk out into my bedroom, and feel my jaw drop.

Beau is propped up in my bed, shirtless, under the covers, and glances up from his phone as I come in the room. On the end table next to the empty side of the bed is a steaming cup of tea. The overhead light is off, and instead the lamp next to him is on, casting the room in a soft, romantic glow.

"You said you're *not* trying to seduce me tonight?" I ask and walk to the dresser where I find some panties and a tank top. I walk back into the bathroom and quickly pull on my clothes, then return to the bed.

"This isn't a seduction, darlin'," he replies with that sexy smile. "Trust me, when I decide to seduce you, it'll be much different than this."

"I don't know, this is pretty sweet."

"Sweet isn't a synonym for seductive," he says and flips the covers back, gesturing for me to join him.

I slip inside, enjoying the way the cool sheets feel against my legs, and slide over to cuddle up with Beau.

This is new. I've never been a cuddler. But in this house, where I know I'm safe, and with this man, it's the best feeling I've ever had.

"You're comfortable." I yawn and rub my nose against his chest. He has a light spattering of hair there.

"Good. I have to send an email real quick."

"This late?" I look up at him in surprise.

"It's not late in Europe. It's morning there." He kisses the top of my head and keeps typing on his phone. I'm so relaxed that I drift in and out of sleep, and the next thing I know, he turns the lamp off and guides us both to lie down, me still in his arms.

"Sleep well," he murmurs.

"*You* sleep well," I reply and sink into slumber.

***

I haven't had this dream before.

I'm sitting on a rock, looking out at a field of bright yellow sunflowers. It's warm, with just a slight breeze to take the edge off the intense sunshine.

And someone is brushing my hair. When I try to turn my head to see who it is, I'm stuck. I can't turn my neck.

But I'm not upset. I like the sunshine and the sunflowers. The breeze. And the gentle hands in my hair. They're braiding it now. Suddenly, a big tractor comes roaring into the field, cutting down all of the flowers.

"Stop!" I yell. I want to stand up and run over to them, and beg them to stop cutting the flowers.

But I can't move. All I can do is watch the beautiful blooms topple under the tractor and feel the hands in my hair.

"I don't want the flowers to die," I whisper and feel a tear fall down my cheek. "Why is he doing this?"

"Because it's time to reap what he sowed," my grandmother's voice says. "He's going to make many people very happy with those blooms."

"But I like them where they are."

She chuckles and smooths the braid on the side of my head.

"It's not always just about us," she says, just as she did many times while I was growing up. "Don't you want him to help others feel better too?"

"I guess." I tilt my head back so I can feel the sunshine on my face. "You never visit me."

"I do, you just can't see me," she says. I can hear the smile in her voice. My Grandmamma had a beautiful smile.

I often see it in my own when I look in the mirror.

"When will I get to see you?"

"When the time is right. You're getting closer. And just like that tractor took away your flowers, you may need to lose your Beau when the time arrives."

"What?" I frown, suddenly remembering Beau. "Why would I lose him?"

"You'll see."

I try to shake my head, to turn around and see her, but I can't.

"Why does the future always have to be so scary? Why can't you just tell me that everything will work out in the end?"

"Well, that's a given, love. It will *work out in the end, it*

just may not be what you expect it to be."

Clouds have begun to form over us, blocking the sun and making me cold.

"I've waited a long time to hear from you."

"I know. I've been here, sweet girl. And I'll continue to be here. You'll see me when you need me the most."

"It's not good enough," I whisper, just as the hands in my hair stop. "Are you safe? Are you happy? Is your pain gone?" I let the questions tumble from my lips.

"Yes to all of those," she says. "But I worry for you. Death doesn't change that. And it certainly doesn't take away my love for you."

"I love you too." She rests her hand on my shoulder, and I can finally move well enough to cover it with mine. "Please don't go."

"I'll be here," she says again and begins to pull the braid free, her fingers brushing through it, the same way she did when I was young.

"Good morning," Beau whispers in my ear. His fingers are in my hair, brushing it. "Did you get up and braid your hair while I was asleep?"

I open my eyes and reach up, feeling the last of the braid at the top of my head, and smile.

"Something like that."

Chapter Seven

~Mallory~

I rest my head on Beau's chest and sigh, happy that not only did I dream about Grandmamma, but I can remember it. Her voice and her touch are two things I've missed very much.

Part of our conversation is starting to slip away. It made me nervous, and I'm not sure why.

"What are you thinking about?" Beau asks softly. His fingertips are making lazy circles on my back, over my tank top.

"I dreamt of my grandmother," I reply. "I rarely do that, so it was nice."

"How long has she been gone?"

I frown and hold onto him more tightly. I don't like to talk about her being gone, and I've never told anyone how she died.

"Since I was a teenager," I reply.

"Are your parents still with us?" I'm relieved he doesn't ask more about Grandmamma.

"No." He rolls me onto my back and props his head on his elbow, looking down into my face.

"What happened to them?"

"They were in an accident," I reply. "I was very little, around three years old. I was staying with Grandmamma at her house in the Bayou, and they had taken my little brother into the city to see the doctor. It was stormy, there was flooding in some places. They probably shouldn't have gone, but he was very sick.

"On the way back to get me, they were in a head-on collision."

"Ah, baby, I'm so sorry." He cups my cheek gently.

I shrug. "I don't remember it. I don't see them, any of them. I never have. They just sort of disappeared from my life. So, I always thought I had it easy because I just didn't remember. My Grandmamma was devastated. She'd been widowed the year before, and then lost the rest of her family so suddenly."

"So it was just the two of you."

"Well, yes, but we also had Lena and her grandmother, Miss Sophia."

"Are Lena's parents also gone?" His brows raise in surprise.

"It's strange, but yes. Not in the same way. Miss Sophia has raised Lena as her own since she was born. Lena's mother was a junkie, an all-around lost person. She never knew how to handle her gifts, and so she rebelled, ended up pregnant with Lena.

"Miss Sophia talked her into not having an abortion, and the day after Lena was born, she left and never came back. No one knows who her father might be."

"I'm sorry," he says with a frown.

"Don't be." I smile and cup his cheek, letting my thumb brush over the light stubble there. "Lena is happy and healthy, and they're my family."

He takes my hand in his before I can pull it away and kisses my palm, sending shivers up my arm and into my back. Not to mention the tingles happening between my legs.

I slide my leg between his, loving the feel of his hair against my smooth skin. He kisses my palm again and leans over me farther, pinning my hand to the bed next to my head and leans in to kiss the ever-loving hell out of me.

He's lazy about it. His lips are soft, moving over my lips, my cheek and jawline, then finding my lips again. My leg is brushing up and down the outside of his, and his impressive erection is pressed into my hip.

Holy fucking shit, he's impressive.

"I'm going to take this shirt off of you," he murmurs into my ear and kisses my earlobe, then drags his teeth down it.

"Good idea."

I feel him smile against my neck, then he rears back and quickly discards the shirt, throwing it aside, and lets his gaze rake over my naked torso.

My nipples are puckered from lust and now the cool air. I'm a curvy woman, with heavy breasts that threaten to fall to my sides when I'm on my back, and he doesn't seem to mind in the least. He grazes his knuckles gently over the puckered nubs, then leans in and kisses them, sucking them into his mouth and my back arches off the bed.

He pushes his leg snugly against my core, and I rub against him, searching for more… More of him.

God, I've never wanted a man so badly in my life!

"You're beautiful," he says, brushing my hair off my cheek. His whiskey eyes are shining as he cups my breast and teases the nipple again, gently rolling it between his fingers. "You have the softest skin."

I can't speak. My back arches off the bed again, and he replaces the leg between my legs with his hand.

"You're so wet."

"Your fault," I murmur, then bite my lip when he slips a finger inside me.

"I'll happily take the blame for this." He presses his thumb to my most sensitive spot. "Look at me."

His eyes are on fire. Every muscle in his body is tight.

"I was going to take this slow," he says. "I wanted to be lazy about it, memorizing every inch of you."

"I'm not feeling particularly lazy right now," I reply and grip his wrist, guiding his wet finger to my mouth so I can suck on it, and that seems to tip the scales to frantic and carnal.

This. This is what I need from him now.

He strips the last of our underwear from us and reaches over to the bedside where a condom is sitting on the table.

"I was a sure bet?" I ask with a smile as he takes care of protecting us both. He covers my body with his and kisses me, biting my lower lip.

"No. But I was very hopeful."

And with that, he guides himself to my opening, and pushes against me, watching my face carefully. When I smile, he presses inside of me, filling me fully.

"Fuck." He grits his teeth.

"Oh my," I breathe, gripping onto his ass, urging him to move.

"If I move, it'll be over before it begins," he growls and opens his eyes. "You're so fucking tight, Mallory."

"Say it again," I whisper.

"You're so fucking tight." He jaw loosens enough for him to smile.

"The other part."

"Mallory."

"Hmm." I roll my hips, loving the way he fills me so completely. Not just physically but emotionally as well. He just fills me up.

"You like that?"

He takes my hands off his ass and pins them both above my head, effectively lifting my bust higher, giving him easier access to the hard peaks.

"I love your voice," I reply and gasp when he pulls out, just a bit. "I fucking love the way you say my name."

"Do you, *Mallory*?" he says with a grin and bites my neck as he thrusts back in me, harder. I can't move my arms, but it gives me leverage to raise my pelvis up against him, grinding, as he sets a hard pace of thrusting in and out, faster and harder, hitting my clitoris with his pubis each time.

"Oh my God, Beau."

"That's right. Look at me."

I open my eyes to see his on me, fierce now.

"Your blue eyes turn violet when you're excited."

"Good to know." He shifts his grip on my hands. "I want to touch you."

I need to touch you.

He lets them free and I immediately grip onto his shoulders, loving the way they flex under my touch.

"I love your body," he says.

"I love *your* body," I reply, surprised to not be self-conscious in the least by the extra thirty pounds I carry.

Beau doesn't seem to care, so why should I?

My hands glide down his back to his ass, but he suddenly raises up on his knees, grips my ankles, and yanks my legs up straight, so my feet are right by his face. He hugs my legs around my thighs, still inside me, thrusting hard, watching me closely.

"Oh my God," I moan, holding on to the sheets at my hips for dear life.

"Too much?" he asks.

"Hell no."

He grins and parts my legs, letting them fall at his sides, and presses his thumb against my clitoris again, and I'm done. I come so hard, I see the stars that everyone seems to talk about.

Beau leans down to kiss me.

"Again."

My eyes whip open in surprise. "I can't."

He narrows his eyes, a half smile on his sexy lips. "Oh, baby, yes you can."

He plants his lips on my neck, his thumb still at my core between us, and I'll be damned if the angle doesn't make me come again.

Holy fucking hell!

He whispers, "Mallory," and tightens, giving in to his own climax, his heart pounding against mine.

We're breathing hard, dripping with sweat, as we stay where we are, coming down from our own highs.

"Not exactly how I planned the first time to be," he murmurs as he rolls to the side and tucks me against him.

"No need to plan," I reply, catching my breath. "We seem to have the wing-it thing down."

He chuckles and tucks my hair behind my ear.

"So we do." He takes a deep breath and kisses my head. "I want to see you tonight."

I'm about to readily agree, but then I remember that I already have plans this evening.

"I can't. Remember when Callie mentioned the girls'

night we have planned? That's tonight."

"Ah yes, the girls' night that I'm not supposed to be privy to." He drags his hand down my back, and then suddenly, I'm on *my* back and he's tickling the hell out of me. "Spill it!"

"No way!" I'm giggling and struggling to get away, kicking and lashing out.

"You're stronger than you look," he says as he barely dodges my fist.

"Hell yes, I am," I reply and decide to fight fire with fire. I cup his balls in my hand and cock an eyebrow.

"Hey now," he says with a laugh. He holds his hands up in surrender. "It's not worth losing the family jewels."

I smirk and let him go, then push him on his back and straddle him.

"I guess I can tell you what we're doing."

"So it's not a state secret?"

"No." I giggle, enjoying him. He's funny. He's laid-back, which surprises me because he always struck me as uptight, despite not being able to read him.

That's what I get for assuming.

"We're going to a strip club." I do my best to school my face.

"Um..." He blinks rapidly, trying to decide how he should react to this news, and I can't help but smirk. "Are you messing with me?"

"No. I'm perfectly serious. We're going to a strip club to find Van a hot piece of ass for the night."

He scowls. "Van's not ready for that shit."

"How do you know?" I slip off of him and sit on my ass next to him. "She doesn't want anything serious, but she wouldn't mind a little...*you know.*"

"No." He shakes his head and sits up. "She's my sister,

so I *don't want to know.*"

"Don't worry. Callie's going to be the designated driver."

"This is out of character for Savannah," Beau says as he puts his boxer-briefs on and paces the room, clearly concerned. Now I'm starting to regret this. "You just don't know who she could end up with. He might be a rapist, or just an asshole."

He stops and stares at me. "Ben is going to freak the fuck out."

"Why?" I tilt my head, enthralled in how he's reacting to this news.

"Because he loves her," he says and reaches for his phone. "He's loved her forever."

"Does Van know that?"

"Deep down, I think so." He's thumbing through his contacts. "I'd better call him."

"Stop. Beau, don't call him." Shit! "Beau, we're not going to a strip club."

"Not when Ben finds out, you won't be."

"No, we're *not going.* We never were."

His hand falls to his side and he stares at me in disbelief. "You *were* dicking with me."

I cringe, then smile. "I was teasing you. There's a difference."

He sets the phone down, then pounces on me, making me yelp and giggle at the same time.

"I had no idea you were this protective."

"Of course I am," he says. "I'm the oldest of six siblings. You just saved some poor dude from being killed by Ben. And maybe me and Eli too."

"Right."

"No one wants to fuck with Ben, sugar. He's a Krav

Maga master, and a general badass."

I smirk. "You were pretty badass there for a minute, too."

"I can be a badass when I need to be," he says and kisses me. "Are you going to tell me where you're really going?"

"We're doing a séance at Gabby's inn."

He pulls back, almost as surprised as he was about the strip club comment. "Really?"

"Really."

He frowns. "Is that safe for you?"

Oh, Beau, be careful. I could fall in love with you.

"I haven't done it in a very long time," I concede. "In fact, after Grandmamma died, I was adamant that I wouldn't *ever* use my psychic abilities. But they're part of me, and I can't ignore them. I tried. I've learned how to protect myself over the years. To brace myself for certain emotions, and to cope with what I see. I've been working on being able to shut the door entirely, so I can control what and when I see things."

"You haven't been able to do that?"

"No, and it's a pain in the ass. Lena can. I think I'm getting better at it."

I hope.

"Be careful tonight. Call me if you need me. In fact, I can come with you and be there on site, just in case."

I smile and cup his cheek again, which seems to soothe him. "I'll be fine. I'll have all of your girls with me, and they're a strong bunch of women."

"That they are." He smiles and kisses my palm. "Just keep *this* girl safe, please."

"I will."

***

"This is so fun," Gabby says as she sets more candles on the dining room table. "Lena, I'm so happy that you were able to come with Mallory."

Lena smiles and nods at me. *I like these people.*

Me, too.

"I'm happy to be here," Lena says. "I've heard so much about all of you."

"I bet that drove you batty," Charly says. "It would me, if my best friend was suddenly friends with someone new."

"Well, I admit I can be protective," Lena says. "Mal is practically my sister, and sometimes people can be—"

"Horrible," Gabby finishes for her. "But you are welcome here anytime."

"I'm surprised you didn't have any guests staying tonight," Kate says and rubs her belly. Kate is about half way through her pregnancy. I pat her shoulder, just so I can take a peek and make sure that everything is still okay. She's nervous, given some problems she's had in the past, but this pregnancy is strong. Both she and the baby are healthy as can be.

"Well, it's the middle of the week in the off season, so tonight was all clear. Rhys took the kids to dinner and the movies, so we have at least three hours to ourselves."

"Perfect," Van replies and sips her tea. I like Savannah very much. I like them all, truth be told, but Van is the one that calls to me. The first time I touched her, I wanted to lie down and sob, and then I wanted to gut the animal that hurt her from crotch to throat.

And I'm not a violent woman.

But what happened to her was horrific. And yet, here

she is, smiling and sipping tea, excited at the idea of hearing from the spirits that are a part of the heritage of her family.

And the spirits are here. There's no denying that. I've already seen two and heard from a third.

The girls won't be disappointed tonight.

"How are things with Beau?" Charly asks me with a smug smile.

"Yes, we want to hear everything," Van says, also smiling widely.

"Well, not *everything,*" Gabby adds with a shudder, "because *ew*, but most of everything else, please."

"He's not my brother," Callie says with a laugh. "I'll take the everything, please."

I sit at the head of the table and smile at these five women who have so quickly become my friends. Lena sits next to me and takes my hand. She's going to be my anchor tonight. I haven't done anything like this in so many years, that I wanted her here to make sure that if something goes wrong, she can bring me out of it.

"Things with Beau are good," I reply.

"And?" Callie asks.

"And I don't know what else to say." I laugh and shrug.

"I know, it's new," Van says. "Would you say you're dating?"

"Yes."

"Would you say you've kissed him?" Gabby asks.

"Yes."

Lena smiles over at me. *Really like them.*

"Would you say he's rocked your world between the sheets?" Callie asks with mischievous blue eyes.

"Affirmative," I reply and press my lips together so I

don't bust out with laughter.

"What?" Lena asks, eyes wide. "You didn't tell me that!"

"It just happened this morning," I reply.

"Wow." Lena sits back, staring at me. "And?"

I glance around again, at all six of them staring at me in rapture and all I can do is bust out laughing.

"I've never had so many people interested in my love life."

"Come on, it's *new sex*," Lena says, looking to the others for support.

"Exactly," Charly says. "Does he make you happy? Is he a jackass?"

"Beau can be a jackass," Gabby confirms.

"He's not a jackass to me," I reply. "And yes, he makes me happy."

My phone buzzes with a call.

"And that's him now. Hello?"

"How's it going?"

"We haven't started the séance yet, but so far things are fun."

"So you haven't seen my Aunt Millie?"

"No, no sign of your Aunt Millie, but your Uncle Cyrus wants to know why you haven't wound his grandfather clock in two years. He says you're going to ruin it."

"Oh my God," Van gasps, and I look up to see everyone staring at me in shock.

And Beau hasn't said anything at all.

"Beau?"

"Wow. Okay. Well, tell Uncle Cyrus I'll get on that. Be careful tonight. I'll talk to you later."

"Okay. Bye." I hang up and look over at Lena. "I

think shit just got real for Beau."

"I think shit just got real for all of us," Kate says.

"So, you told Beau," Charly says with a smile.

"Yeah, we had a visit from Miss Louisa last night at his place, so I had to talk to him about it all earlier than I'd planned."

"Charly filled us in, Mal," Van says. "I hope that's okay."

"Well, we're here for a séance, so it's totally okay."

"Shall we get started?" Lena asks.

"Yes." I take a deep breath and let it out slowly, closing my eyes and opening my mind wide open. "Wow."

"Are you okay?" Lena asks aloud.

"Yes, I just haven't been this open in a long time," I whisper, letting my mind reach out through the house and the whole property. "There have been hundreds of people who lived here. Slaves." I scowl at the sight of someone being whipped, but then cared for immediately by who I assume is a family member.

"There are many spirits on this land," Lena says, her grip on me tightening.

"Yes, but they're not in distress," I reply in relief. "I don't sense any evil here."

"I agree," Lena says and we both open our eyes to the others. "We're safe."

"Your eyes are so dilated," Kate whispers.

"Because our minds are open," I reply and look at the man standing behind Gabby. "There's a man named Cyrus here."

"So you weren't bullshitting Beau," Van says.

"No." I smile at Cyrus, who smiles back. He's tall, with dark hair and eyes, and he's wearing clothes from at least a hundred years ago. "Do you know him?"

"He was one of our great grandfather's brothers." Charly looks at Van and then back to me. "And Beau has his grandfather clock."

Cyrus winks at me. "Well, that I knew. Do you want me to say anything else to them?"

He shakes his head, tips his head to me, and disappears.

"Let's hope they're all as gentlemanly as Cyrus," Lena says softly.

"There's only one other who's coming forward," I reply and close my eyes again. "I can't see her, but I can feel her."

The room is quiet as I clear my mind, opening myself up to a young woman, only in her teens. "She's young."

I like it here. Please don't make me leave.

"She says she doesn't want to leave. She likes it here."

"I don't mind if she stays," Gabby says with a smile. "I'm just curious about who she is."

I close my eyes again, listening.

Larissa.

"She says her name is Larissa."

I don't know why I'm here. I've been here a long time.

I frown and silently ask her, *do you know that you're no longer alive?*

"What is she saying?" Gabby asks.

"That she doesn't know why she's here."

Yes. I died on a cliff.

"She never lived here when she was alive," I say and squeeze Lena's hand. I'm okay, I just like feeling her. "She says she died on a cliff."

"Holy shit," Van says. "Is she the French girl who was ripped from her slave lover?"

Yes.

"She says yes."

"Holy fucking shit," Gabby says.

Are you trying to transition? I ask her.

I just want to stay here until Douglas can find me.

"Poor girl," Lena says. "She says that she wants to stay here until he finds her."

"Oh, how sad," Kate says.

I'm so sorry. I don't know how to find him for you. I can help you move on though, Larissa.

Maybe he's there? she asks.

Maybe. I don't know for sure.

"She's asking Mal if Douglas might be waiting for her in the next life," Lena says. "She's quite sad."

"I don't know where he is," I say aloud, "but I can help you move on, Larissa. You don't have to stay here."

I won't leave without him.

And then she's gone. I can't sense her.

"What is she saying now?" Gabby asks.

"She's gone." I let out a long sigh and open my eyes. "She said she doesn't want to leave without him, and she's not talking to me any more."

"Poor girl," Van says. "She said her love's name is Douglas?"

"Yes."

Gabby's tapping her chin thoughtfully. "I have all of the slave records. If he was sold to our family, I can look for a boy named Douglas. He would have also been a teenager, or just a little older."

"That would be great," I reply, but I'm exhausted. "Maybe you could look for that, and we can try again another time."

"Are you okay?" Charly asks.

"I'm fine, just tired."

"You should stop," Lena says.

"Yeah, I'm done." I close my eyes, ready to close all of the doors, when I suddenly feel something...*different.*

Lena's hand tightens on mine.

"What the hell?"

I can't answer her. It's a being, but it's not a spirit.

This person isn't dead.

CHAPTER EIGHT

~Beau~

"Yellow stripe in the corner pocket," Eli says as he leans over Ben's pool table and taps the ball in the hole.

While the girls are having their séance, Eli and I decided to hang out at Ben's house, raid his beer fridge, and kick his ass at pool.

"What's new?" Ben asks and sips his beer.

"Beau's been bouncing on the psychic chick," Eli replies and taps another ball into the pocket.

"How old are you?" I ask him, scowling.

"Well, you have been."

"I've been *seeing* Mallory," I reply.

"I'd already heard," Ben says and claps me on the shoulder. "She's pretty hot."

"Don't make me kick your ass." I narrow my eyes at him, but Ben just smirks.

"Right. 'Cause that could happen."

"How did you already know? I've barely been on two dates with her."

"News spreads quickly in the Boudreaux family," he says with a shrug. Ben's last name may not be Boudreaux, but he's been a part of our family since middle school. One of Eli and my best friends, Ben's always been around, and we were always welcome at his house too.

"By the way," Eli says, "you need to tell Mama."

"I need to tell Mama that I took a girl out on two dates? That hardly constitutes a proposal."

Eli holds up his hands. "All I'm saying is, the girls have been talking, and we all know that they're talking to Mama too. So you might want to talk to her yourself before she's convinced herself that the proposal is just around the corner."

"You know, the bad thing about big families is they can't keep their noses out of your fucking business."

"We love you too," Eli says with a wink. "I have to say, I was surprised that you're interested in Mallory. I didn't know you were into all that hocus pocus phooey stuff."

I cock a brow. "She doesn't cackle while stirring a cauldron at midnight," I reply dryly. "And she's not a witch. She says she's psychic. Which I didn't think I believed in either."

"But you've changed your mind?" Ben asks.

"I don't *understand* it," I reply, choosing my words carefully. I know they want to rib me; they're my brothers, and that's just what we do. But they also care about me. This isn't an interrogation, it's a conversation to make sure I know what I'm getting myself into.

But does anyone understand what they're getting themselves into when they start a new relationship?

"How could she know about the grandfather clock?" I ask.

"Maybe one of the girls told her?" Eli suggests.

"I don't think so. It was an off the cuff comment," I

reply. "So, no, I don't fully understand it, but I believe that *she* believes it, and she's not crazy."

"I totally believe it," Ben says casually.

"Really?"

He looks at both of us like *we're* nuts.

"Don't you know who her grandmother was? Her last name is Adams."

Eli and I look at each other and then back to Ben. "So?"

"Olivia Adams was a super famous psychic. She helped find dozens of missing kids. My mom was obsessed with that stuff. Hell, she still is."

"I don't remember her," I reply, shaking my head.

"Well, even so, we live in New Orleans. There's some crazy stuff that happens in this town."

"Regardless of all of that," I say, interrupting him, "I like her. *Her.* Mallory, the woman. She's sexy and smart. She's a good businesswoman. Being psychic is something she does, but it's not who she is."

"I get it," Eli says with a nod. "I just wonder, is it weird that she reads your mind all the time?"

"She doesn't," I reply, getting tired of this conversation. "She says that I'm the one person she *can't* read, and I think we both prefer it that way. Now, are you going to play pool or keep asking me about a woman that I've just started dating?"

"Both," Eli says with a grin.

"Hey, I think it's great," Ben says, his face totally sober. "If you like her, you should spend as much time with her as possible."

Fuck.

"Ben, Savannah's single. You know we wouldn't mind in the least if you—"

"We're not talking about me," he says. "Just spend time with your girl. Now, let's play some fucking pool."

***

I haven't seen her since yesterday morning when we both went to work. I wanted to go to her place after she got home from the séance last night, but she called and said she was tired and headed to bed.

She sounded out of it, and I didn't argue. For Christ's sake, I'm acting like I can't live without her, and I still barely know her.

But I'm drawn to her. I can't deny it.

So, on my way to work, I stop into Bayou Botanicals to say good morning and make sure she's okay after last night.

I walk in and smile at her employee, Shelly.

"Hi, Mr. Boudreaux," she says in greeting.

"Good morning. Is Mallory in her office?"

"No, I'm sorry, she's not in today."

I stop short and frown. "Is this her usual day off?"

"No, she called and asked me to cover for her today. She's out ill."

I want to ask a hundred questions that I'm sure she won't know the answer to, so I simply don't and thank her, then leave the shop and immediately dial Mal's number.

She doesn't answer.

"Good morning, it's Beau. Shelly said you're out sick, so I wanted to call to see if you need anything. Just let me know if you do. Feel better, sugar."

I hang up and head for the office, but then decide to go see her myself. I don't have any meetings today, which is rare.

I pull into her driveway and ring the doorbell.

She doesn't answer.

I try calling again, and then curse myself a fool. She's probably asleep and I'm just disturbing her.

But I *need* to see her.

When one more ring of the doorbell goes unanswered, I turn to leave but the door opens.

"Beau?"

She looks…*exhausted.*

"Hi, sweetheart. Shelly said you were sick, so I came to check on you."

"Oh, that's nice." She smiles, but she can barely keep her eyes open. "I'm just so tired."

"I see that. Do you want me to stay?"

"No." She shakes her head and scratches her cheek. Her red hair is all over the place, as if she's been thrashing about in bed. Her half-open blue eyes are dull, and surrounded by dark circles.

She looks *horrible.*

"You should go," she says and reaches out to pat my chest. "Your muscles are ridiculous. I'm just going to sleep. That's boring."

I can't even bring myself to snicker over the muscles comment.

"Do you mind if I work from here today, while you sleep?"

She frowns, but it looks like she's going to fall asleep on her feet, so I scoop her up and carry her up the stairs.

"This is a weird dream," she says and lays her head on my chest. "But a nice one. I haven't dreamed of you before."

I kiss her temple and set her down on the edge of the bed. Her clothes are soaked through with sweat.

What the fuck is happening?

"Don't lie down, sweetness; we need to change your clothes."

"Too tired."

"I know." I quickly rummage through her drawer and find an old tank top and panties. "I never thought I'd be trying to get you dressed," I murmur and turn back to find that she's fallen back on the bed, her feet still on the floor, and she's snoring lightly.

Poor woman.

I manage to get the soaked clothes off of her, and get her into the fresh clothes, then tuck her into bed.

I'm not leaving her here alone all day. She's just too out of it. So, I run out to my car and gather my briefcase and the work I had with me that wouldn't fit in the briefcase, go back inside, and set up shop on her dining room table.

My phone rings in my pocket. "This is Beau."

"Hello, Mr. Boudreaux, this is Hillary."

"Yes, Hillary." Hillary has been my administrative assistant for five years, and knows what my schedule is every minute of the day.

"I was just going to remind you that you have a phone conference with Japan in fifteen minutes, sir."

"Thank you." *Shit.* I'd forgotten. "I'm not coming into the office today."

"I'm sorry, I don't think I heard you correctly."

I smile. "I won't be in today, Hillary. But I am working remotely. Please set the call up through my cell phone, and email me anything that I don't already have."

"Yes, sir."

No matter how many times I've told her over the years to call me Beau, she still calls me *sir* or *Mr. Boudreaux.*

And she's only three years older than me.

But I do appreciate her professionalism.

"Is everything okay, Mr. Boudreaux?"

"I understand that I'm a workaholic and that this is unusual, but I'm perfectly fine, Hillary. Thank you for asking. I trust you can handle things there, and I'm available all day. Just call or email if you need me. As if I was on a business trip."

"Of course, I'm sorry. You've just never called out before."

"Thank you."

I hang up and briefly check email and my notes on this phone call. If the contract goes through, this will be a three billion dollar deal for Bayou Enterprises. I hope we can wrap it up today, and that I don't have to go to Japan to do it in person. A month ago, it wouldn't have bothered me. But now, the thought of being on the other side of the world, away from Mallory, is unacceptable.

So, while the woman who has shifted everything else in my life out of focus recovers upstairs, I prepare to do what I do.

Work.

***

The call went well. There will be no trip to Japan in my immediate future, and a very lucrative agreement was cemented.

It's been a good morning.

There's also been no movement upstairs, so I take a break, fetch a fresh bottle of water, and go upstairs to check on Mal.

She's kicked all of the covers onto the floor, and she's

sweaty again. Her damp hair clings to her forehead and face, which is scrunched up as if she's in pain.

"Shh." I sit next to her and press my cool hands to her forehead, then hurry into the bathroom to get a clean, cool cloth to wipe her face off. Her face immediately relaxes and she sighs in relief.

"Thank you," she whispers without opening her eyes. "I missed you, Grandmamma."

She's dreaming. What in the hell is wrong with her? Does she have a virus? Should I take her to the doctor?

Despite the sweat, she doesn't seem to have a fever. I manage to barely wake her, enough to get her to take some sips of the cold water and switch her pillow, and then she falls back onto the clean pillow with a sigh.

I leave the room, and pull my phone out to call my mother—who else am I supposed to call?—when there's a knock on the door.

"Hi, Lena," I say when I open the door.

"Well, hello," she says in surprise. "I didn't realize you were here."

"I came by this morning after I'd been to the shop and Shelly said Mal had called out sick."

"She texted me to tell me," Lena says as she walks inside and looks up the stairs toward Mal's room. "Is she still sleeping?"

"Yeah, but I've never seen anything like—"

Suddenly Lena's eyes go wide with concern and she sprints toward the stairs. "Oh my God."

"What's wrong?" I run behind her and we both come to an abrupt halt at the doorway. Mal is writhing on the bed, as if she's in pain. She's making high-pitched mewling sounds, and crying, "Stop. Please stop!"

"It's okay," Lena says and takes her hand, then falls to

her knees. "We didn't know this would happen."

"*What* is happening?"

Lena looks up with sad eyes. "Mallory is a powerful empath and medium. Most people think a séance is a game, but for a powerful psychic, it's not a game at all. It's why she took me with her, so I could be her anchor.

"There wasn't anything dangerous there," she says, but then frowns, as if she's remembering something, but she keeps talking. "She did great, talking to the dead, and relaying the messages to the girls. But it takes *so much* out of her, and not only is she exhausted, but she'll dream about those spirits, and experience things they experienced in life."

"You're kidding."

"This isn't fucking funny," she replies, her eyes hot now.

"No, it isn't." Mal's head is still thrashing back and forth, so I reach down and brush my knuckles down her cheek. She immediately settles down, letting out a soft sigh.

"Well." Lena's watching me, blinking rapidly.

"What?"

"Nothing. She should be okay by tomorrow. We didn't know how much it would affect her because she hasn't done anything like that since she was a kid. But now she knows, and she'll be well rested by the morning."

"What should I do for her?"

"Just what you're doing," she says with a smile and stands to leave the room. "It looks like she's in good hands."

"I don't like these nightmares," I reply as I follow Lena down the stairs.

"I'm sure they're not fun for her either. But they

won't last. Thanks for staying with her."

"There's nowhere else I'd rather be."

She waves, and then she's gone, and I can't help myself from climbing the stairs again to watch Mallory sleep.

Her breathing is soft and even now, and she's sleeping peacefully, so I run downstairs to fetch the laptop and my phone. I'm going to work in Mallory's room for the rest of the evening. Her nightmares are scaring *me*.

When I return to her room, she's rolled over to her side and kicked one leg out of the covers, showing me her perfectly round ass, barely covered by red cotton. I lean on the doorjamb, watching her. I want to kiss her there.

I want to kiss her everywhere.

But even more than that, I want to protect her, and that's surprising to me. I am a protector, always looking out for my siblings and my mother, but I didn't know that I could feel so deeply for someone that I've only just met.

Yet, the thought of anything happening to her makes my heart jump in fear. She's come to mean a lot to me in just a few short weeks. She makes me happy.

She makes me happy.

When was the last time I could say that? When was the last time something or someone besides work and my family fulfilled me in any way?

I don't remember.

Mallory whimpers, throwing herself onto her back again, struggling to grab onto something.

I cross to her, put my electronics aside, and climb onto the bed next to her so I can brush her hair off of her face, then take her hand in mine and kiss her knuckles.

"It's okay, baby."

She immediately calms, falling back into a dreamless

sleep, and I'm reminded of what she said the other day. She can't read me, and when I touch her, she calms down.

Well, that certainly seems to be true right now.

I literally calm her. What an honor that is.

I kiss her temple and whisper, "I'm right here, Mallory. There's no need to be afraid. Just sleep."

And with her hand still in mine, I open my laptop and struggle through one-handed typing. The emails may take longer to compose, but Mallory is at peace this way, so there's no way I'm letting her go.

I don't ever want to let her go.

After an hour, and only three emails, I close the computer and set it aside, then release her hand so I can use the restroom and order some food. When I return, Mallory is still sleeping peacefully, just where I left her.

I hope the nightmares are gone for a long, long while.

Chapter Nine

~Mallory~

I'm thirsty, and I have to pee, *right now.*

I throw the covers aside, and without opening my eyes more than slits, walk into the bathroom and sit on the toilet.

When I'm done, I wash my hands and ladle some water from the tap into my mouth, dry off, and march back to bed.

And see Beau, sitting on the bed, watching me with an amused smile.

I stop short and stare at him for several seconds.

"Am I still dreaming?"

"If you are, I am too," he says. "How are you?"

"Thirsty," I reply and climb back into bed, frowning as I realize what I'm wearing. "I don't remember putting this on."

"That's because you were conked out when I put it on you."

I sigh and don't argue at all when he urges me to lay my head on his leg. He pushes his fingers through my hair, and I smile, remembering the dreams I had of him.

At least, I think they were dreams.

"Did you come to the door today?" I ask.

"Yes."

"And were you here, saying nice things and sweeping my hair off of my face?"

"That was also me," he replies.

"And Lena was here too."

"Yes."

"I thought I'd dreamed it all. What time is it?"

"It's about midnight."

I sit up and stare at him in the moonlight, open-mouthed. "Midnight on Wednesday?"

"You slept all day, Mal."

"Damn, I lost a whole day." I shake my head, relieved that it's finally clearing.

"Have some water." He hands me a cold bottle of water and I greedily drink half of the bottle down. "How do you feel?"

"Better," I reply and pass the bottle back to him. "It was a weird sleep."

"Tell me about it. I've never seen anyone have nightmares like that."

And just like that, it comes flooding back to me. Being whipped, raped, thrown off of a cliff. Grandmamma's voice, but not being able to see her.

"Oh, I'm glad that's over," I mumble and bury my face in Beau's thigh.

"What happened, exactly?" He asks quietly, still brushing his fingers through my hair.

"Well, I guess the séance, and having so many active spirits around me, opening myself up so completely, took a toll on me. I've never done it like that before. I was too young before, so I always observed. I'm glad I thought to invite Lena so she could be an anchor."

"Do you plan to do this often?" he asks, his voice deceptively calm.

"No," I reply and pull his hand to my lips so I can kiss his palm. "I don't plan to do it often at all. I didn't like the way it made me feel, and I think I opened myself up too widely. It could have been dangerous."

And there was someone else there at the end, and I still don't know who, but they weren't friendly.

They were scary. Dangerous.

Not that I'm going to tell Beau that.

I really don't want to talk about psychics or spirits or any of that anymore. I've talked about it more in the past three days than I have in the past ten years combined.

And I'm sick of it.

"How was your day?" I ask.

"It was fine." He shifts, urging me onto my back so he can look down at me. "Why do you ask?"

"Because I want to stop talking about me and talk about you. What did you do today?"

He tips his head to the side, as if he's trying to figure me out, but then he starts talking. Lord Jesus, how I love the sound of this man's voice. It's deep, and his New Orleans drawl is laced through it beautifully.

I hardly notice the drawl, given that I have one of my own and I've lived here forever, but in Beau's case, you can't *not* recognize it. It's as sexy as the rest of him.

"I was here, at your place, and I did some work. Lena stopped by to check on you."

"What kind of work did you do?" I ask, keeping the subject on him.

"I spoke with a high ranking official in Japan who is interested in having Bayou Enterprises build him several yachts for his private fleet, and then I looked over some staffing issues in the yard."

"In my yard?" I ask around a wide yawn.

"No," he says with a smile and leans down to kiss my cheek. "At the shipyard, where the boats are built."

"I've never been on a boat." Beau's eyes widen. "Does that surprise you?"

"You lived in the bayou."

"And didn't need to be on a boat to avoid the critters." I smile and cup his cheek. I love touching him.

"Well, I think we should get you on your first boat."

"In the bayou? Like, on one of those swamp tours?"

He laughs, and it flows over me like a salve, healing the remnants of the nightmares.

"I was thinking of something a bit more…well, substantial."

"Bigger?"

"Yes."

I smile up at him. "Okay, you choose the boat and I'll go on it."

"You're very easygoing," he remarks as he drags his fingertips up and down my arm, giving me goosebumps.

"Not always." I shrug. "But I trust you."

Please don't make me regret trusting you.

"Thank you." He kisses my hand. "Now, what can we do for you? Shower?"

"I have been sweating." My clothes are sticky, and I don't smell fantastic. "Give me fifteen minutes?"

"Take as long as you need," he says and returns to his laptop. "I'm finishing up some business."

I nod and walk to the bathroom, stripping out of my clothes on the way, unfazed by Beau being here to watch me. He's seen me naked. I have nothing to hide from him now.

But I toss a sassy look over my shoulder, and he's watching me avidly.

Which does amazing things for my ego.

I turn on the shower and gather a towel, washrag, and some clean pajamas, then step into the hot water and sigh in happiness. It feels damn good to wash away the rest of the bad dreams.

Someone else's bad memories.

I let the hot water hit my back for a few extra moments after I've finished washing myself, then turn it off and go to grab my towel, but it's missing.

"Beau?" I call out, just as he walks through the doorway, holding my towel.

"Sorry, I tried to be quick." He holds the towel out and I walk into it, feeling the heat coming off it as he wraps it around me. "I put it in the dryer so it would be warm for you."

"Are you human?" I ask and let him pat me down. When I'm dry, he wraps his arms around me, and gives me the best, strongest hug I've had in years.

"Flesh and bone," he replies softly. "Did that help?"

"The shower or you?"

"Both."

"Yes," I smile up at him. He's so much taller than me, and when he holds me like this, he makes me feel *safe*.

And very turned on. I'm surprised I have enough energy to feel this turned on, but Beau's sexy as fuck body is pressed against mine, and well, I'm a red-blooded woman, after all.

"What are you thinking?" he asks as his hands glide down my back to my ass.

"You feel good."

I can feel him smile against the top of my head.

"Do you want to watch TV?" he asks. I shake my head no. "Do you want to talk some more?" Again, I shake my head no. "Hmm."

"What ever shall we do?" I ask and bat my eyelashes up at him, enjoying this little flirty moment, and suddenly I'm in his arms. He's carrying me back to the bed, Rhett Butler style.

"I have an idea," he says with a sexy grin.

"You do?"

"Oh yeah."

"A card game?" I ask and giggle when he drops me onto the bed, my towel falling off, leaving me stark-ass naked.

"Not much of a gambler," he says, his eyes raking over me as if he's starving and I'm his favorite entrée.

"Hmm, would you like to—"

"Why don't I just show you what I want?"

"I'm really a show-don't-tell kind of girl," I reply and gasp when he grabs my ankle and yanks me to the edge of the bed, my ass almost hanging off the side. He sinks to his knees, presses my thighs open wide, and lays wet kisses on the sensitive skin that leads to my core, licking and nibbling all the way, until he can circle my clit with his tongue.

"Holy shit," I groan and collapse back, my hips arching, searching for more of his mouth. He shifts his hands to my hips, and he holds on as I go crazy, grinding myself on his face, soaking in every quiver, every amazing feeling that he's giving me.

So this is what all the fuss is about!

He licks down to my lips, and then he groans as he kisses me intimately, making me come apart at the seams, thrashing about like a wild woman, unable to control myself.

I'm still quivering when he kisses his way up my stomach, between my breasts and up my neck. Finally, he kisses me on the mouth and I can taste myself there, which only turns me on more.

"You're amazing," he whispers against my mouth.

"Let me return the favor."

"Oh no," he says, shaking his head slowly side to side. "Tonight is all about you."

"Okay, *I* want you to let me return the favor."

He chuckles. "Sorry, sugar, but that's one wish I can't grant. I'm taking care of *you.* We have plenty of time ahead of us for you to do me any favors you like. But not tonight."

Where did this guy come from? He's true to his word. Now that I've had the most amazing orgasm of my life, he lathers me up with my favorite lotion, helps me into my usual sleep attire of a clean tank top and panties, then undresses himself and slips into bed with me.

He pulls me against him and kisses my head. "Are you tired?"

"I shouldn't be," I reply. "I slept for about twenty-four hours. But yeah, you wore me out."

"Better me than anything else," he says with a smile and reaches over to turn off the side light. "Sleep, Mallory. I'm right here."

"Okay." I take a deep breath, reveling in his arms wrapped securely around me, and I know that I won't dream at all tonight.

And I have Beau to thank for that.

***

We've spent the better part of the past week together. Whenever we weren't at work, we've been at either my place or his, always spending the night at mine. I should offer him some closet and drawer space at my house, but I don't want to jinx it.

I'm falling in love with this man. I'm nowhere close to being ready to tell *him* that, but I feel it. He knows all about me, and he accepts it all. Not to mention, he's amazing in bed, and he makes me laugh like crazy.

It's Monday, my first full day off since my snooze fest last week. Beau has decided to start taking Mondays off as well, and I have a feeling his family and colleagues are all completely flummoxed by this new development.

Beau is a self-proclaimed workaholic. But maybe it's doing him good to keep a more normal schedule, and to spend time with me.

I hope that's the case because I love all of the time he gives me. I don't take one minute of it for granted.

"Wow, they've come a long way." We pull up to Beau's new house, and I'm stunned to see that the outside has all been painted, making it look like he could move in at any moment.

"Yes, there has been a lot of progress this week. It's funny because it goes in spurts." We both exit the car, and instead of leading me into the house, he takes my hand and guides me around to the back of the house. "Some weeks it feels like nothing changes, and then others, *BOOM!* Everything changes and it feels like it's almost done."

"It looks fantastic. I like the soft butter yellow color you chose for the outside."

"Thanks." He flashes me his sexy grin. "Now, I need your input on something back here."

"Okay. What's up?"

"Where should I plant the rose garden and the herb and vegetable garden?"

I stare at him like he's just asked me to explain the Pythagorean theorem.

"Excuse me?"

He takes my hand and leads me farther into the backyard.

"I have landscapers coming tomorrow, and I need to finalize where I want my gardens to go. What do you think?"

"I'm not sure why you're asking me. I kill everything, Beau."

He stops and stares back at me. "Everything?"

"Well, if it has roots, it probably isn't going to survive if I'm around. I forget to water and feed everything, including myself sometimes."

"But you sell herbs in your *botanical* shop."

"Yes, and I buy them from someone else who has grown them." I shake my head and laugh, wandering around the yard, that at this moment is just brown dirt and weeds. "Besides, aren't you going to hire a gardener?"

"No. I'll hire groundskeepers to come mow and keep the grass looking good, but I plan to tend to the gardens myself."

"I thought billionaires hired people to do this stuff."

He smirks. "And I thought botanical shop owners grew their own botanicals."

"Touché." I laugh again, and then trip in a hole, falling on my ass. "That's gonna leave a mark."

"Are you okay?"

"Oh yeah, I just—"

Before I can say more, he falls on top of me, pinning

me to the ground, and kisses me in that way he does that makes my knees weak and my heart beat faster.

It's a good thing I'm already on the ground.

"You never stop surprising me, Mallory."

"That's the plan," I reply with a wink. "I have to keep you on your toes."

"It's working," he replies and helps me stand. "Okay, so I'm going to be the green thumb in this relationship. I can live with that. But at least show me where you think we should put the gardens."

I look around, not having the slightest clue what should go where.

"Why do you want my opinion?"

"Because if I get my way, and I usually do, you'll be spending some time here with me. And I value your opinion."

And there he goes, being all sweet and wonderful again.

How is this man single?

Women are clearly dumb.

"Okay, I think the herbs and veggies should be closer to the house because you might want to run out to clip some oregano, or grab a cucumber for the salad and whatnot."

"Smart," he says, nodding. "I like it. Okay, vegetable garden should be over here." He's gesturing with his hands, his whiskey eyes lit up with excitement.

He loves this home.

And that makes me happy for him.

"Now, roses need to be in the sunshine," he says and wanders away from me toward the middle of the yard. "This is really the most well-lit part of the property. I'm thinking six feet by eight feet."

"How many bushes are you planting?" I ask, getting into the spirit of things.

"Six. That's always been a good number for my family."

"That will give them plenty of room to establish their roots and grow."

He smiles at me like he just couldn't be more proud. "And you claim to not be a flower person."

"I like flowers," I clarify. "I just can't be trusted to grow them."

"We'll see about that," he says. "If you wouldn't hate it, you can help me, and I can teach you. It's really easier than you think."

"I wouldn't hate it."

He picks up a shovel and begins to dig, just a little bit, as if he's outlining the area for the roses. During the third time of shoving the shovel into the dirt, he unearths a bone. His gaze whips to mine.

"I sure hope this is someone's beloved pet, and not their beloved family member."

I've kept my shields up since the night of the séance, and I've been doing a good job of blocking any unwanted feelings and emotions. But I crack the door, just for a moment, concentrating on the bone.

"It's a dog," I reply and slam the door shut again. "Not human."

His eyes squint as he watches me for a moment. "You okay?"

"Yes." I nod. "I'm great, actually. And you don't have to have the county shut down your construction while they investigate those bones."

"Thank God," he says and walks to me. "You're handy to have around."

"Well, I'm so happy that you think so." He's advancing quickly, mischief written all over his handsome face, and I begin to walk backward away from him. "What are you planning to do?"

"Whatever do you mean?"

"You're not fooling me. You're going to—"

And before I can say or do anything, he's smearing his dirty hands down my cheeks and laughing like a kid.

"Got you."

"This dirt touched a decomposing dog," I remind him and wipe my cheek on my sleeve.

"Well, that's not a good way to think of it."

"Is there a good way to think about dirt being all over my face?" I demand.

"Well, it could be worse. It could be mud."

"You're going to pay for this."

"Oh, sugar, I hope so. I truly hope so."

Chapter Ten

-Mallory-

"I think we need to talk about this," Lena says a few days later as we sit in my living room and eat ice cream, waiting for our favorite show to come on.

"I don't see what there is to talk about," I reply and squirt more whipped cream into my bowl. A girl can never have too much whipped cream.

"Seriously?" She lowers her spoon and stares at me like I've lost my mind. "I think we need to talk about *everything.*"

"I think you're being dramatic," I reply and wither just a bit under her ice-cold glare. "Right, because you're never dramatic?"

"I'm not being dramatic about this. My Nana wouldn't say so either, and I know damn well that if Miss Olivia was alive, she'd think it was a big deal."

"Well, she's not alive." And oh, how that still hurts!

"You're a stubborn ass," she says, as if that's going to hurt my feelings in the least.

Because it doesn't.

"Look, I've been fine since the séance, Lena. Sure, it wiped me out for about twenty-four hours, but I'm fine now. No weird things have been happening."

"Weird as in a living person breaking into your

thoughts the way they did that night? Because that wasn't normal, Mal. I've only ever heard of that happening with your grandmother, and you know it."

"It's never happened before."

"That doesn't mean it won't happen again."

"What do you want me to do?" I stand and pace my living room. "I've got everything locked down as tight as I possibly can, and you know that I've never been able to lock it down completely. But I'm not seeing anything right now. I haven't even seen Miss Louisa at the shop, although I think she's still mad at me from that night at Beau's."

"Do you hear yourself? The spirit is mad at you."

"It happens." I shrug as if it's no big deal and keep pacing. "I'm barely picking up on emotions too."

"You can't keep it all under lock and key forever. You'll let your guard down eventually."

"So what? I let my guard down all the time, Lena. Nothing like that has happened before. You're the only one who's freaking out about it."

"Somebody has to," she says. "It wasn't just that the person is living and knew how to get into your head. He, or she because I couldn't tell what it was, wasn't friendly. It was...*evil*, for lack of a better word."

"I know." I sigh and sit back down, returning to my ice cream. "But I honestly haven't sensed anything like it since then. It could have been someone in a neighboring property, or who knows? But I can't dwell on it. If I sat around and dwelled on all the weird shit that happens in my head, I'd be in a hospital by now."

"True. Because you *are* weird. You don't like chocolate ice cream."

I laugh. "Yeah, that's cause for being institutionalized right there."

Suddenly, my phone rings. I check the number, but I don't recognize it.

"New York?"

Lena shrugs and I answer.

"Hello?"

"Is this Mallory Adams?"

"Yes."

"My name is Debbie Williams, and I'm calling because I used to work with your grandmother."

"I can stop you right there," I reply, shaking my head.

"Please," she says, desperation in her voice. "Please just hear me out before you hang up."

I put the phone on speaker, gesturing for Lena to listen as well.

"Go ahead," I say.

"I sent you an email a couple of weeks ago, but I didn't hear back from you, so I thought I'd call to at least speak with you one-on-one.

"I'm a lieutenant with the New York Police Department. I was a detective when I worked with your grandmother. I'm in homicide and missing persons."

"I remember hearing your name," I reply. My grandmother admired Detective Williams, and enjoyed working with her. "But I can't help you."

"I think you can," she replies immediately. "There have been a string of young girls going missing, all about a month apart, all thirteen years old. At first, we assumed that they were runaways, but they all have too many similarities to think that it's anything other than abduction, and by the same person."

"I'm so sorry," I reply, holding Lena's gaze. "I really am. My heart aches for their families. But I'm not gifted like my grandmother was, Lieutenant. It's not that I don't want to help you; I don't have the experience or capabilities to help you. But I do know others who can, and I'm happy to send you their contact information."

She quiet for a moment, and I think I've lost her.

"Ma'am?"

"I heard you," she says, her voice heavy with disappointment. "I have other resources. If you change your mind, please call me. Thank you for your time."

She hangs up, and I just sit and stare at Lena for a long moment.

"I don't want it," I finally say softly. "I've never wanted it, Lena. And I can't help her the way Grandmamma could."

"I know," she replies and covers my hand with hers, squeezing it. "You haven't nurtured your skills in over a decade. I was shocked that you agreed to the séance last week."

"I was too," I murmur. "And look at what it did to me. I don't want to live my life like that. There are plenty of psychics out there who are qualified to help her. I'm *not* one of them."

"Okay." She nods vigorously. "You're right. It's completely your decision, and if you're not comfortable with it, then you should not do it."

"Thank you." A tear slips down my cheek, surprising me.

"What is it?" she asks.

"I feel guilty," I reply. "Like I'm being selfish."

"You don't have the skills." She shrugs again and offers me a small smile. "There's nothing you can do about that. And even if you *did*, it wouldn't be selfish to choose to not help. You have the right to do what you think is best for you."

"I do," I agree. "What Grandmamma did wasn't safe."

"I know."

"I just want to enjoy this new relationship with Beau, and run my store, and love my friends. That's all I've ever wanted."

"I know that, too, and you deserve that. We all do. You're not doing anything wrong. But what happened last week scared me. It was new."

"Are we circling back around to this?"

"Yes, because I want your word that if *anything* like that happens again, you'll call me and we will take it to my Nana."

"Okay." I nod reluctantly. "If it happens again, we will talk to her about it. But in the meantime, let it go. Please."

"Fine." She scowls at her bowl. "My ice cream is all gone."

"Well, then let's get some more."

***

"This is pretty." I hold up a scarf that I've found in one of the shops in the Quarter. Beau and I are wandering around on this sunny fall evening, ducking in and out of stores, galleries, and just spending time together.

"The blue would look pretty on you." He takes it from me and wraps it around my wrists, shielding me with his body so no one can see what he's doing. He leans in and whispers, "See? It's lovely against your skin."

He cocks a brow, and all I can do is lick my lips and think about all the ways he could use this scarf on me when we're both naked. A slow smile spreads over his wicked mouth and he walks over to the cashier and buys the scarf, then takes my hand and leads me out onto the sidewalk.

"Thank you."

"Oh, I think this is for both of us," he says, New Orleans hanging heavily in his voice. I'm pretty much perma-turned on when I'm around him. The chemistry between us is simply off the charts.

Halle-freaking-luia!

As we walk, Beau is quick to shield me from anyone who might accidently brush against me, or guide me around areas that he thinks are dangerous. It's sweet, but I also just want him to treat me the way he would any other woman.

Finally, when he pulls me out of the way of a family walking past us, I pull us around the corner, where there's less traffic, and stop him.

"What are you doing?"

He frowns and looks around, as if he's looking for the person I'm *actually* talking to.

"Yes, you. What's going on in your head?"

"I'm walking through the Quarter with you."

"Beau, I'm not fragile. You don't have to constantly make sure that no one touches me. I understand why you feel this way, but it's not necessary."

"I want you to be comfortable. I want you to have a nice evening without all of the other stuff."

"Thank you for that." Not wanting to sound ungrateful, I reach up to brush my fingertips down his cheek. "Thank you *so much.* But I'm okay." I smile widely. "I'm having a great time. You don't have to protect me against any of those people. Just treat me the way you would any woman. I seem to be getting better at shielding myself lately."

He frowns and cups my face in his hands, the carefree man gone, replaced by this serious one, and I'm sorry that I said anything at all.

"I can't do that, Mallory. If I treat you the way I do other women, I wouldn't be with you right now." He shakes his head. "I wouldn't take the time to get to know you. Not because you're not beautiful and smart, but because my priority is my career and my family. So, we would enjoy a mutually satisfying evening in bed, and then I probably wouldn't call you again."

Whoa. Talk about swoon!

"Why am I different?"

"That's the million dollar question," he replies. "And the answer is way more complicated and personal than what can be discussed in this public place. But I will say this, you *are* different, and I'm different with you. I'm not going to stop seeing you."

"Well, that's good." I smile, not regretting this conversation now in the least, and boost myself up on my tiptoes to kiss his lips. He wraps his arms around me and hugs me close while he extends the kiss, then lets me slowly slide down his body.

I wish we were somewhere private, and that we were both naked.

But that's just going to have to wait.

He pulls away and takes my hand again, leading me back in the direction we were headed before: to Café du Monde.

I've been craving beignets all day.

We grab a seat under the green and white awning, and place our order of two plates of the delicious sugary doughnuts and frozen coffees, then I pull my new scarf out of the bag and wrap it around my neck with a sassy wink at

Beau.

"I had no idea you were a scarf fan."

He smirks, rubbing his fingers over his lips and watching me fuss with the blue fabric. It's soft and feels good against my skin.

Finally, he leans over and presses his lips to my ear. "I'm going to take you back to your place this evening, strip you naked, and tie your hands with this scarf. Then I'm going to fuck you blind."

He leans back in his chair, a proud smile on his handsome face, and I surprise us both by saying, "Promises, promises."

He busts out laughing just as our drinks and beignets are delivered, and I take a bite of the piping hot pastry, then sigh in absolute delight.

"These are the most delicious things on the earth."

"They're close," he says.

"What's better than this?" I take a sip of my frozen coffee before taking another bite. He doesn't reply, he just cocks a brow, and I know he's talking about *me.* "You're on a roll today."

"I haven't had you in three days," he replies, deceptively calmly, and meets my gaze with his. "Which is exactly three days too long."

"And what are you going to do about that?"

"I just told you."

I cock my head to the side, surprised.

"Oh, I wasn't kidding. That scarf has a very important job to do in roughly sixty minutes."

"Wow. That's a lot of pressure for a scarf."

He chuckles and offers me a bite of his last beignet, and I open my mouth, then suck his fingers as he pulls them away.

"We'd better change the subject before I take you on this table, sweetheart."

"Ew." I wrinkle my nose. "I don't think they wipe these tables down very well. That's just not sanitary."

He busts out laughing. "You're probably right. Well, I have something else to talk about anyway."

"Okay, shoot."

"I have to go to Miami on Thursday."

"Thursday as in two days from now Thursday?"

"That's the one."

"Wow, that's short notice."

"It happens a lot," he replies and wipes his mouth with a napkin.

"That must cost you a fortune in airline tickets," I say, immediately overthinking it the way I always do.

"We have a company jet," he replies with a smile. "I can travel pretty much anywhere on the planet at the snap of my fingers."

"Of course." *I'm a moron.* He may be just a normal man with me, but Beau Boudreaux is filthy rich and a powerful man in our community. Of course he has a private jet.

"I want you to go with me," he says, completely stunning me.

"Excuse me?"

"I'd like for you to join me in Miami, and once my business is finished Thursday afternoon, we'll spend the weekend there. Or, near there."

I blink at him for several moments.

"You want me to leave in two days."

"Yes." He takes a sip of his coffee, as if he just asked me to go to the movies with him.

"I have a business to run," I remind him, already

trying to figure out how I can make it work.

"When was the last time you took a vacation?"

"I was twenty-two." I smile, remembering the trip Lena and I took right after college. "Lena and I went to Paris. It was Miss Sophia's gift to us for graduating from college."

"Well, I'd say you're overdue then," he says. "We'll be back by Monday evening."

"I guess I can ask Shelly to cover for the weekend, and Lena can help her too."

"Is that a yes?"

I smile and nod, not bothering to cover my excitement. "As long as Shelly isn't sick or dead, yes."

"I will fervently pray for Shelly's well-being," he says. "Now, let's get back to your place. I have plans for you and that scarf."

I laugh, slipping my hand into his as we walk back to the shop, and to my car.

"What should I pack for this weekend?"

"It's hot in Florida."

"That doesn't help me. Will there be swimming?"

"Probably."

"Will we be going out to dinner?"

"Definitely."

"What else will we be doing?"

He thinks about this for a moment. "Boating, sitting on the beach, shopping. Pretty much anything you want to do."

"Oh, the beach!"

"I guess the beach is high on our priority list."

"I love the beach," I reply. "I need to go shopping tomorrow for a new bathing suit."

"Now we're talking."

I snort, and he scowls down playfully. "What? I love your body."

"And only you know why."

"Remind me later that we need to work on your self-esteem."

"No, we don't. I'm not shy around you. You're attracted me, that's obvious. And I'm happy that you are. But I'm a woman, so I see the flaws."

"You're a human being, sugar. We all have flaws."

"You don't. At least, not physical ones."

He shakes his head and chuckles. "I'm happy you think so. But my arms could use some more definition."

"I like your arms."

"See? We're attracted to each other. No need to question it. I say we just enjoy it."

"Good plan." He's a smart man.

***

The drive home has taken *forever.* We took his car, leaving mine at the shop, because Beau will spend the night, and he'll just give me a ride to work in the morning. He hasn't stopped touching me. He's dragged his fingers up and down my thigh, held my hand, then returned to my thigh.

I'm so hot and bothered, I could fry an egg on my chest.

I have the scarf in my fist, holding on with a death grip, excited to see what he has in store for us.

Sex with Beau is never boring.

Finally, we pull into my driveway, and he leads me calmly to the front door, waits patiently as I unlock it and walk inside, and the next thing I know, the door is shut and I'm pinned against it, my arms above my head, and Beau's face pressed to my neck, kissing and biting me like a man starved.

"You smell so fucking good," he growls against my ear, sending shivers down my entire body. "You look at me and I'm hard. You smile at me and I want to do exactly this to you, no matter where the fuck we are."

He pulls us away from the door and up the stairs to my bedroom, strips me naked in a flash of flying colors, then grabs the blue scarf, and with lust in his eyes, he slowly urges me back to the bed.

"Not yet," he says as I move to lie down. "I'll tell you when I'm ready for that."

I cock a brow. "You're very bossy today."

"I'm bossy every day, Mallory." He chuckles and steps back so he can admire me from head to toe. My nipples pucker under his scrutiny, so he reaches out and brushes the soft material over them, making me gasp and bite my lip. "You're—"

"I'm?"

He just shakes his head and lets out a long, deep sigh. "You're everything."

He steps to me and drags the knuckles of both hands down my chest from collarbone to nipples, then he turns me away from him and pulls the scarf up over my eyes.

"This is what we're going to do tonight," he whispers against my ear as he ties the scarf. He gently spins me back around and tips my chin up to tickle my lips with his, then guides me onto my back on the bed. "I want you to put your hands over your head."

I comply, frowning.

"Is there a problem?"

I love this take-charge bossy side of Beau.

"I like to touch you."

"I know." I can hear the smile in his voice, and suddenly he's sucking on my nipple, not touching me anywhere else. "But you don't get to touch me right now."

"Okay."

"I want you to tell me if I do anything that makes you uncomfortable."

I nod, not able to find my words.

"I need you to speak out loud, please."

"I hear you."

"Good."

And suddenly his lips are moving down from my nipple to my stomach, around my navel and even farther south, over my smooth pubis. He's not touching me with his hands at all, and I can't see him to know where his lips will be next. My entire body is on high alert, covered in goose bumps, and my pussy is wet, pulsing with anticipation.

Instead of moving down further to kiss me, his lips are on my hip, then my side, licking over my ribs.

"Holy shit," I mutter and squirm under him, unable to keep my hands over my head, I reach down to grip his hair in my fist, but he snatches them before I make contact and pins them above my head again. I can feel the length of him over me, his hard cock pressed to my center. "I want you."

"I'm right here," he replies before softly biting my chin. "Keep your arms where I put them."

"It's not easy."

"I know." His voice is softer now as he brushes a lock of hair off my cheek. "You have to trust me. Do you trust me, Mallory?"

"You know I do."

"I want to hear you say it."

"I trust you," I reply.

"Good. Lift your hips." I comply, and he slips a pillow under them, tilting my pelvis up. I'm sure he's going to start kissing me there, but instead I feel his fingers gently pet me, slipping through the wet lips, and then he's inside me, thrusting in and out at a hard pace. "You're so fucking tight."

"You're so fucking *hard*," I reply and clutch the bedsheets in my fists above my head so I don't try to reach out and touch him. This isn't going to last long, for either of us.

He pulls out, then flips me over, jerking my hips into the air and slips back inside me once more. His hands are firmly holding my hips, controlling the speed and the depth of his lovemaking. He slips his thumb down the crack of my ass and lays it lightly over my anus, barely touching me, but it's enough to send me into overdrive.

"Fuck," I groan.

"Too much?"

"No." I shake my head. "Don't stop."

Not only does he not stop, he picks up the pace, thrusting harder and harder, until all I can do is cry out with my climax, and smile as he also cries out, then kisses his way up my spine until he reaches my neck.

"We're not done."

"No?"

"No." He takes the blindfold off and collapses next to me, brushes my hair off my face, and I'm finally able to look around.

It's all a mess. My hair, the bed, my thoughts.

Life.

It's a wonderful, glorious mess.

Chapter Eleven

~Mallory~

The blue scarf is tied around my head, holding my hair back from the whirl of the wind as Beau drives me down Interstate 1, from Miami to Key West.

"How long will we be over the water?" I ask again, slipping my sunglasses on.

"For a while," he replies and squeezes my hand, as if to comfort me.

"That's not natural," I reply and take a deep breath. "What if the bridge gives out?"

"It won't," he says.

"How do you *know*?" I demand.

"Well, I'm quite sure it was engineered by intelligent people, not to mention, it's been here for a long time, and it's designed to *not* give out."

"All bridges are designed to not give out. Doesn't mean they don't."

He squeezes my hand again and tosses me a cocky smile. "Take a breath and enjoy the view, sugar. Most people don't ever get a 360 degree view of the ocean without being on a boat or in a plane."

"It is pretty," I concede and watch the water zoom past us. Beau rented a convertible Mercedes. At least, I assume he rented it. It was waiting for us at the airport this morning. I settle back against the soft leather seat and watch as a school of dolphins swim past, as if they're popping up out of the water to say hello. "I've never seen dolphins before."

"You'll see plenty of them this weekend," he replies. "Our cottage is on the beach."

"Thank you for bringing me," I say for the fiftieth time since this morning. We've only been gone for nine hours, but every part of this trip has been something new and fun. Riding in the private jet, being sent shopping with his credit card while he was in a meeting—even though I didn't buy anything, and now driving down to a cottage on the beach in Key West.

"Thank you for coming along. I know it's not easy to drop everything on a moment's notice."

"It wasn't as difficult as I thought it would be. Shelly and Lena jumped at the chance to cover for me." I smirk. "I guess I needed a little time away more than I realized."

"Is there anything specific you'd like to do while we're here?"

"I've always heard of Ernest Hemingway's house, and all of his polydactyl cats. I'd like to see that."

He smiles over at me, then turns his gaze back to the highway.

"I know, not a very sexy thing to do. I'm a book nerd."

"You are?" He grins, surprised.

"Oh yeah. The things I've seen are nothing compared to what's in fiction."

"And I have a feeling that you've seen quite a bit."

I smile and shrug, enjoying the way the wind feels on my face, and not doing too bad at forgetting that I'm hovering over the deep, blue ocean.

"I've seen my fair share. But it's fun to lose myself in a book. I just don't get the chance to as often as I'd like."

"Okay, Hemingway's house is on the list. What else?"

"Why do I have to make all of the decisions?"

"Because this weekend is for you."

I blink and glance over at him as he switches lanes, enjoying his sharp jawline and the way the wind ruffles through his thick, dark hair.

"I thought it was a work weekend?" I shift in my seat, facing him.

"It was a work *day*," he says and smiles over at me, making my heart lurch just a bit. "And then you agreed to join me, making the rest of the time about you."

"Hmm." I don't know what else to say. I don't know if there's ever been a time in my life that a man has made *anything* about me. And I don't know if that reflects on me, or the men I've been with in the past.

"What are you thinking?" Beau asks.

"That I don't know what else to put on our list."

He pulls my hand up to his lips, still watching the road. "Well, you just think about it and let me know. We don't have to do anything at all, if you don't want to. We can sit on the beach and soak up some sun all weekend."

"Well, I think at least one day of that is important," I reply, thankful that I found a super cute swimsuit to bring with us.

"I was thinking that we could take a short cruise this evening."

"Like, on a big cruise ship?"

"No, on a sailboat. We keep one down here."

"*We* do?"

"The family."

"Wait. You didn't rent the cottage, did you?"

He shakes his head. "No, we own it."

"Your family owns it."

"Yes." He frowns over at me. "What's wrong?"

"Nothing." I sigh and tip my face up to the sunshine. "I'm just still getting used to how wealthy you are. You're down to earth, fun, sexy, and then we go somewhere or you say something, and it's like a glass of cool water in my face."

"The money is just a result of generations of hard work," he says reasonably, completely comfortable with this conversation.

"I understand that, and I don't begrudge you or your family your wealth. That's not what I mean at all. I just come from a very different background, so it's new to me."

"That's just one more reason that I'm so attracted to you," he replies.

"You're attracted to me because I grew up poor?"

He smirks. "No. I'm attracted to you because the money isn't what attracts you to *me.*"

"Well, it doesn't suck," I say, teasing him. "But no. I think that I would be intrigued by you whatever your tax bracket was."

"So back to the subject at hand, how do you feel about the sailboat idea?"

"I'll try anything once," I reply and brush my fingers over the scarf on my head, remembering all the ways the pretty blue material could be used. He glances over and laughs.

"That's an excellent outlook, sugar."

***

I don't think I'm much of a sailor. We've barely set foot on this huge sailboat, and I can't seem to find my sea legs. But there's a whole crew of four people to sail the boat, and I'm not going to chicken out in front of them or Beau.

"We're going to push away from the dock," Beau says, excitement written all over his face. I don't want to be the party pooper who says, *I don't feel so good*, so I just smile and nod, holding on to the rail at the side of the boat tightly.

Do not throw up, Mallory. You've got this.

The engines start, surprising me.

"I thought this was a sailboat."

"It is." He wraps his arms around my middle and kisses me on the head. We haven't even been to the cottage yet to settle in. Beau brought us straight here, he was so excited to take me sailing. "But there are engines in case there is no wind, and to get us away from shore, then to guide us back in again."

"Gotcha." I nod, watching the horizon. The sun is just beginning to set, throwing a riot of color across the sky.

If I didn't feel so damn nauseated, I would be enamored with it.

I take a deep breath. *In through my nose, out through my mouth.*

"The water is nice and smooth this evening," Beau says. He's so *happy*. I nod again, but inside I'm freaking out. This is *smooth*? It feels like…I don't even know what it feels like.

Like I'm in a bounce house for kids with about thirty kids going crazy inside.

And this is smooth.

Lord help me.

Suddenly, the engine quits, and the sails are raised, and they catch the wind, pulling us across the water. It's a bit smoother now, amazingly, and I start to relax back into him.

"Are you okay?" he asks.

"I think so." I reply.

"Look how far out we are already," he says, pointing back to land. I look, and being okay flies right out of the window.

"Oh, God."

"What, sweetheart? It's hard to hear you over the wind."

Good. Because I'm going to hurl. Looking back wasn't a good move. I close my eyes, but that doesn't help at all.

It just makes it worse.

I'm going to die.

"Mal, you're shaking," he says and leans around so he can see my face. "God, are you okay?"

"No," I reply. "I think I'm going to be sick."

"Okay," he says, rubbing circles on my back. "It's okay if you need to be sick."

I'm quite sure it's never *okay to be sick in front of the man you're currently having sex with.*

I shake my head, so angry at myself. He's still rubbing my back, and I know he's trying to help me feel better, but *nothing* is making me feel better right now.

"Deep breaths," he croons into my ear. "Just breathe, Mallory."

"If I didn't feel like I was going to lose my very expensive lunch right now, I'd find that very sweet."

"Ah, baby, I'm so sorry."

I shake my head, and that's it. I lose it.

All over the side of this beautiful sailboat.

And I can't stop. It's like the floodgates have been thrown open, and there's no slowing it down.

"We're turning back," he says, and I pray that he can't see what's happening. He's pulled my hair back and instead of circles, he's just patting my back gently. "We'll be back in just a little while."

"I'm so sorry," I say, then heave again. God, my stomach is empty, but I can't stop the heaving.

"No, I'm sorry," he says.

"Didn't know." I rest my forehead on my hand, as there's a lull in the super sexy throwing up. "Now we do."

"Now we do," he says. "I wish they had ice chips on board."

"Why? I'm not in labor," I reply, not understanding.

"Chewing on ice chips helps the nausea," he says. "Or peppermint oil."

"Oh!" I whip my head up and immediately regret it. "I should have thought of that. I have peppermint oil in my handbag."

"Excellent." He reaches for my bag and hands it to me. I find it, shove my bag back in his hands, and rub a drop under my nose, then on my pulse points, hoping it helps quickly.

"I don't know why I didn't think of this."

"I don't know about you, but I don't think well when I'm throwing up."

I nod and breathe deep, beginning to feel just a bit better. Not all the way, but it is lessening the urge to heave.

Thank God.

Finally, we reach the dock and Beau immediately leads me off the boat and to dry land.

"Just stand here," he says, taking my shoulders in his hands so he can watch me. "Take a deep breath."

And just like that, the nausea disappears as quickly as it showed up on the boat.

"Amazing," I whisper, and then I feel my shoulders drop.

"What's wrong now?"

"We have to break up," I reply and lean forward, until my forehead is resting on his chest.

"What? Why?"

"Because I can't sail!"

"Okay?"

"I can't be on boats, Beau. I should have known I'd get seasick because I get motion sick doing almost anything. I can't ride rides at carnivals. I can't ride in the backseat of the car for very long. I'm a mess."

"I'm not following you, sweetheart."

"You build boats for a living!" I look up at him now, and am shocked to see him smiling. "You build boats, and just the thought of being on one now makes me—"

"Okay, okay," he says and pulls me in for a hug. "Shh. It's okay."

"It's not okay that we have to break up."

"We're not breaking up." He kisses my head again. "Just because my family builds boats, doesn't mean that I spend my life on them. I can still sail with my family. It doesn't mean you have to join us. Gabby isn't particularly fond of it either, and my parents didn't disown her."

"She doesn't like it either?" I ask, hope blooming in my chest.

"Nope. So you're stuck with me, Mallory." I pull back, and he plants his lips on my forehead. "You have no idea how important you've come to be to me, and I don't know how to explain it. But I will say that I'm not going anywhere, certainly not because you have a queasy stomach."

And now my stomach is moving again, but with butterflies now.

"You say the sweetest things," I whisper.

"I don't say anything that I don't mean," he replies, his eyes on my lips. "Now, let's get to the cottage so you can get more comfortable."

"Okay." I smile as he slips his hand in mine and leads me back to the car.

***

"This isn't a *cottage.*"

I've just stepped from the car, and am staring at the beautiful home we just pulled up to. It's a full moon tonight, so there's a bright glow cast around the white building with black wrought iron balconies. This *cottage* is bigger than the home he's building in New Orleans.

"We call it the cottage," he says with a smile, pulling our luggage behind him. "Come on, I'll give you the tour. Are you feeling okay?"

"Much better," I reply with a smile. "I'm sorry again."

"There's nothing to be sorry for. Come on, this is one of my favorite places, and I'm excited to show it to you."

"It's lovely on the outside," I reply, silently making sure all of my walls are secure, just in case there's something, or someone, here that I don't want to feel.

"It was built about a hundred years ago," he says. "It's survived its share of hurricanes and bad weather over the years."

"How long has your family owned it?"

"They built it," he says with a smile. "And my mother and I are the only ones who use it now. For the most part, anyway."

He leads me into a beautiful grand foyer, with a double staircase, on either side of the room, leading up to a landing.

"The bedrooms are all upstairs, as well as the ballroom."

"Ballroom?" I ask.

"We have one," he confirms. "It's empty. It hasn't been used in, hell, I don't think it's been used since my parents got married here."

"They married here?" I ask, then realize I'm repeating everything he says. "I bet it's a great spot for a wedding."

"Wait until you see the view in the morning," he replies with a smile. "There's a back patio with lounge chairs and cabanas, so we can sit out and enjoy the view all day if you like."

"I like," I say with a smile.

"I can also seduce you out there."

"I noticed you don't have close neighbors."

"We're alone," he confirms and leans down to kiss me, but I duck out of the way.

"I need to brush my teeth before you kiss me," I say, cringing. "I hurled."

"Ah, yes. That. Okay, let's get this tour finished so you can freshen up and I can get you naked."

My eyebrows climb. Surprisingly, despite the way I felt earlier, just the way he's looking at me right now makes my body heat and spine tingle.

"This is the kitchen."

"This has been recently remodeled," I comment, in love with the black and white color scheme. It's clean, with pops of teal and yellow, giving it a beachy feel.

"About a year ago," he confirms. "We have to have modern kitchens."

"That's what I always say," I reply, then wink at him and he slaps me on the ass.

"You're sexy when you're sassy."

"I'm glad you like it, because I don't plan to change any time soon."

"Good." He leans in, and rather than kiss me on the lips, he plants a wet kiss on my neck, sending my already humming nerves into full sparks.

"You're good with your mouth."

He just smirks and pulls me through the rest of the downstairs, showing me a parlor, formal dining room, home theater and massage room.

"Nice," I say. "I've never had a massage."

"Ever?"

"Ever. I don't like to be touched by strangers," I remind him and shrug.

"We'll see what we can do about that."

He leads me upstairs, and shows me all six bedrooms, with attached baths. I don't know how an upstairs can be bigger than the downstairs, and it probably isn't, but it feels like it goes on forever.

"I don't use the master bedroom because Mama still uses that room. This is the room I use." He opens French doors into a room with a massive four-poster king bed, and another set of French doors that lead out to a balcony.

"I can hear the ocean," I say, walking to the balcony and opening the doors. The air swirls around me as I step out and lean on the railing. "Oh, this is lovely."

"Yes, it is."

I turn to find him staring at me, pure lust and

happiness in his whiskey colored eyes.

"I can see why this is your happy place."

"And you just got here," he replies with a smile and crosses to me, pulling me into his arms. "Thank you for coming with me."

"Oh, I'm the one who should be thanking you," I reply and hug him tightly. I love how small I feel in his arms. He's a big man, tall, with broad shoulders.

I feel safe here. In this place, and with this man. I let my guard down, cautiously and a little at a time. There are spirits here. Two. No, three.

"What do you feel?" he asks quietly, as if he knows what I'm doing.

"I feel a few spirits here," I whisper. "But I don't sense that any of them are malicious. They're attached to the house, not a person."

"Do spirits attach themselves to people?" he asks with surprise, as if he's truly beginning to believe in what I do.

"Oh, yes," I reply. "And that's not always bad either. But it can be."

"Interesting."

I nod and lean against the railing again, breathing in the salty sea air. The palm trees around the home are moving with the light breeze, and I can see the white caps of the waves in the moonlight.

I glance back at Beau, and am surprised to see a woman standing behind him.

"Hello," I say cautiously. She's not living. She's short, and as round as she is tall, it seems. She's dressed in a maid's uniform, with a white apron tied around her ample waist. Her mocha skin is soft and lovely, her black hair pulled up under a white hat.

Beau spins and looks in the direction I'm looking, but

can't see her.

"Who's here?" he asks.

"I'm Liselle," she says softly.

"Liselle."

His brows climb into his hairline, and he's blinking rapidly, like he's seen, well, a ghost.

"I'd like her to leave."

Chapter Twelve

~Beau~

Mallory's eyes widen, and then she frowns. "She doesn't want to hurt you in any way."

No, she wouldn't. I shake my head and rub my fingers over my mouth, not sure how much to tell her. I trust her, implicitly, but I'm not used to feeling vulnerable.

And this is one of the things I feel most vulnerable about in my life. It certainly ranks in the top five.

"I can ask her to go," Mallory says and reaches out to touch my arm, gently rubbing my bicep. She says I calm her, and I believe her, because I've seen it. But she's come to calm me just as much. Her eyes are on me, not on the spirit standing behind me.

And the fact that I just thought that sentence surprises the hell out of me. A month ago I would have scoffed and brushed off the thought. But now, being with this woman, it feels almost normal.

"Beau?"

"Liselle was our housekeeper here when I was a little boy. It was only me, Charly, and Eli then. The twins and Gabby hadn't been born yet.

"I loved her," I whisper and then shake my head, surprised that a memory from so damn long ago could shake me. "She was sweet and fun, and she loved to snuggle us while she read to us before our afternoon nap."

Mallory smiles and says, "Curious George was your favorite."

Jesus.

"I'd forgotten that," I reply and turn, but still can't see her. "She died here, in this house, while she was reading to us. Charly and Eli were still too little to know what was happening, and so was I, really, but I was old enough to know that something was *wrong*."

"Oh, you poor baby," Mal says and immediately walks into my arms, hugging me around my middle.

"Heart attack," I say, surprised to feel emotions that I'd long forgotten course through me. "My dad told me many years later that she'd had a heart attack that killed her instantly."

"That must have been traumatic," Mal says.

"My mama had me in therapy for a couple of years," I confirm. "I kept asking for her, and didn't understand why she wasn't coming back."

"That's an awfully young age to learn about death."

"Indeed. I hope Liselle isn't suffering."

Mal pulls out of my arms and looks to my left, then smiles softly.

"She says she's not suffering, but that she's waiting to move on because she wanted to apologize to you, and tell you that she loved you."

I nod and feel my throat close up with the flood of emotion that's suddenly sitting on my chest.

"She has nothing to apologize for. She didn't do anything wrong. She should move on and be happy."

And then, just like that, my chest is light again, and Mallory takes a deep breath and glances about, then smiles up at me. "She's gone."

"Good." I take Mal's hand in mine and lead her into the bedroom, leaving the French doors open so the salty sea air can drift inside. "Are you okay?"

"I'm actually just fine," she replies with a smile. "Almost energized."

"Really?"

"Mm hmm," she says and begins unbuttoning my shirt, her fingers moving slowly but surely down my torso until she reaches my pants. "You made some promises earlier."

"Promises? I don't remember making any promises."

I love it when she gets flirty.

"There was some strong flirty language," she says and pops the button on my fly, then lets my pants pool around my ankles.

"That's a promise?"

"Oh yeah." She takes my already throbbing cock in her fist and pulls up, then down, firmly gripping me. The breath hisses through my teeth as I sink my fingers in her hair, careful not to force her to me, but needing something to grab onto. "I'm fond of this."

"So glad you approve," I mutter, then let my head fall back as she licks me, from balls to tip, then wraps those fucking sexy lips around me and proceeds to give me the best blowjob of my goddamn life.

"Jesus, Mallory."

"Hmm," she purrs, and it's almost enough to make me explode. Her hands, working me over firmly, and that mouth wrapped around me is the sexiest thing I've ever seen.

But I want this to last.

So I grip her by the shoulders and bring her to her feet, spin us around, and guide her down to the bed.

"I wasn't done," she says with a pout.

"Unless you want this to be over before it really starts, I had to stop you, sugar." I pull her skirt up around her waist and just about swallow my tongue when I see that she's not wearing panties.

"I ditched them earlier," she says with a sassy smile, as if she *can* read my mind. "What with you making promises and all."

Her sassiness both delights me and makes me want to slow things down a bit, draw it out longer.

Make her writhe in pleasure.

So rather than plunge inside her and have my way with her the way I want to, I kiss her exposed navel, then bite the soft, slightly rounded flesh beneath it. Mallory isn't stick thin, and I prefer her this way.

She wears her curves like most women would wear a fancy gown, proudly and confidently, and it's fucking sexy as hell.

She's comfortable in her skin, which makes me comfortable too.

I can't stop touching her, dragging my fingertips up and down her sides, over her hips, and to that smooth apex of skin just above the promised land.

"You're so damn good with your hands," she moans and bites her lip as she grips onto the quilt on the bed to anchor herself.

I'd much prefer she grab onto me.

Slipping my fingers through her slick lips, I bury my face in her neck and kiss her, then bite the sensitive skin just below her ear.

"Shit," she whispers, then contracts tightly around my fingers, almost making me lose control.

I want to fuck her. Hard.

"Please," she pleads, raising her hips off the bed.

"Please what?"

"Inside me." She grips my cock, and I can't hold back any longer. I let her guide me to her, and slip just the head inside.

"Look at me."

She opens her violet eyes and watches me avidly as I sink balls deep and brush a lock of hair off her cheek.

"You're beautiful, Mallory."

She bites her lip again, unable to reply as I begin to move in a long, slow rhythm, taking us both on the ride of our lives.

"And this? This moment, this woman. All of this is mine."

Her eyes widen in surprise, and then she cups my face sweetly in her hands.

"It's ours," she says with a smile and tightens around me, almost making my eyes fucking cross.

"Yes, baby, it's ours."

***

"The Hemingway house was fantastic," Mallory says the next afternoon as we sit on lounge chairs under a cabana, lazily watching the water. "I had no idea there were so many cats."

"He was the original crazy cat lady."

She smiles over at me and my heart catches.

"I don't think they were all his. They've reproduced quite a lot since his day."

"True." I reach over and take her hand in mine, kiss her knuckles the way I always do, then rest our hands on my thigh. She's enthralled with watching the water, and I'm enthralled with watching *her*. She's in a black two-piece suit, a matching cover thing, and her hair is in a ponytail, high on her head.

She looks young and vibrant and *happy*.

And fuck me, she makes me so happy I hardly recognize the feeling.

Because I've never felt it before. I've always been dedicated to my family and my business, and women were a fun distraction from time to time.

And now I can't imagine my life without her in it.

I'm love with her.

"Why are you staring at me like that?" she asks.

"Like what?"

"Like you're not quite sure what to do with me."

I snicker and gather my wits about me. "I'm not quite sure what to do with you."

"Oh, you knew exactly what to do with me last night."

Her smile is sexy and fun, exactly like last night. It *was* fun and sexy.

"True. But I was just wondering if I should feed you."

She tips her head to the side. "I could eat. The sea air makes me hungry."

"We have water in New Orleans."

"It's the river," she says with a shrug. "It smells, looks, sounds different. Although, you're right. I'm always hungry at home too. As you can see." She holds her hands out to the side, gesturing to her curves, and then laughs.

"You look perfect to me," I reply honestly.

"Well, good," she says. "Let's go in and eat."

"I could run in and put something together, then bring it back out here."

She thinks it over, then stands and holds her hand out for mine.

"I'd like to go in out of the heat for a bit."

She pulls me out of my seat and we walk inside, sighing in delight when we hit the air-conditioned house. The air here by the ocean isn't as hot as if we were away from the water, but it's still warm.

"What should I make us?" she asks and opens the fridge, staring inside. I grip her waist and pull her away from the appliance, boost her onto a stool at the island, and shake my head.

"You can sit there and look beautiful while I throw something together."

"You can cook?"

"Of course I can cook."

"Do you *like* to cook?"

"Good question," I reply with a chuckle. "I guess they're two different things. I don't mind it. My mama made sure that we all knew how to cook."

"I'm surprised you didn't have people to do that for you."

She plucks a grape from the bowl I just set on the counter and takes a bite, then holds the other half of it out to me.

"Mom and Dad were pretty traditional," I reply and pull out the fixings for grilled cheese with ham and tomato sandwiches. "We did have a housekeeper who came twice a week to spruce the place up. I mean, there were six kids, and Mom is no glutton for punishment."

"Good plan," Mallory replies. "Hell, I have a girl who comes in once a month just to deep clean for me, and I'm only one person."

"Exactly. But they gave us all chores to do, and Mama had us help with the cooking all the time. So, all of us can cook. Not all of us love it."

"Gotcha," she says with a wink. "I think that's a great way to raise kids. It ensures that you're not all spoiled brats who can't live in the real world."

"Well, Gabby was pretty spoiled because she was the baby, but she's not a brat, and she can definitely live in the real world. She had her son at nineteen years old."

"Wow," she replies, not with censure or judgment. "That must have been rough."

"She had us," I say and set the sandwiches in the pan to grill up. "And Sam is amazing. And then she met Rhys, and he is a good father."

"That's wonderful. I didn't meet Rhys or the little ones when we were at the inn, but Gabby is a really great woman. I like her very much."

"I'm glad." I grin and flip the sandwiches. "She and I were always the closest. Not that I don't love all of my siblings, and surprisingly we all get along very well, but Gabby and I have a special bond. Until she married Rhys, I lived on the inn property so I could look over everything."

"I love that," she says with a sweet smile. "It sounds a lot like Lena and me. We don't live far from each other."

"Have you always known each other?"

"Yes. Our grandmothers were best friends when they were small too, and stayed friends their whole lives. So Lena and I grew up almost like sisters. And because of what we can do, there were many times that we were each other's only friend. She's a great person."

"I like her," I reply honestly. "I like that she's so loyal to you, and she's pretty funny."

"No one like her," Mal agrees with a laugh. "And this looks delicious. Thank you."

"My pleasure," I reply and stand on the other side of the island while we eat. She's leaning on her elbows, casually eating, and my hips are leaning against the countertop.

We can't take our eyes off each other.

"So you bring up an interesting topic," I begin and reach for a dill pickle, then pop it in my mouth.

"Okay."

"What are your thoughts on children?"

She stops chewing and stares at me for a moment, then sets her sandwich down and wipes her fingers on her napkin.

"In what context?"

"As in, do you want to have children one day?"

She sighs and also reaches for a pickle. "Honestly, I don't know."

"What are your concerns?"

"Are we really having this conversation?"

I just smirk and raise a brow, waiting for her to continue.

"I have *genetic* paranormal abilities," she says slowly, not looking me in the eyes anymore. "That concerns me because it's not something easy to be saddled with."

"I can see that," I reply, trying to keep the light tone to our conversation. "What if that wasn't a factor?"

"It's always going to be a factor."

"Humor me."

She shrugs and takes a bite. "*If* it wasn't a factor, I would say yes. I want kids. Not six," she says with a smile. "But a couple. You?"

"I like kids," I reply honestly, also surprised that I

brought it up, but finding myself wanting to know *everything* about her, and I love her. I don't see myself without her. "Kate is about to have a baby, and Gabby has two already. I'd like to have some of my own."

She smiles and rests her chin in her hand.

"What?"

"You're cute," she says.

Bullshit.

"No, I'm not cute."

"You are when you talk about having kids," she says and then laughs when I glare at her. "You get this sweet, excited look in your eyes. It's cute."

"Say that again, and I'll bend you over that counter and show you how very *not cute* I am, sugar."

She just shrugs without concern and takes another bite of her lunch.

"You don't scare me. I think it's awesome that the idea of having children makes you happy. I'm sure that whomever is lucky enough to give them to you will love it too."

She stands to set her empty plate in the sink, washes her hands, then turns back to me with a forced smile.

Shit.

"Did I just upset you?"

"I don't know why you would," she stutters, and I know it's a lie.

"We agreed at the start that this isn't a game, Mallory. No lies."

She sighs and rubs her temple. "That was a stupid thing to agree to."

"No, I don't think it was." I stay where I am, not touching her, just watching her. "What's wrong?"

"Really, nothing's wrong."

"Something is bothering you."

"Okay, here's the truth: I don't want to tell you."

I nod and cross to her now, nudging her face up with my finger under her chin. "That's better. I didn't mean to upset you."

"I'll be just fine," she says and smiles in earnest now. "Shall we go back outside and watch the water until the sunset?"

"Is that what you'd like to do?"

She nods happily.

"Then sit by the water for the rest of the day it is, sugar."

We grab fresh bottles of water and walk out to our seats under the cabana. The wind has rustled our towels, so we take a moment to straighten everything out and then relax, watching a school of dolphins play not far offshore.

"I can see why you love to come here," she says softly. "I would be here all the time."

"We can come whenever you like," I reply, not missing the fleeting frown that crosses her beautiful face. I wish she'd talk to me. "I like to come a few times a year."

"Do you own homes in other places?"

"The house I'm renovating in New Orleans is the only property I own in my name," I reply. "But my family owns places all over the world. Travel is a big part of our jobs, as our company is globally sought after, and my father, and let's be honest, Eli, wanted a home base rather than hotels. So we own apartments in London, New York, and San Francisco. There's this property here in Florida, and that's it for now."

"That's a lot," she says, hugging her knees to her chest. In the past twenty minutes, she's withdrawn from me.

This won't be tolerated.

But she's stubborn, like me, so I can't just demand that she speak.

Why are women so difficult?

We sit in silence for a while, watching the waves and the sea birds.

"I can't change the fact that my family is wealthy," I say at last. She whips her gaze to mine.

"I'm not—"

"I understand that it's unusual, and I can see where it could be intimidating for many people, but damn it, I work very hard. I won't apologize for being successful."

"No." She stands and straddles my lap, holding my face in her hands. "I'm not asking you to apologize for that, and I never would. You're right, it's a lot to take in, but it's who you are, and I respect you very much."

I plant my hands on her back, holding her close.

"Then tell me what's wrong. Why did you pull away just now? What did I say that's bothering you?"

"Are you sure that you're not the psychic?" She asks, trying to smile. I wait, watching emotions roll over her face. Finally, her shoulders drop and she looks at me with tear-filled eyes. "It's dumb."

"No, it's not dumb, baby."

She nods. "Yeah, it is. But I can't help it."

I brush a tear away with my thumb. Seeing her cry is killing me.

"What is it?"

She bites her lip and then says, "I don't want to think about another woman having your babies. It just makes me sad and jealous and then I get pissed, and that's dumb because you want babies and someone should have them for you."

I try to speak, but now that she's talking, she's not stopping, so I decide not to interrupt.

"I know that I'm not the woman who will have kids with you, and some day I won't see you or your family any more, and that's sad to me because I really *like* all of you. But when you decide to move on, it'll be awkward for me to still be friends with the girls, and I'm really going to miss them."

"Wow, this is a lot of thinking," I say with a sigh and pull her down into my arms, cradling her. "Shh, Mal. You're getting worked up over things that aren't happening."

"But they will. I don't have to be psychic to know it."

Bullshit. I'm completely in love with you. I'm not going anywhere, and when the time is right to have children, it's going to be with you.

But she's not ready to hear those words yet, and frankly, I'm not ready to say them.

"This is ours," I remind her. "And it's right here."

She nods, and fists her hand in my shirt, holding on. I tighten my hold on her and kiss the crown of her head.

"I'm right here, baby."

Chapter Thirteen

~Mallory~

I loved being in Florida with Beau, but it's good to be home. The shop ran well without me, and I don't know if that makes me proud, or feel a little like I'm useless.

I'm going to choose pride.

Beau is sound asleep beside me, resting peacefully. He doesn't snore, at least not that I've ever heard. Although, I'm usually asleep too. I've found that since I've been with Beau, I rarely have insomnia.

I think it's because I feel so safe when I'm with him that sleep comes easily.

But not tonight. I'm physically exhausted. It's been a busy week at work, and I started going to the gym with Lena. I'm not sure why, other than she begged because she doesn't like to go alone, and that way I get to see her more.

But she likes to go at six in the morning, before school, so basically she hates me.

I snort and shake my head at myself. I guess I'm a bit dramatic when I'm tired and I can't sleep. Maybe I should wake Beau for a round two?

I glance over at him and feel myself soften. He's so relaxed, I don't have the heart to wake him. And, round one was something to write home about, so I really have nothing to complain about.

So I reach for my journal and begin writing about my day. I like to keep a gratitude journal, where I talk about all of the positive things that happened that day, or whenever I have the time to spend with it. We always remember all of the bad things that happen. I certainly don't have to write those down.

But I want to remember the good as well.

I'm only one page in when my eyes are too heavy and unfocused to continue, so I set it aside, lie down, and give in to sleep.

I blink my eyes open and reach over to turn out the light, but movement from the corner of the room has me sitting upright and scowling.

"I don't allow spirits in this house."

The tall man, sitting in my grandmother's rocking chair, simply smiles and pats his knee in time with the rhythm of the chair.

"I know, and I'm sure sorry for intruding, but you're a tough woman to catch up with."

I tilt my head to the side, no longer afraid, but interested to know who this is.

"I'm Beau's Papa, Beauregard Boudreaux." He smiles and nods his head toward me. "And you're the beautiful woman who has captured his heart."

"Beau's daddy is a romantic?" I ask with a smile and leave the bed. I glance back at Beau to see that he's still asleep.

"This is a dream, Mallory. He can't hear us. But we're

leaving anyway. I have some things to show you."

He winks and stands, holds his hand out for mine, and when I slip it in his grasp, we're suddenly not in my house anymore.

"Where are we?"

*"*When *are we," he replies with a wink. "I thought I'd show you some of my memories."*

"Why?"

"Because I love my family, and it seems that you're going to be a part of them now. You're a lucky girl."

"I know that they're wealthy—"

"For Christ's sake, child. You're way too focused on the money. That's not why you're lucky." He shakes his head, and I feel like a scolded child. "These people are the most loving, supportive, caring people you could ever have in your life."

"But you're not biased," I reply with a laugh, and then look where he's pointing. There's a woman, about my age, chopping vegetables and giving orders to three children.

"Charly, that's perfect. You're sure learning my gumbo recipe quickly. Your daddy will love it."

The little girl's smile shines with excitement. "It's special."

"If you want to know why I'm a romantic," Mr. Boudreaux says as he watches the woman, "it's because of her. The love of my life. We were married for almost four decades when I left. I would have been married for a million more, if it meant I got to be with her."

I glance away from the children and watch him. "She's beautiful."

"Inside and out," he agrees with a nod. "Much better than I ever deserved. But she gave me six gorgeous children, was by my side through thick and thin. And let me tell you, there was a lot of thin, and no, I don't mean financially. I'm human, so I wasn't perfect, but I loved her the best way I

knew how."

"Who are the other two children?" I ask.

"Eli and Declan. Charly and Eli were always inseparable. They're still close."

"You watch over them."

"Of course I do," he says with a smile. "They're my crew. And now you're part of that crew as well."

"I love him," I whisper, surprised that I said it aloud. "It's been hard to admit that."

"Why?"

"Because I think he deserves better than me," I reply and watch Mrs. Boudreaux with her children. They're smiling, laughing, enjoying their time together. "I don't think I can give him what you had."

"Nonsense," he replies. "If you love each other, you make the rest work. I'm going to tell you what I told my own children all of their lives; you can't control the wind, but you can adjust your sails. You'll set the right course for you as a couple."

"I threw up on the boat," I reply in horror. "I'm not a good sailor."

He tips his head back and laughs, right from the belly, making me smile too. "Our Gabby doesn't have the stomach for it either. But the analogy works all the same."

I sigh, nod, and follow him when he leaves the kitchen, headed toward the living room. We're still in their home, but time has passed because the children are older.

"Is that Ben?" I ask, pointing at a skinny boy who's sitting with Savannah. They're reading together. I'd recognize her anywhere.

"It is," he says with a nod. "I loved that boy as if he were my own. He's grown into a good man, on his own path, just like all of my children."

"He looks at Savannah with a lot of love in his eyes," I remark.

"He still does," he agrees. "I wish my daughter would open her eyes and see it. That she would accept *it. They need each other."*

"She'll accept it when she's ready," I reply. "I've felt it when she and I are together. I can't tell the future, but I know that you're right. They're for each other, but it won't happen until she's ready for it. I don't think she'd know what to do with those feelings quite yet."

I look up at him and see the sadness in his eyes, and I know that he knows.

"Her ex-husband hurt her," I say simply.

"And I wasn't here to kill him," he replies, then glances down at me. "He's going to try to hurt her again before it's all done."

"And Ben will be there," I reply, then rub his arm, wanting to reassure him. "He'll be there."

He nods and leads me to another room again, and I can see that more time has passed.

"Is that Gabby?"

"Yes, my poor sweet girl." His face is soft with love as he looks at his youngest daughter. "She's a good girl, who made a bad decision and got herself into trouble."

We're in Gabby's bedroom, and she's sitting at the head of the bed, her knees drawn up to her chest, and she's crying.

"What's wrong?"

"She's pregnant with our Sam," he says. "She was so frightened to tell me, afraid of what I might think of her." He shakes his head, as if the thought bewilders him. "I could only ever love her, Mallory. Our actions don't just affect us, and I won't say that it wasn't hard on the family to have Sam arrive when he did, but we adjusted those sails and went where the

wind took us."

"She's a great mom," I reply, remembering what Beau told me about her.

"She really is," he agrees and leads me down the hall to another bedroom. We walk inside, and many years have passed now. Mr. Boudreaux is lying in the bed, and Beau is a grown man, sitting next to him.

"Here," he says to Beau, holding up a coin. "This was one of two of the first dollars made in our company. I'm going to give the other one to Eli, since the two of you are running it now."

"Papa," Beau says, his voice cracking with emotion. "You're going to get well. You'll be back in your office before you know it."

"We both know that isn't true," his father says as he gently lays the coin in Beau's hand. "So I need to say some things to you."

"I won't say goodbye to you," Beau says adamantly.

"I understand. I'm not quite ready for that either. But I do want to tell you how damn proud I am of you, son. You and all of your siblings are exceptional people. I couldn't want more. I know that you will take care of your mother and the others."

"Papa—"

"Thank you, Beau. Thank you for being my son, and my friend. I admire you. Great things are in store for you, my boy."

Beau simply nods, unable to speak, and my heart breaks for him. I know what it is to know that the person you love and admire most is about to leave you forever.

"I'm so sorry," I whisper.

"It was hard on all of us," he says to me and pats my shoulder. "I wasn't ready to leave, and they weren't ready to

say goodbye. I don't know if it's fair to say it was hardest on Beau, because it was difficult in different ways for each of them. But, he definitely shouldered a burden, as the eldest of the family, to step into my shoes."

"They're big shoes to fill," I reply with a smile.

"All my boys wear the same size," he says and leads me out of the room, away from a crying man, grieving for his father. "And they're doing quite well filling the shoes."

We pass a room where the music from a saxophone plays loudly.

"And that's my Declan, always losing himself in music. It's how he copes."

"He's amazing. I got to hear him at his wife's bar not long ago. He's a talented man."

"That he is. I will sometimes go listen to him when I'm lonesome for him. It helps me feel better."

"Mr. Boudreaux, why are you still here? You can move on. You don't have to stay and miss them all so much."

"I won't leave my love," he replies and when I look around, I see that we're back in my bedroom, and I'm fast asleep in my bed. "I want to look in on my family, Mallory. I sometimes come to them in their dreams, and I can see them live their lives, marry their own loves, have children. I wouldn't miss it for the world."

"They miss you," I reply, then rise up on my tiptoes to kiss his cheek. "They miss you just as much."

He smiles gently. "I know."

I wake slowly, blinking against the bright sunshine coming through the window. Beau's not in the bed anymore, and the linens are cool where he was, so he's been up for a while.

I glance over to see the rocking chair barely rocking

and I smile, remembering my time with Beau's father.

What a special gift, to be introduced to his family through his eyes.

I leave the bed, wrap a robe around me, and go in search of Beau. I find him down in the living room, his laptop on his lap and his phone pressed to his ear.

"Yes, I can make that deadline. Make sure my assistant is cc'd in the email so she can add it to my calendar. Thank you."

He ends the call and I curl up next to him, rest my head on his shoulder, and hug his arm.

"Are you okay?" he asks.

"Oh yes." I kiss his shoulder, then hug him again.

"Funny, I can smell my father."

I glance up and smile at him. "We just had a lovely chat."

"Did you?" He tucks a lock of my hair behind my ear. "You must have been dreaming."

I lay my head back on his shoulder. "Is the coin in your pocket?"

He stills. "Excuse me?"

"The coin. Is it in your pocket?"

He reaches in his pocket and pulls out the dollar coin, holding it up for me to see. "This coin?"

"That's the one. Your father is a smart man, Beau."

I feel him sigh, and his hand is a bit shaky when he returns the coin to his pocket.

"Jesus, Mallory."

"I'm sorry. I don't want to scare you."

"Not scaring me," he mutters and kisses my head. "But you're full of surprises."

***

"It's so nice to finally meet you, Mallory," Beau's mother says the following Sunday. "I'm glad you could join us for dinner. I've heard a lot about you."

"Thank you for having me," I reply. Mrs. Boudreaux is petite like her daughters, with salt and pepper hair and a warm smile. I immediately like her. "I've heard quite a lot about you as well."

"Well, then, we should chat and get to know each other better." She loops her arm through mine, and I'm immediately hit with feelings of deep love. This woman *adores* her family. "Are you from around here?"

"Yes, ma'am. My best friend's grandmother said she went to school with your eldest sister."

"Really? What is her name?"

"Sophia Turner," I reply and raise my chin for the blow to come when she remembers her. She tilts her head for a moment, trying to remember, and then her eyes light with the memory.

"I think I remember her. Did she have pretty blonde hair? About my height?"

"She still does," I reply with a nod.

"Oh, we must have them join us for dinner sometime," she replies with a genuine smile. Not one ounce of disgust in her voice.

"I'm sure she and Lena would enjoy that."

"Lena's a hoot and a half," Charly says from the stove. "I'm making Mama's gumbo tonight, sugar. I hope you like it."

"You've been making it for years," I reply before I can stop myself, and then decide to roll with it. "I'm sure it's great."

The house looks pretty much the same as my dream,

aside from some updating and color changes through the years. It's inviting and homey, and I can feel Mr. Boudreaux here, but that's it. No other spirits are here.

"I don't like green beans," a young boy says with a frown.

"This is Sam," Gabby says and ruffles his hair. "You liked green beans just fine last week when we had them."

"Geen," the little girl in Gabby's arms says with a smile, showing off a mouth full of tiny teeth.

"You like green beans, baby girl," Mrs. Boudreaux says as she kisses the baby's head and takes her from Gabby's arms. "This is Ailish. She's almost a year old now, and likes to repeat everything her brother says."

"She's beautiful." I smile at the little girl, who suddenly gets shy and hides her face against her grandmother's neck.

"Where are the boys?" Van asks as she tosses a salad.

"They're out back," I reply. "Beau said they had some work to talk about."

She rolls her eyes. "Clearly not because *I'm* not out there with them. They're talking about you."

"What?" I glance around in surprise. "Why?"

"Because the boys are nosier than a henhouse full of hens," Charly replies with a laugh. "And they want the scoop."

"I think I'd like the scoop too."

Van tilts her head, watching me. "You know the scoop. My brother's in love with you."

"He's never said that."

The women all look at each other, then start laughing.

"Oh, darlin', it's written all over his handsome face," Callie says and pats my shoulder. "Trust us. He's smitten."

"Well." I don't know what to say, so I just don't say

anything at all. Suddenly, Ben walks in through the back door, and stops short when all of us are staring at him.

"What did I do?"

"Nothing. Are you guys talking about Mallory?" Gabby asks.

"Psshh," he says, completely lying. "No. We have other things to talk about than women."

"Right." Charly rolls her eyes. "Tell Simon that I'll fill him in later."

Ben grabs a few beers from the fridge, glances at Van with the same lovesick eyes he had as a teenager, and walks back out of the house.

"Speaking of someone being smitten," Gabby says, but Van pins her with a glare.

"I'm not discussing this again. Stop it."

"Sorry," Gabby says, holding her hands up in surrender.

Mrs. Boudreaux passes the baby back to Gabby. "I should get the bread in the oven."

"Do you have a moment to talk privately?" I ask her.

"Of course, darlin'," she says and nods at Callie. "Can you put the bread in the oven?"

"Sure thing." Callie winks at me as I lead Mrs. Boudreaux to the living room, and turn to see her eyebrow cocked.

"Have you been here before?"

I bite my lip and curse myself. I shouldn't be walking around in here like I own the place.

"Of course not, I'm sorry." I clasp my hands at my waist, wondering if this is a huge mistake.

"You can say whatever is on your mind."

I nod and take a deep breath.

"I don't know if anyone has told you that I have some

abilities that are, well, different."

"Yes, I heard all about the séance," she says with a smile. "Sounds like it was mighty interesting."

I nod, relieved that she doesn't seem to think I'm a basket case.

"Well, I would like to pass along a message. I spoke with your husband the other night."

I expect her to go pale, to sink into the nearest chair, to act shocked. But instead, she just smiles at me, so I keep going.

"He's with you quite often."

"Oh, I know that, dear."

"You can see him?"

"No, but I feel him. I smell him. I talk to him all of the time."

I relax more, relieved that I'm not going to be thrown out on my ass.

"Well, it seems my message isn't needed, but he loves you very much."

She nods and reaches out to hug me tightly. "This may not be news to me, but it sure is wonderful to hear. Thank you, sweet girl. Now, let's go eat."

CHAPTER FOURTEEN

~Mallory~

I'm standing in an unusually chilly rainstorm with Lena and Miss Sophia, next to my Grandmamma's grave two weeks later. Today is the worst day of the year for me. I grieve, just as if it happened last week.

"I can't believe it's been ten years," Lena whispers and loops her arm around my shoulders. I lean my head on hers as Miss Sophia steps up to my other side and gently takes my hand in hers.

"It's been a blink of an eye," Miss Sophia says and gives my hand a squeeze. "Do you see her?"

My head whips around. "No. I can never see her. Can *you* see her?"

She looks over at me with sad eyes. "I can always see her."

"So unfair," I mutter and let all of my psychic walls down, opening myself up completely, hoping with everything in me that I might catch just a glimpse of her. "Can you see her, Lena?"

"Only in dreams," Lena says. "Seeing the dead isn't one of my gifts, and I'm perfectly okay with that."

"You should be, especially when we're in a cemetery," I reply and look around us, at all of the spirits that seem to drift between the headstones. It looks like something out of a movie.

But it's not. It's real. And I don't like cemeteries in the least. It's the one place that creeps me the fuck out, because I can see *hundreds* of spirits all at once.

But never Grandmamma.

"You can close it up," Lena says softly. "I can feel the tension, Mal. You don't have to keep yourself open here."

"I might see her," I reply and tighten my hold on Miss Sophia's hand. "So, on this day, I'll keep myself open."

"Well, then we'll stay with you," Miss Sophia says with a nod. "She loved you fiercely."

"Not fiercely enough to stay."

Her gaze whips over to mine. "Do you think she chose death over you?"

"She chose to continue to use her gifts, knowing that it could one day be too much and take her away." I shrug, surprised that I'm still harboring so much bitterness. "And it did finally do just that."

"Children," Miss Sophia mutters with a deep sigh. "Mallory—"

But before she can continue, I'm suddenly drowned by darkness. I can feel Miss Sophia and Lena, but I can't see them.

I can't see *anything*. But I can feel the evil that has washed over me. It's absolute and painful. A bright red light rises into the sky, casting everything in the deep, blood red.

Menacing red.

Fucking horrible red.

The other spirits have fled, and I'm trapped where I stand as a dark mass begins to take form.

"Darkness be gone, this child I protect." It's Miss Sophia chanting. "Touch her no more, as I command it, so mote it be!"

She repeats the words, getting fiercer each time, until the black mass retreats, and suddenly we are standing in the cold, wet cemetery again, just as we were before.

"It's gotten stronger," Lena says, holding on to me like her life depends on it.

"Thank you," I say to Miss Sophia, still clutching her hand. What in the actual fuck was *that*? I've never felt anything so strong, never experienced anything like it in my life except when we were at the inn for the séance. But this is a hundred times stronger.

"Are you going to finally talk to me about this?" Miss Sophia asks, her eyes fully dilated, her blonde hair still swirling in the breeze that the spell conjured.

My mouth opens and closes, as I'm completely dumbfounded. I turn to Lena. "Did you tell her about before?"

"Oh, I should have," she replies and rolls her eyes. "I sure should have."

"How did you know?" I demand.

"Darling, that's what I do. I cook and I know things."

"Wasn't that a Game of Thrones line?" I ask my grandmother's headstone, trying to lighten the mood while I also try to figure out what in the hell I'm going to say.

"Why didn't you bring this to me immediately?" Miss Sophia demands.

"Because it wasn't important enough to tell you," I reply and wither under her glare. Miss Sophia is the gentlest soul I know.

And the most powerful witch in the south.

She's kind of a big deal.

I'm prepared for her to let loose with a rare moment of yelling, so I'm shocked when she simply takes a deep breath, closes her eyes to let it out, and says softly, "I should have told you this long ago."

"Told me what?"

"Yeah, told her what?" Lena adds.

"First, tell me exactly what happened the first time you encountered this being."

I frown and glance at Lena. "We were at the séance."

I pause and stare up into the sky. It's still raining, soaking us, but we don't run for cover. We hardly feel it at all as I keep talking.

"I had just finished talking with the spirits who had something to say, and I hadn't put my guard back up yet." I glance over at Lena. "She was holding my hand to ground me, since I hadn't done anything like that in years."

"At least you thought to do that," Miss Sophia replies.

"It had gone well," I continue, "and the girls seemed happy with what they heard. And then suddenly there was a…a darkness. That's the best way to describe it."

"Did it speak?" she asks.

"No, I slammed the door and it was gone. It happened in less than two seconds."

"That's plenty of time." She sighs and shakes her head, paces away to stare off for a moment, then nods and returns to me. "I should have talked to you about the circumstances of your grandmother's death years ago. But, I was trying to spare you any fear and pain that would come with the knowledge."

"I know how she died," I reply with a frown.

"You know some of it," she says and turns to walk back to the car. "I'm cold and wet, and so are you. Let's go back to the house where it's warm, and I have my things around us to keep us safe, and I'll explain it all."

"I don't think I'm going to like this," I mutter to Lena.

"I can guarantee you won't. I don't know what she's going to say, but she's got her stern look on, and that always scares me."

***

"Have a seat," Miss Sophia says when we're settled in her kitchen with hot tea. We take our places and sit, waiting anxiously to hear what is going through her head.

"First of all, I want to tell you that I'm very disappointed that you didn't come to me sooner with this."

"I truly didn't think it was important," I say again. "It was so fast, and after I shut it out, it hasn't come back until now."

"It is important," she replies adamantly. "Did you feel it too?" she asks Lena.

"Oh, yes," Lena says, nodding. "And she's right, it was fast, and then it was gone. Otherwise, I would have told you myself."

"If this *ever* happens again, you come to me right away. Do you understand?"

We're both flabbergasted as we nod in agreement. I've never seen her like this. She looks *scared*, and that makes me shiver to the bone.

"What is going on?" I ask. "And how does this have anything to do with my grandmother?"

"You know that she died because an evil presence

embedded itself inside her head so deeply that she couldn't defend herself."

Lena and I both nod.

"But you don't know *how* or why that happened."

"It happened because she chose to help the police find missing children," I reply. "And she did. Hundreds of them. I may not love that it eventually took her away from me, but she helped families and she was proud of that."

"Yes. And she chose to do that because her own daughter had been kidnapped and killed when she was a little girl, and *she couldn't find her.*"

I gasp and sit back, my jaw dropped, and feel the world fall out from under me.

"That's not true."

"I'm so sorry, sugar, but it is true." She reaches over to pat my hand, but I sit back out of her way.

I can't be touched right now. I don't want to feel the pain or see the memories going through her head.

"She never mentioned it."

"No, she never spoke of it. And your parents died when you were so young, there was no one else to tell you."

"Except *you.*"

Lena hasn't said anything. Her eyes are glassy with unshed tears, and she's staring across the room, as if she's trying to process it all.

"It wasn't my place to tell you when your grandmamma was still alive," Miss Sophia replies gently. "And then when she was gone… Well, how does one bring up that conversation?"

My mouth is suddenly dry. I take a sip of tea. "Why are you telling me *now*?"

"Because it's what put everything into motion. That

sweet little angel Melissa—"

"Melissa was my aunt's name?" I ask.

"Yes. She was only five when she was taken. And your poor grandmamma tried so hard to be able to see where she was. But it was no use. She couldn't see it, and a week later, Melissa was found. She didn't survive.

"And then your grandmamma was a woman on a mission. She wasn't going to let other families go through what she and your grandpapa did. Her only goal in life was to help children come home safely, and later, to take care of you."

"But how could it *kill* her?" I demand, still not fully understanding. "She would never tell me, she just said that it was dangerous, and she was willing to do it if it meant she helped even one child be reunited with their family."

"Evil is strong," Miss Sophia replies. Her voice is strong again, almost emotionless as if she doesn't want to give the word any power at all. "My sweet friend was the strongest psychic I knew. Well, until you."

I stare at her in horror. "Me?"

"Oh, yes. You." She nods sadly, then continues. "She was powerful, and she was just so *good.* She had trained herself to translate symbols, to listen, to *know.* It was years in the making, but she was the best there was. She didn't even need to hold a piece of the victim's clothing, or go to where they lived. She could reach out and search from her living room."

"I can travel that way." I think of the dream a couple of weeks ago, and how I often travel to different places in my dreams.

"Yes, you have many of the same gifts," she replies with a smile. "And many other different ones. The dangerous part of opening your mind to find evil is that you're essentially giving that evil a door to walk into if you're not careful."

"So, a living person, also psychic, walked into her head and killed her?"

"I know it sounds impossible, but essentially yes. Another powerful, evil psychic living man did just that."

"And what does that have to do with what happened today?"

"I believe it's the same man," she replies, completely throwing me.

"What? No. That man went to jail."

"He was admitted to a hospital for the criminally insane because he was given an insanity sentence," she replies and everything in me goes dead cold.

"He's out?"

She nods.

"And how do you know it was him?"

"Because I can see him," she replies and that's it. That's all I can handle.

I stand and begin pacing, tears streaming down my face.

"I don't psychically see living people," I say, feeling everything in me begin to break. "I see them once they're dead."

"Yes, and that's one of your differences."

"So why is this happening?"

I'm just lost. I don't understand, and I don't *want it.*

"That detective called you," Lena says, as if she's just woken up and joined us.

"What detective?"

"I think her name was Detective Williams? Wait, she's a lieutenant now."

"In New York?" Miss Sophia asks, her eyes wide and

not a little frightened.

"Yes," Lena replies. "Remember, Mal?"

"Of course I remember," I snap.

"He's back at it," Miss Sophia says and closes her eyes, letting out a long breath. "He's hurting people again."

"I can't help," I reply. "And yes, that makes me feel like an asshole, but I don't have the same abilities that Grandmamma had, and I can't help!"

"I'm not telling you to help," Miss Sophia says. "But he's worried that you *will* try to help, and he's targeted you."

"How does he even know about me?"

"He might have read the obituary," Lena says. "You were mentioned in it."

I shake my head and continue to pace back and forth, too wound up to sit down. "I didn't ask for any of this."

"None of us ask for it," Miss Sophia replies.

"Some do. Some search it out. I never wanted it. I just want to be a normal woman, who owns a store and has an awesome boyfriend."

"But that's not all you are," Lena says and shrugs. "I'm sorry, but it's the truth. You've always had a hard time admitting it, accepting it, but it's who you are, Mal. You need to start seeing the glass as half full."

"Really?" I demand and snort out a laugh. "The glass is half full because I can see dead people and a crazy psycho psychic is trying to kill me? Seems like the glass is half empty to me."

"You're missing the point," Miss Sophia interrupts. "The point is, the glass is refillable. Fill your glass with the love of your man, and your successful shop, and your family and friends. And when the glass empties because of the unpleasantness of your gifts, go back to those places to fill it up again."

"Stop being smart," I pout and swipe the tears from my cheeks. "Why didn't Grandmamma tell me all of this when she was still here?"

"Because you already didn't want it," Miss Sophia responds with a resigned shrug. "She knew you were resistant to it. She didn't want to push you into embracing something that you didn't want."

"But I don't have a choice," I reply.

"She loved you," Lena adds and pats my shoulder. "She was also being a parent. She wanted the best for you. Maybe if you embrace some of your abilities, it will enhance your life."

I smirk. "Right."

"Something to think about," Lena says with a shrug.

"In the meantime, what do I do about the asshole trying to get inside my head?"

Miss Sophia's eyes narrow. "I have to do some research, make some calls, and think. You keep your door shut and your walls up, at all times. I'm sending home some fennel, agrimony, and osha root."

"I hate the taste of that stuff."

"You're not going to drink it, you're going to bathe in it," she replies as she fills bags. "This should protect and repel. Stay guarded."

"Okay, I get it. I'll protect myself."

"You've gotten better at that lately," Lena says thoughtfully.

"I think part of it is Beau," I reply, hesitant to say too much. "He makes me stronger."

"Yes, he does," Miss Sophia agrees. "Keep him close."

"Yes, ma'am."

***

It's later than I expected when I get home. I had to text Beau to tell him I'd be late, and now I'm just exhausted.

And frankly, I want to be alone.

Rather than text him again, I dial his number and smile when he answers on the second ring.

"Hello, beautiful."

"Hi. I think I'm going to have to cancel on you tonight."

"Is everything okay?"

Fuck no, it's not okay.

"I just don't feel great, and I'm super tired. I might be coming down with something. I thought I'd just go straight to bed."

"I can come over and take care of you," he offers. "My nursemaid skills are stellar."

"I remember," I murmur with a smile. "Thanks for the offer, but I'm okay. It's nothing like before. I'm just going to go snuggle down in bed and sleep this off. I'll see you tomorrow."

"You're sure?"

"Positive. Don't worry about me. Have a good evening."

"You too, sweetheart."

We end the call and I do collapse on the bed, staring at the ceiling. What is going to happen? With Beau, the shop, these *gifts* that won't go away, no matter how much energy I put into ignoring them.

I'm in love with him. I'm sure of it. He's...*everything.* And I'm afraid that when he learns everything that I, myself, have just learned, when he has a firm understanding of what I am, that he won't want to stick around.

Those aren't his words. No, his words and actions have been the opposite. But for how long does a person want to have to deal with someone else's oddities? It's taken me years, and I'm still struggling.

But, for tonight, I'm just exhausted, right down to the bone. I don't want to think about dead people, or emotions that aren't mine, or psychotic crazy people worming their way into my head.

I don't even want to think about Beau.

I want to sleep a dreamless sleep, and wake up tomorrow refreshed and ready to face this all head on. Because I have a feeling I'm in for the fight of my life.

CHAPTER FIFTEEN

~Beau~

"Why aren't you with Mallory tonight?" Callie asks me from behind the bar at the Odyssey. Ben and I ended up here a couple of hours ago.

"She's not feeling great," I reply and sip my beer. "I offered to go over, but she sounded exhausted, so here we are."

"I'm glad. We don't see as much of you these days."

I frown at my sister-in-law just as Ben nods.

"You see just as much of me now as you did before Mallory."

"Negative," Ben replies but shrugs good-naturedly. "But it's okay. That's normal."

"Do you guys need something?" I ask, concerned that I've been slacking off on my family since Mal came into my life.

"No, big brother," Declan says as he takes the stool on the other side of me. "We're fine, and you're happy. Just keep doing what you're doing."

"I like her," Callie says with a grin. "And I can see that you like her. A lot."

"Are we in the ninth grade?" I ask the room at large and then take another sip of my beer as they all dissolve into laughter. "She's great. We're great. Everyone is great. Change of subject, how are you, Dec?"

"I'm great too." He smiles and gazes over at his bride. "I have to go up to Nashville for a couple of days next week for some studio work."

"Nice," Ben says. "Working with anyone I would know?"

"Of course," Declan replies. "But I can't tell you who. I had to sign an NDA on this one."

"Fancy," Callie says with a wink. "He won't even tell *me*, and I even offered lots of sexual favors."

"I'm hoping I still get those," Declan replies. "You'll all know soon enough.
Artists are all different, and this one wants absolute confidentiality."

"Huh," I reply and shrug. "Well, have a good time."

"I will; it's only for a couple of days."

"If you need anything while he's gone," Ben offers, "just give one of us a call."

"You know, there are perks to being married into this family," Callie replies with a wink. "I have access to a whole gaggle of handsome men to save me."

Declan smirks. "You don't need saving, sugar."

"Of course not," she agrees. "But it's nice to have lots of handsome men at the ready, just in case."

"How are things with you, Ben?" Declan asks.

"Good. Business is good at the dojo." He passes his empty bottle to Callie, and just asks for water for the next round. Ben is a healthy guy, but as a Krav Maga master, he has to be. "I hired two more masters to help with classes. I prefer to do them all myself, but apparently people want to beat the crap out of each other in New Orleans, so I added more help."

"You're as much of a workaholic as the rest of us," I reply.

"That's why he fits into our family so well," Dec says. "He gets us."

I nod, watching Ben thoughtfully.

"So when are you going to ask Savannah out on a real date?" Callie asks, in pure Callie fashion. No beating around the bush with this woman.

Ben's eyes widen and he takes a sip of his water and frowns.

"We're friends," he says.

"Friends who look at each other like they want to tear each other's clothes off and go at it against any available surface."

"That's how she looks at me," Declan says with a smug smile.

"I've actually been wanting to talk to you about this," I say to Ben, whose shoulders hunch just a bit in defense. "Stop brooding."

"I'm not fucking brooding," he replies. "And I'll take that second beer now."

"Sure," Callie says with a happy, innocent smile.

She's not innocent in the least.

"The thing is," I begin, "Van's been single for a couple of years now. She's doing so much better, and we all know that's partly because of *you.* You've been a good friend to her."

"Exactly," he says, cocking a brow. "She's made it clear that I'm squarely positioned in the friend zone. I'm up to my fucking ears in the friend zone. So no, I won't be taking her out on a date any time soon. Or ever."

"Jesus, men are dumb," Callie says, rolling her eyes.

"Hey!"

"Sorry, but you are. I see the way you look at her, Ben. And frankly, she looks at you the exact same way."

"Bullshit."

"No. It's not bullshit."

"Look," I say, interrupting. "All I'm saying is, it's okay with us if you decide that you do want to date her. Or whatever."

"No," Declan says, "no *whatever* without dating her. You're our best friend, but she's our *sister.* If you *whatever* and don't date her, we'll all kick your ass."

"I'd like to see that," Ben says with a smirk. "You don't have anything to worry about."

"Beau's always worrying about someone," Declan says, clapping me on the shoulder. "If there's nothing to worry about, he panics."

I roll my eyes and take the last sip of my beer.

"Another?" Callie asks.

"No, thanks. I'll take the water too. Okay, let's leave Ben alone. How are you, Callie?"

"Never better," she says, her smile bright. "My bar rocks."

"*Our* bar!" her business partner, Adam, calls down from the other end of the bar.

"Whatever!" she calls back and winks at him. "Declan is healthy and happy, you guys don't suck. Kate's going to have a baby for the rest of us to spoil, and we don't have to have one ourselves, which is really selfless of her."

"Yes, I'm sure that's what she and Eli were thinking when he knocked her up. Let's help everyone else out and have a baby," Ben says with a laugh.

"I agree," Callie says. "They're selfless."

Declan and I share a glance, then laugh.

"So, yeah. Things are good," she says with a nod.

"Well, now that we're all caught up, I should head out. I have an early class tomorrow." Ben stands and pulls out his wallet to pay, but Callie shakes her head and waves him off.

"I'll walk with you," I reply and throw down some money, despite Callie's protest. "I'm paying for my damn beer."

"You might be the best looking family in Louisiana, but you're also the most stubborn."

"We'll take that as a compliment." We wave and leave, walking back toward the loft. Ben met me there earlier and we walked to The Odyssey together. "I'm sorry for all the questions about Van," I say as we set off down the street toward my place.

"I know y'all wish we'd just pull our heads out and get married and have babies, and all of that, but it's not going to happen, Beau. We've known each other all of our lives."

"But she's no sister to you," I reply.

"No, I don't think of her like a sister."

"Like you do Gabby and Charly and the rest."

"True."

I look over at him. "So?"

"So fucking drop it," he says and rubs his hand over his face.

"Consider it dropped."

"Good."

Meow.

Just as we reach the top of the steps to my flat, we see a little black kitten huddled by my front door.

Meow.

"You got a cat?" Ben asks.

"No, I have no idea where it came from."

"I wonder if it's Mallory's familiar," Ben says.

"Excuse me?"

"You know, a familiar."

I simply stare back at him and he sighs in disgust. "Jesus, you live in fucking New Orleans. How do you *not* know this shit?"

"Maybe I don't want you to date my sister after all."

He reaches down and picks up the tiny little fluff ball.

"She has the same blue eyes that Mallory does."

"Are you implying that Mallory, in the form of a black kitten, is hanging out by my door?"

"It could happen," he says and lets the kitten burrow down into his neck, purring loudly.

"If Mallory ever snuggles up in your neck and purrs like that, we're going to have issues."

He laughs. "True. Probably not Mallory."

"But…" I pause, looking at the little kitten, a plan forming in my head. "Mallory might like her."

"I don't know if you should give a woman a cat as a gift," Ben says with a frown.

"Let's go to the pet store to get supplies," I reply, ignoring him and excited to see the look on her face tomorrow.

"Don't say I didn't warn you."

***

The kitten kept me up most of the night. There were several times that I questioned my judgment, but then it would curl up next to me and purr, and well, turns out I'm a softie.

What the fuck is happening to me?

I slip the sleeping kitten inside my jacket and walk down to Mallory's shop, worried that she might not be there again, but when I walk inside, there she is sitting behind the counter. She glances up, and takes my fucking breath away.

She's just so damn beautiful.

And mine.

"Hey there," she says with a welcoming smile. But she has some dark circles under her blue eyes, and she looks…unsettled.

"Hi."

Meow.

She blinks rapidly. "Is that a cat in your jacket, or are you just happy to see me?"

I smirk and pull the baby out, and Mallory's face melts the way most women's faces do when they see a baby of any species.

"Oh my goodness, look at you!"

I can only stare in surprise at the silly baby talk voice coming out of her mouth as she takes the kitten from my hands and snuggles him.

"Oh, he's so cute." She kisses his face, and he pats her cheek with his fluffy paw. "Hello, little love. Oh, you're just precious, aren't you?"

"I'm sorry, is Mallory here?" I ask with a laugh. "Because I don't recognize this woman."

"It's a *baby*," she says, as if that explains it all. "A super cute baby."

"Well, I'm glad you like him. Or her. I'm not sure which."

"Are you keeping him?" she asks hopefully.

"No. You are."

Her gaze whips up to mine and she looks between me

and the kitten, as if the little ball of fur is going to confirm what I just said.

"Excuse me?"

"I brought him for you."

She frowns and sets him on the floor when he squirms to get down and props her hands on her hips.

"What if I don't like cats?"

I nod. "Yes, because clearly the way you just fawned all over him indicates that you can't stand him."

"Well, what if I was allergic?"

Oh God. "Are you?" I ask in horror.

"No." She watches as the little terrorist bats at a piece of plastic on the floor. "But you should have asked me if I wanted a cat. It's a living thing, which requires attention. I don't have any of the supplies."

"They're upstairs," I reply and walk behind the counter to pull her into my arms. "I haven't seen you in a couple of days."

"So you bought me a *cat*?"

"No." I kiss her forehead, loving the way she fits in my arms.

I love you.

"I missed you. But the cat was on my doorstep last night, and I didn't have the heart to leave him outside. I thought you might like to keep him. If you don't, I'm sure Gabby would take him out at the inn. He could be a mouser."

"Hmm." She leans her head against my chest, the way she does when she's had a rough day and just needs a hug. "I'll keep him."

Her words are muffled against my chest, but I smile and pat her back.

"Good."

"He's really cute."

"Ben thought he was your familiar."

Her head jerks up so she can look me in the face. "Really? Ben believes in that stuff?"

"It was a surprise to me," I reply with a shrug. "I had no idea. You think you know a person."

"Well, he's not my familiar," she says with a chuckle and returns to hugging my chest.

"Do you believe in familiars?" I ask, only knowing what I read about it last night on a Google search.

"I've never seen one," she says. "I think it's lore, like vampires and such. But who knows?"

"Who knows, indeed?"

"This is nice," she says and hugs me tighter.

"How do you feel today?"

She's silent for a moment, then shrugs one shoulder.

"I don't know what that means," I say with a laugh and kiss her head. "I need words, please."

"I'm okay."

I tip her chin up so I can see her face.

"You look tired."

"I'll sleep better tonight."

"I'm not leaving you alone tonight."

She smiles widely. "Good."

"What can I do to help?" I ask softly, hating the sadness in her eyes.

"You're doing it. I'm really okay, Beau. Yesterday was the anniversary of my grandmother's death, and that's always a hard day for me."

"I get it," I reply immediately. I dread the anniversary of my dad's death every year. It's a shitty day. "I'm sorry."

"It'll pass. I found out some stuff yesterday, but I don't want to talk about it. Is that okay?"

"Of course." Suddenly, there's a crash from across the room and Mal winces.

"Looks like he won't be a shop cat. He'll put me out of business."

"Yes, it's probably best if he's a house cat."

She nods and smiles as the little kitten brushes up against her leg, purring.

"He's quite...*active.*"

"Of course he is," she says with a smile. "He's a baby. I'll keep him here with me today, and take him home later."

"Good idea." I brush my thumbs under her eyes, not liking the dark circles there in the least. "Are you sure you're okay?"

She pauses, as if she's trying to decide what to say, but she just kisses my palm and nods. "I'm okay. Shelly is going to come in this afternoon to close for me, so I'm only working half of the day."

"Do you mind if I make us dinner this evening?"

She shakes her head. "Not at all. What's on the menu?"

"Well, I confess that although I *can* cook, I'm not the best cook. But I make a fantastic spaghetti."

"Spaghetti it is then."

***

"He so cute!" Mallory says from the couch in her living room. She's been home with the kitten for a couple of hours. I just arrived with groceries for dinner, and some forget-me-nots the same color as her eyes. "And he's already figured out the litter box."

"What are you going to call him?" I ask.

"I've narrowed it down to Binx and Kat with a K."

I stop stirring the sauce and stare at her for a moment, then bust up laughing.

"What? I like them both!"

"I didn't say anything. Besides, you're really not a "fluffy" kind of person."

"He *is* fluffy," she says and takes a sip of the red wine I poured her when I arrived. "But fluffy is really a girl's name. I think I'll go with Binx."

"Binx it is." I let the pasta fall into boiling water, give it a stir, and join her on the couch. "You look better this evening."

"Did I look horrible earlier?"

"Not horrible, but troubled. I don't like it when you're not well. I would much rather trade places with you."

"Trust me, you don't want to trade places with me."

"Want to tell me about it?"

She shakes her head no and takes a deep breath. "I'm sorry, but I don't want to get into it."

"I don't like feeling shut out."

"I'm not shutting you out. Trust me, if that was the case, you wouldn't be here tonight. I want you here, and I want to be with you. But I don't want to talk about yesterday."

"I do trust you," I reply gently. "And I don't say that lightly. Trust isn't easy for me."

"Me either," she says, lacing our fingers. "But I trust you."

"That's the most important thing. However, I have another important subject to bring up."

"Oh?"

"Yes. This could be a deal breaker for one or both of

us."

She frowns and shifts in her seat, facing me. "What is it?"

"What movie are we going to watch tonight?"

She rolls her eyes and slaps my arm. "Damn it, Beau! I thought there was even *more* drama to deal with!"

"Well, there could be if you tell me you're going to make me watch all of those sad movies that make girls cry. They're a snore fest, Mal. I can't do it."

"What if we work out a trade?"

"So you're saying you *do* like those movies?"

"Well, sometimes," she says with a grin. "What kind of movies do *you* like?"

"Action. Lots of action."

"So, blood and guts and sex?"

"Yes. All of that." She cups my cheek in her hand, laughing up at me.

"How about if I pick one, then you pick one? We'll trade."

"Oh God. I'm going to have to watch sappy Sandra Bullock movies, aren't I?"

"Some of her stuff is really funny," Mal says defensively. "Have you seen The Proposal? It has Ryan Reynolds."

"Reynolds is in Deadpool. That's better."

"Looks like those are our picks for tonight." She smiles smugly and scratches Binx behind the ears when he jumps into her lap. "Your water is boiling over."

"What? Oh!" I jump up to stir the pasta, surprised that I shifted my focus so completely to Mallory that I didn't hear the hissing from the overflowing pot.

But then, when I'm with Mallory, all I see is her.

CHAPTER SIXTEEN

~Mallory~

I didn't dream last night. I mean, if I did, I don't remember it. That almost never happens, and when it does, I wake refreshed and rested.

And I want to lie here, for just a while longer, enjoying the warm sheets brushing over my naked body, and the sexy man currently spooning me. He's still asleep, but even subconsciously he has a vise grip on me and his face is pressed to my back, just below my neck.

I'm a small woman, generally speaking, just shy of five foot three. I have more curves than I'd prefer, but compared to Beau I'm tiny.

And it feels fantastic.

Not to mention, I can't keep my hands off of him. My fingertips drag up and down his arm, and after a moment, he presses a sweet kiss to the base of my neck, then higher, just below my hairline.

Cue the shivers.

"Good morning," he whispers, just as his hand starts a journey of its own, traveling first up over my breast, making the already semi-hard nipple pucker right up. He tweaks it gently twice, and then his hand glides down my side to my hip. He grips me firmly and pushes his hard cock against my ass suggestively.

"Someone's happy to see me this morning," I murmur with a sleepy smile. He bites my earlobe and slips his hand over my belly and then lower, where I'm already wet and ready for him.

"I'm always happy to see you," he whispers and slips his fingers over my clit and down to my slick lips. "And it looks like it's reciprocated."

"Mm."

He rolls me onto my back and latches onto my nipple, sucking in tiny pulses, exactly the way he does to my clit.

It drives me out of my fucking mind.

His hand is playing my core like an instrument, and I can't handle it. My world splits in two with a beautiful orgasm, surprising me.

Before my feet are firmly back on solid ground, Beau covers me, slips on protection, and slides inside me. He stops when he's balls-deep and stares down at me with more than just lust in his whiskey colored eyes.

He loves me.

I don't have to read his mind to see it. To *feel* it. It's coming off of him in waves as he begins to move his hips, taking us both on the ride of our lives.

I grip his shoulders, digging my nails into his smooth skin, and arch my back, needing to feel him even deeper.

"More," I murmur.

"I don't want to hurt you," he replies, and I smile up at him.

"You're not going to hurt me." I lean up to kiss him, then bite his lower lip. "And if you do, well…a little pain never killed anyone."

He cocks a brow and moves faster, and much deeper, making me gasp.

"You like it a little rough, baby?"

"Sometimes," I reply and squeeze his ass, inviting him even deeper. "And I fucking love the way you feel."

"I love your dirty mouth," he says and grips both of my wrists in his big hand, pinning them over my head. "But I want you to tell me if it's ever too much."

"Deal."

He grins and moves harder, watching my face with every thrust for any discomfort, but it doesn't hurt at all.

It's so goddamn good.

Everything about this, every time, is just amazing.

Also, I'm not sure I could tell you my name right now.

"God, you're beautiful," he groans and finally closes his eyes in pleasure. "I can't get enough of you."

"I love your mouth, too," I say, panting. "Beau?"

"Yes, baby."

"Flip us over."

He frowns down at me, but I push against his shoulder, and he rolls to his back, staying inside me as I plant my knees and begin to ride him like fucking crazy. He plants his hands on my hips and holds on tightly.

"So good," I moan. My hands are braced on his chest as I grind down hard, loving the depth with this position.

"Jesus, Mallory, slow down."

"I can't." I shake my head and keep the pace, my hips moving fast, my muscles squeezing around him. I want to tell him I love him, but all I can do is show him.

"Mal, I'm gonna—"

He sits up, wraps his arms around my back, and kisses me fucking mad as I bear down on him and we come at the same time, staring into each other's eyes.

"Damn," he murmurs, resting his forehead against mine.

"Yeah."

"As soon as I can feel my body, I'll get out of bed."

I smirk. "You can't feel your whole body?"

"No. I'm pretty sure I just had an out-of-body experience."

I kiss him and slip off of him, then collapse onto my back so I can catch my breath.

"Do you want breakfast?" he asks.

"Sure."

"What do you have down there that I can fix us?"

I cringe. "I might have a jar of pickles."

He stops scratching the sexy stubble on his cheek and stares at me for at least three seconds. "That's it?"

"I'm hardly here for meals," I reply. "I guess I'm going to have to start keeping some food here."

"Maybe some staples," he says, and just as I'm about to roll away, he tugs me back into his arms and hugs me close. I can hear his heart, still beating hard. He kisses my forehead, and then my cheek, and there it is again: love.

I swear he's going to tell me he loves me.

Am I ready for this?

Fuck yes, I'm ready for this!

He drags his knuckles gently down my cheek, and suddenly, he jerks back, shouting in pain.

"What the hell?"

Binx has jumped on his shoulder, digging his claws in so he wouldn't fall. I reach out and pull the kitten to me.

"Bad kitty."

Meow.

"I forgot all about him," Beau mumbles, and just like

that, the moment's gone. "Let's get ready for the day, and I'll take you out to breakfast."

"Okay." I nuzzle the kitten's face. "Are you hungry too, Binx? Come on, baby, I'll feed you."

"I've never been jealous of anyone before," Beau says, an odd look on his face.

"What could you possibly be jealous of now?" I ask.

"That damn cat," he says, scowling. I crack up laughing, still holding Binx to me.

"Come on, Binx." I kiss his furry face and carry him out of the room, still naked. "I'll feed you."

"I'm smacking your ass for that later!"

"Promises, promises," I reply.

***

"These purple wedges are awesome," Gabby says later that week. We are at Charly's shoe shop, trying on shoes and getting ready to go out for happy hour. "Are these new?"

"I've had them for about a month," Charly replies and reaches for another pair of wedges, in red this time. "Look at these beauties."

"I have those," Kate says and lowers her growing frame in a nearby chair. "They're super comfortable, and I can even wear them pregnant."

"Which means I should be able to wear them around the inn," Gabby says with a smile. "How are you feeling, Kate?"

"I'm told that I'm going to survive this," she says and pats her belly. "But I have my doubts. My ankles are the size of tree trunks."

"I remember those days," Gabby says with a wince. "It

sucks. But don't worry, after the baby is born, it won't happen anymore."

"I have two whole months left of this," Kate says and looks up at us with tears in her beautiful green eyes. "Did you hear me? *Two. Months.*"

"Okay," Callie says and squats next to her, patting her hand. "I know it feels like it's going to be forever, but it's not. It's going to be here so fast, and then you're going to have her here in your arms."

"Yeah, yeah." Kate rolls her eyes and leans her head back on the chair. "I know. But I'm already the size of a house. Eli says I'm still sexy, but *I'm the size of a house.*"

"You're actually a sexy pregnant woman," I reply honestly. "You may not feel like it, but I'm an unbiased third party, and I can tell you that I think you look amazing. Your skin is clear and glowing, and you're very healthy."

"I'm glowing because I'm always sweaty," Kate grumbles.

"Well, aren't you just a little ray of pitch black?" Van says with a saccharine sweet smile. Rather than be offended, Kate giggles.

"I know. I'm sorry. I *am* thankful for this baby, and that we're both healthy. I know she'll be here sooner than I think. I just get tired more easily, and the stretch marks are ridiculous. Not to mention, you guys get to drink crazy amounts of booze tonight and I don't."

"But we're glad you came because you're fun and it wouldn't be the same without you," Charly replies and kisses her cheek. "Cheer up, sugar."

"Okay." Kate takes a deep breath. "Thanks for letting me vent. I feel better."

"Good. We won't make you walk much tonight."

"Where are we going, anyway?" I ask. "The Odyssey?"

"No," Callie says, shaking her head adamantly. "I practically live there. If we're going out for fun, I want to go somewhere else."

"I heard a fun spot just opened up a few blocks over," Van says. "Let's walk down and check it out."

"Fine, but I'm not walking back later," Charly says. "I'm going to be too drunk, and we're all wearing pretty shoes."

"We'll call the guys," Gabby says. "Rhys will have to come get me anyway. It'll work out."

"Fun. Let's go," Callie says and the six of us set off, walking two by two down the heart of the French Quarter.

"I've been meaning to call you, Mal," Gabby says. "I would love it if you and Beau could come out to the inn for dinner one night this week."

"Oh, thank you! That would be fun. I think we're open just about any night, but I'll ask Beau to make sure."

"Great," she replies with a grin.

"I hear that you're a *we*," Van says, tossing a smile over her shoulder. "I like that."

"I think I like it too." I grin as we walk through the door of the bar. Like most bars, it's dark, but the furnishings are new, and it's clean. The music is classic 80's.

"I love Cyndi Lauper," Gabby murmurs, nodding her head in time with the song. "It's pretty in here. Not cheesy."

"Thank you," a tall brunette says as she approaches, a wide smile on her pretty face. "We just opened last month. I'm Alice. Six of you tonight?"

"Yes," Callie replies. "If you could put us in a corner somewhere, that would be great. And I apologize in advance for our shenanigans."

"Sugar, we welcome shenanigans," Alice says with a sassy wink and leads us to the back corner of the bar. The booth is massive, with rich gold and purple leather. It's typical New Orleans colors, but not at all cheesy.

We order our first round of drinks and get settled, taking in the scene around us.

It's not packed, but there are several other full tables. The dance floor is empty, but it's still early.

"I'm so happy we're doing this," Gabby says. "I don't come into the city to see you guys nearly enough."

"Agreed," Van says. "But it's a long drive, so I get it."

"We should try to do this once a month," Charly suggests.

"Sure, until I have this baby and never feel like leaving the house again," Kate says, then smiles. "Because I won't want to leave her."

"Oh, trust me," Gabby says, "you'll want to leave her. Not for a few months, but you'll eventually need a break."

"I want to know about Mallory and Beau," Charly says, suddenly changing the subject. "Spill it."

"I'm seeing him," I reply, not sure what she wants to hear, exactly, but positive that it's probably more than I want to say.

"Duh," Gabby says, rolling her eyes. Our drinks are delivered. "You can go ahead and get round two going now," she tells the waitress.

"Not for me," I jump in. "I am a one drink girl."

"Why?" Van asks. "Can't hold your liquor?"

I smile and shrug. "It's a safety thing. It's harder to keep a grasp on my head when I'm drunk. And I say way too much."

"An honest drunk," Callie says with a wink. "I think

we want you to be honest, Mal. Plus, there are six of us. Safety in numbers and all that jazz."

Just then my phone pings with a text.

"No chatting it up with my brother during girls' night out," Charly says and sips her cocktail.

"It's Lena," I reply with a grin. "Do you mind if I have her join us?"

"Not at all!" They all nod good naturedly, so I shoot Lena a response, tell her where we are, and to get here STAT.

"Thanks, guys."

"I like her," Kate says with a smile as she sips her Sprite.

"We all do," Callie adds. "Bring her along anytime. In fact, we'll get her number, and include her in group texts."

"She'd like that," I reply, surprised to find tears near the surface. "You're all so nice."

"Oh, we have bitchy moments," Charly replies. "But on the whole, yeah, we're good people."

I nurse my drink for the next twenty minutes, feeling not a little overwhelmed by these funny, successful women, and the fact that they've befriended me, bringing me—and my best friend—into their fold.

"You summoned me, and I'm here," Lena says when she finds our table.

"Yay!" Gabby says and scoots over to give Lena space in the booth. "We're happy you came. You need to give us all your number so we can just include you in the group texts for stuff like this."

"Oh good, group text hell," Lena says with a wink. "Thanks for including me. Is Mal shitfaced yet?"

"Whatever," I reply and throw my lemon wedge at her. "I'm not a boozer."

Lena smiles, and I can hear her thoughts clearly: *I'm here. Go ahead and have fun. You're safe.*

I shrug one shoulder and reply: *thank you.*

"Why do I think that a whole conversation just took place between you two?" Callie asks.

"Because it did," Lena says. "Let's flag down that waitress."

***

"So, back to you and Beau," Callie says an hour and several drinks later. "Talk to us."

"So sexy," I gush, then clamp my hand over my mouth. "See? I talk too much."

"Never," Charly replies and leans her chin on her fist, either listening intently or too drunk to hold her own head up. "I'll talk about Simon if you want."

"Yes!" I clap my hands and nod. "Tell us about Simon."

"Sexiest man ever," Charly says, but the rest of us shake our heads. "I know, you all think *your* men are the sexiest ever, but I'm related to most of them, so just… no. Simon has the British sexy factor going on."

"I love a British accent," Lena says with a sigh. "Can we meet him sometime?"

"Of course!"

"There, she shared," Kate says. "Now you, Mal."

"So, he's really sexy," I begin, watching a few couples shake their asses on the dance floor. "And he's so *nice*."

"That's not what we want to hear," Van informs me helpfully. "Get to the good stuff, but remember he's our brother, so leave out the naked parts."

"But the naked parts are fun," I reply and blink my

eyes several times because I'm starting to see two of each of them.

"Ew," Gabby says, wrinkling her nose. "But I'm so happy that you like him because we like him and he likes you."

"I do like him. I like both of him," I reply, then snort. "I'm seeing two of everything right now."

"Right on," Lena says and raises her glass in a toast. "I haven't seen you shitfaced in a very long time."

"It's kind of fun."

"Do you see more spirits when you're drunk?" Gabby asks.

I glace about the room and frown. "I don't think so. It's just the normal amount of dead people."

"Oh good," Callie says. "Hey, I wonder if there are spirits at The Odyssey?"

"There are," I reply. "But they're harmless."

She swallows hard and takes another sip of her drink. "I think I liked it better when I didn't know for sure."

We spend the next hour laughing and talking, enjoying our drinks and each other. I had no idea that friendships like this, with a whole group of women, were possible.

"Beau got me a kitten," I say. "I forgot to tell you. He's soooo cute!"

"Awe, a baby," Van says with a sigh, her eyes glassy from too many cocktails.

"What time is it?" Gabby asks and stares at her phone. "Holy shit, we've been here for four hours!"

"Time flies when you're having fun," I murmur.

"I should call it a night," Van says. "I have work to do in the morning."

"We all do," Charly reminds her. "But you're right, I

can't drink anymore. I'll be on my ass, and I'd rather be on my back while Simon takes advantage of me."

"Atta girl," Lena says with a laugh.

"I'll see if Beau can come get me," I murmur and send him a text.

Can you come pick me up?

A few seconds later, he replies: *Of course. Where are you?*

I tell him and look up to find that everyone is texting someone for a ride home, except Lena.

"Lena, we can take you home," I offer.

"I have my car," she says with a smile. "I only had one drink. I'm sober."

I nod and sling back the last of my fourth cocktail just as Beau walks in.

"Hi," I say with a smile. "You must have been close by."

"Well, hello there," he says. "I live just a few blocks away. How are we?"

"Drunk," I reply, then giggle. "I have to tell you something."

"Okay."

"You're lovely." I cup his cheek in my hand and love the stubble as it scratches my palm. "Like, really pretty."

"I'm a man, sugar."

"Yes. You are. I've seen all of your man parts." That last part is said in a whisper, so the others can't hear.

"Ew," Gabby says. "We weren't going to talk about him naked, remember?"

"I whispered it," I say in my defense.

"No, you didn't," Beau says with a laugh. "It looks like girls' night out was a success."

"It was." I nod and rub my nose. It's the only part of

my face that isn't numb. And it's itchy. "And I have to tell you that I like you. Like, I *really* like you."

"I like you too, drunk girl."

"No, I mean, like, I *like you* like you."

"Got it." He brushes my hair behind my ear.

"I wonder if she likes him?" Charly asks. I turn to her, nodding.

"I really do like him."

"Maybe she should use a different L word," Van says, tapping her lips with her finger.

"Like *Loser*?" Gabby asks.

"Maybe he's a *Lemon*," Charly suggests.

"No, he's lovely," I reply and kiss his cheek. "And I like him. Like, a lot."

"Now that we've established that you like me, I think I should take you home," Beau says.

"Your smile is ridiculous." I frown and watch his face. "Your whole gene pool is just ridiculous. Why are you all so pretty?"

"She's ready to go home," Lena says. "Keep an eye on her. She doesn't have as much control when she's this drunk."

"I've got her," he says and takes my hand, leading me out of the bar.

"My handbag," I say.

"I have it," he says.

"You do have it," I reply just as he opens his car door. "You have all of it. My bag, my heart. Just don't break it."

"Your bag?"

"No, my heart." I lean back in the leather seat and close my eyes, suddenly so tired.

"Don't fall asleep, sweetheart; we'll be home in a few minutes."

"I'm just resting my eyes," I reply. "Talk to me."

"Did you have fun?"

"So much fun." I smile and rub my itchy nose again. "I love your sisters. They ask a lot of personal questions."

"Of course they do," he says with a laugh. "I'm glad you like them."

"Yeah." I sigh, sleep tickling the edges of my mind. "I almost spilled the beans and told them I love you. I mean, I'm not ready to say that to anyone yet. But my mouth runs away with me when I'm drunk."

I feel the car stop, and Beau's hand on my leg.

"We're home."

"Okay. Good. So tired."

"Come on, baby. Let's get you into bed."

"Always trying to get into my pants." I giggle and bury my face in his neck when he picks me up and carries me inside the house and up to my bedroom. "I like it when you're in my pants."

"Nowhere else I'd rather be," he says. "But for tonight, you're going to just sleep."

"Only if you'll be in my pants tomorrow."

"Deal."

Chapter Seventeen

-Mallory-

"It was nice of Gabby to invite us out for dinner," I say as I fasten an earring in my left ear. "I haven't met Rhys yet."

"You'll like him," Beau replies. He slides his wallet into his back jeans pocket, and rolls the sleeves of his blue button down to just below his elbows, showing off the muscles in his forearms.

"You have great arms." His gaze whips up to mine. He gives me a slow, wide smile that would melt the polar ice cap. "Don't smile at me like that. We don't have time for any hanky panky."

"Hanky panky?" he asks and slowly walks to me, like a predator stalking his prey. Except, I love it when he catches me. He can catch me all damn day. "We have a little time."

"No." I giggle and hold my hand up, but it doesn't stop him. "We really don't, Beau. We have to get on the road or we'll be late."

"Then we'll be fucking late," he says as he cages me in against the wall, that sexy as fuck arm pinning me in place. "Do you have any underwear on under that skirt?"

"I guess you'll just have to investigate and find out." I cock a brow and every nerve ending in my body is on high alert as he squats before me and glides his fingertips over my ankle, up my calf and the backside of my knee, which makes me bite my lip.

There's a new erogenous zone.

They keep climbing up my inner thigh, and then brushes over my naked lips, almost making my knees buckle.

"Oh my God," I gasp and grip onto his shoulders for support.

"Well, look what I found," he says, looking up at me with pure mischief and lust. "No panties."

I shake my head, unable to release the death grip my teeth have on my lip.

"This is a big turn on, sugar."

Yes. Yes, it is.

"Should I fuck you, or should I eat you?"

That question, added to the music his fingers are making, almost sends me over the edge.

"Answer me," he says. His voice is quiet, but stern.

"Want you inside me," I manage to say just before he stands, unbuttons his pants, then spins me to face the wall and pins my hands above my head.

My skirt is around my waist, legs spread, and I'm expecting him to be inside me any moment. The wait is killing me.

"Do you know what you do to me, Mallory?" Beau whispers in my ear.

"No."

"No?"

I shake my head, and sigh when he drags his nose along my neck.

"You make me crazy," he says, then plants a wet kiss just under my ear. "You have totally disrupted my life, in every way possible."

"Not sorry," I mutter, and he chuckles, sending shivers up my arms.

"I'm not sorry either," he replies. "And I'm not sorry for this." He bites my neck. "Or this." Slaps my ass. "And definitely not this." Finally, quickly slips on protection and slides inside of me, and without pause, fucks me blind, right here against the wall in the middle of the day.

I can't think. All I can do is feel the way his free hand roams over my body, through my clothes and then under my skirt. He reaches around to plant his finger on my clit, and that's it. That's all I can take.

I cry out as the current of the orgasm pulls me under.

"Yes, that's it. Come for me, baby."

As if I could stop it even if I wanted to.

Which I definitely don't.

Just as the tremors start to settle, he grips my hips and pushes hard, just one more time, and comes, whispering my name.

After a few moments of catching his breath, he slips out, lets my skirt and hands fall, and moves away from me.

"Now we can go."

"No, now I need to clean myself up."

He smirks and slaps my ass one more time. "Make it quick, or we'll be late."

"Smart ass."

***

Thirty minutes later, we're zooming down the interstate, driving out of town and toward Inn Boudreaux.

"So, you made this commute every day?" I ask, watching the swamp move past us in a green and brown blur.

"Yes," he replies. "I could make the drive with my eyes closed."

"Well, let's not do that." I grin and reach over to take his hand in mine. "But I will borrow this hand."

"You can borrow anything you like."

"We haven't been to your house in a while. How's it coming along?"

"Great." He smiles, his eyes lighting up. "I should be able to move in by the end of the month."

"Oh, Beau, that's fantastic. Congratulations."

"Thank you. I'm ready."

"I bet you are."

"I'll be closer to you, too."

"True, your new neighborhood is only a five minute drive from my place."

"I actually wanted to talk to you about the living arrangements," he says cautiously.

"Okay." And just when we're getting to the good stuff, my phone rings. "Oh, sorry. It's Miss Sophia. I should take it."

"Of course."

"Hello?"

"Hi, darlin'," she says. "Is this a bad time?"

"Not at all, but I might lose my signal in a few minutes. Beau and I are on our way out to Inn Boudreaux for the evening."

"Oh, how nice," she says. "I just wanted to check in

with you and make sure you're okay."

And that what happened at the cemetery hasn't happened again.

"I'm great," I reply honestly. "Everything has been business as usual."

"Good."

"And how are you?"

"I don't have anything to complain about. I've gathered some information about our project, so if you'd like to come over for dinner in the next few days, we can go over it together."

"Oh, that would be wonderful. I'd love to have dinner with you. You and Lena choose a time and I'll be there."

"We will do that. Stay safe today, baby girl."

"I'm safe every day," I remind her. "I'll talk to you soon."

As I end the call, Beau pulls up to the inn, and I'm struck again by how beautiful the property is, with massive oak trees surrounding the pretty white plantation house.

"This is such a lovely place."

"I think so, too," he says.

"You wanted to talk about something before that call came through."

"It'll keep until after dinner," he replies and exits the car, then walks around to my side to open my door. "I'm a very patient man."

"That's a virtue I don't have much of." Rather than walk to the house, I walk into his arms and hug him close.

"What was that for?"

"You're just my favorite person, and I wanted to hug you."

His eyes soften as he tucks my hair behind my ear. "Mallory—"

"You're here!" Gabby exclaims from the front door. "Come on in. It's getting cold out there."

"It's going to be a chilly night," I agree and lead Beau up the steps of the wide front porch. "It's so pretty out here, Gabby."

"Thanks." A tall, broad man joins her. "This is Rhys."

"Pleasure," he says, reaching out to shake my hand. I pull my walls more tightly around me and am relieved when we touch and I don't feel anything but welcome and the love this man has for his family.

"Nice to meet you."

"Where are the kids?" Beau asks as we walk into the main living area of the house.

"With Mama," Gabby says with a wink. "We get a whole evening without the kiddos. The guests have been fed, and they're newlyweds, so they've already gone back up to their room."

"That's sweet," I reply with a smile. "This would be a great honeymoon location."

"Well, they rented out the whole inn for the week because they wanted privacy," Rhys says.

"Wow. Good for them."

"Would you like a glass of wine?" Gabby asks.

"No, thanks, I'm still detoxing from the other night. I'll just have some water."

"We can do that. Your shoes are fab."

I glance down at the blue ballet flats I bought at Head Over Heels and grin. "Your sister is a shoe goddess."

"And thank the lord above for it," Gabby replies. "I hope you're hungry because dinner is pretty much ready."

"I'm starving. I've been waiting all day for this, so I didn't eat much."

"A woman after my own heart," Gabby says with a

wink. "The guys are always hungry."

"Guilty," Rhys says and kisses his wife's cheek. "And you're an excellent cook."

"Thanks, babe."

The dining room table is already set, and Gabby begins bringing hot dishes in from the kitchen.

"How long have you lived here, Rhys?" I ask and ignore my growling stomach.

"For a couple of years now," he replies. "I'm Kate's cousin."

"Really? I didn't know that."

He nods happily. "She suggested I come down here to the inn for some R&R, and it turns out it was the best thing I ever did in my life."

"So you enjoy it, then?"

"I do. It's different from where Kate and I grew up in Denver, but it has it's own charm. There's plenty to do, and Gabby's family is here. It made sense to relocate."

"How do your parents feel about that?"

Larissa, the spirit I spoke to during the séance, has walked into the room and is standing in a corner, watching me. She's not speaking.

"My parents both passed away when I was very little. Kate's parents raised me."

"I'm so sorry to hear that," I reply, keeping Larissa in my peripheral vision. "I also lost my parents when I was a baby. My grandmother raised me."

"Interesting," Rhys replies. "Well, Kate's folks live in Ireland now, so it's just Kate and me here in the states."

"And you have each other here, with a wonderfully big extended family."

Rhys and Gabby both smile widely. "That's a beautiful way to put it," Gabby says.

"I need to talk to you, Mallory," Larissa says, but I try to ignore her. Tonight is about Beau and his sister, spending time with them. I don't want to have to deal with this tonight.

Not today, Larissa.

She shakes her head adamantly. "It's important."

I take a bite of a Brussels sprout.

"Mal?" Beau says, frowning down at me.

"Yes?"

"I just asked how the Brussels sprouts are."

"Oh, they're good." I can't taste them. Larissa is agitated, and won't go away.

"What's wrong?" he asks, just as my phone rings. Lena's calling, probably to talk about dinner with Miss Sophia. I send her to voice mail and do my best to smile at Beau.

"Nothing. I love Brussels sprouts."

"What do you see?" he asks, setting down his fork.

And then he's gone, along with Rhys and Gabby, and the food on the table. Only Larissa is here with me.

"What's happening?"

"I don't know," she says. "It just feels different now."

I frown and turn my head, listening. Despite coming in here with my walls up and door shut, I'm seeing and hearing more than I ever have before. I can hear a man's voice, calling from behind the house.

"Do you hear that?"

"Oh, yes," Larissa says. "He's been calling out for as long as I've been here. That's normal."

"Do you know who it is?"

"No." She shakes her head and looks around the room, as if she's expecting someone to walk in. "Sometimes I think it sounds like my Douglas, but it can't be him."

"Why can't it be him?"

"Because if it was him, I'd be able to see him, wouldn't I?"

I blink rapidly, not sure how to answer. *I don't know.* But I want to help her. And if it's Douglas outside, I want to help him, too.

"I'll go see."

"Be careful," she says. "It's different today."

"Can you leave the house?"

"I can only go out to the back steps, but I can't go further."

I nod and stand, heading out the back of the house toward the loud voice of a man, yelling. I can't make out what he's saying.

I walk through the back door, and Larissa is still with me. She stays on the steps, wringing her hands at her waist as I walk down the path lined with oak trees toward what I assume is the old slave quarters.

"Hello?" I call out. There are several spirits here. Two children are playing hopscotch on the sidewalk. An older woman is rocking in a chair on the porch of one of the small slave quarter buildings. Her dark skin is wrinkled, her hair white and standing up on end.

"You shouldn't be here," she says. She's not mean, or angry. She's trying to warn me.

"Who is yelling out?" I ask, opening my mind wider so I can search out. Miss Sophia told me to keep myself closed up, but I *want* to help Larissa. I know I can help her.

"That young man has been yelling out in torment for a century," she says, her face turning sad. "Poor boy."

"Where is he?"

She frowns. "Why, he's right there. You can't see him?"

I turn in a circle, looking around me. The voice is getting louder, more frantic.

And then, there he is.

"Are you Douglas?"

He's out of breath, panting as if he's just run a hundred miles.

"Yes'm." He nods. "I can't find Larissa. She's lost."

"I know where she is," I reply, excited that there is finally something good that I can do with my gift. "I can take you to her."

"You can?" His eyes fill with tears. "I've been looking everywhere."

"She's in the house."

His face falls. "I can't go in there."

"What do you mean?"

"I've tried to look in the house, but I can't go up the back steps."

Oh, God.

This is heartbreaking. Why would this happen?

But before I can try to help further, absolute darkness falls around us. I can't see my hand five inches from my face.

"What is happening?"

The red glow is back. The same one from the cemetery.

"I have to help you," I say to Douglas, who is looking in the direction of the house, his face a mixture of pain and longing.

"It's her," he whispers. I follow his gaze, and sure enough, Larissa is walking carefully toward us. She's scared and hopeful, and then I'm suddenly standing in front of my grandmother.

"Oh my God."

"Hello, my love," she says.

"You're here. Why are you here?"

"Because you need me." Her eyes are sad, belying the smile on her beautiful face. "He's here to hurt you, darlin'."

"Who?"

"He was here before," Larissa adds, her voice trembling. "When I saw you before, with the other women."

"The séance," I say, and she nods.

"I've never seen anyone else in the house before then."

"She can't see the living?" I ask Grandmamma, who shakes her head slowly.

This is so fucking weird.

"Watch your language," Grandmamma says sharply.

"Did you find Douglas?" Larissa asks.

"I did," I reply. "He's right here."

"Oh." Her eyes fill with tears. "I can't see him. Why can't I see him?"

"Why can't she see him?" I ask Grandmamma.

"Because she's being punished for throwing herself off of that cliff. They're both being punished."

"Well, that's horrible."

The red glow intensifies. "He's coming."

"Who?"

"You know who. Remember your talk with Sophia."

And then it all comes back to me in a rush. The day at the cemetery, and the story Miss Sophia told me after.

"He wants to kill me."

"Yes."

"The way he killed you."

"Yes."

"Do you see him?" I ask her. She tilts her head to the side, as if in surprise.

"You can't?"

I glance around again. "I only see the dead."

"Oh no," Larissa says.

"He's coming," Douglas says at the same time.

"What is happening?" I shout, terrified.

"They can help you," Grandmamma says. "Larissa and Douglas can help, but you have to open yourself up completely. You have to accept what and who you are."

"But I want to help *them.* This isn't fair!"

"She's right," Larissa says to me. "Your grandmother is right. We can help." She's calm now, as if she understands something that once eluded her. "That's why we've been here all along."

"It wasn't to find each other," Douglas adds, as if he can hear Larissa. "It was to help *you.*"

"They should get each other," I say softly to Grandmamma, who simply smiles and pats my hand.

"That's not meant to be, child."

"You're living, Mallory," Larissa says. "You have your love, who is also living, and ready to spend that life with you. Our love is already lost. Let us help you."

"All you have to do is open your mind," Grandmamma says. "But once you do, there is no going back. You'll be permanently open, and you'll have to learn to live with it."

"But the alternative is to die," I reply.

"Yes."

I glance between Larissa and Douglas, then to my grandmother.

"It's cold."

"He's so close," Douglas says. He's not afraid anymore. "I want to end this. I don't want to be here anymore."

"Live your life, child," Grandmamma says and takes my hand. I feel her fear, her love.

"I miss you."

"I know. And you'll be with me, but not now. Not like this. Embrace it, and fight back. Don't let him win again."

"No." I square my shoulders, tip my head back, and open my mind completely, then fall to the ground as the wind swirls around us. Larissa and Douglas vaporize, turning to blue mist that moves in a flash to the red, surrounding it completely, and then the red takes over again.

"They're not strong enough," I shout, trying to be heard over the roar of the wind.

"They are," Grandmamma insists. Her hair is a riot around her head, her silver cloak swirling in the wind.

"We're here!"

Miss Sophia and Lena?

"Evil be gone!" Sophia shouts, and takes Grandmamma's hand as Lena takes mine. They chant, loudly and growing in volume, words I've never heard before. It makes the red light dim and the blue intensify, and just when I think the red will die, it explodes in anger, filling the sky and air around us, surrounding us, knocking us on our backs.

I can't see the blue at all now.

"Join them," Lena yells.

"I don't know the spell!"

"Just say what we say!"

And so I do, listening carefully and learning the spell.

By the third time they begin to chant it, I have it down and join in, my voice strong and loud. The four of us levitate off the ground, a storm of wind, railing against the red darkness that shrieks in pain and retreats.

The blue lights are back, stronger and brighter, and together we advance until the red light explodes, like fireworks, into a million sparks.

The wind is gone. It's dead still as we return to the earth. The blue lights fly above us, then merge together and fly away.

"They're finally together," I murmur.

"And he's finally dead," Grandmamma says. She blinks fast, and falls to her knees. "Oh God, Sophia. I see the girls. I see the house. I know where they are."

"Tell us," I say, holding onto her hands. But she doesn't have to. Instead, I can see everything that she sees. A dozen girls, maybe more, chained to the wall in a dark basement. They're naked and cold.

One is dead.

The vision pulls back so I can see the whole house, and the street signs.

I know where they are.

"How?" I ask.

"Because you've opened yourself up," Grandmamma says. "But don't worry. This is not your life's work, it was mine. And you've just helped me finish. You call Detective Williams and tell her where the girls are."

"And that's it?"

"That's it. For now." She hugs me tightly. "You'll always see the dead. You're a medium and an empath, Mallory. You can help them, the way you just helped Larissa and Douglas."

"They saved me."

"You saved them, too." She smiles softly. "And you're about to help me."

"You? Why do you need help?"

"I need to move on," she says and brushes a lock of hair off my cheek.

"Beau does that," I say.

"I know. I like him."

"You've seen him?"

"Of course. I told you I would be here."

"I've never seen you."

"You didn't need me until now." She cups my cheeks in her hands. "You are a beautiful, talented, wonderful woman, Mallory. I want you to live every moment of your life. I want you to enjoy it all."

"I don't want you to go."

"I know." She smiles gently and looks over to Miss Sophia and Lena. "But just like before, you're in good hands. And your Beau will be a wonderful, worthy partner for you, darlin'."

"I didn't want to say goodbye before. And I don't want to now."

"It's time, love. It's time to let go. If you'll let me go, I can move on, to be with your grandfather, and your parents."

"And your Melissa."

Tears fill her eyes and she nods, hope shining through her. "I've waited a long time to hold her again."

My heart sinks. "I'm selfish."

Miss Sophia and Lena are on either side of me now, and I can feel Beau with me, too. I take a deep breath and brush the tears from my cheeks.

"I love you, Grandmamma."

"I love you, Mallory."

I look up at the light that's appeared behind her. "There it is. There's the way."

She turns to look and her face lights up. "Oh, look at that. Thank you, darlin'."

And with that, she walks away. I can see the shapes of people waiting for her. They greet her with hugs and love, and then the light closes, and it's gone.

"You're brave," Beau whispers in my ear. I glance around, but I'm alone.

Yet, I'm not alone.

And it's time to go home.

Chapter Eighteen

~Beau~

"Where is she going?" Gabby asks as Mallory stands and slowly leaves the dining room.

"I don't know," I reply.

"She has the same dilated eyes that she had the night of the séance," Gabby says as we all stand and follow her through the kitchen to the back porch.

She's talking to someone, but I can't make out the words. All I know for sure is, she's not here. She's somewhere else.

And I'm terrified.

The phone in Mallory's pocket rings, so I reach for it and answer.

"Lena, something's happening."

"I know, my grandmother and I are on our way. Stay with her. What is she doing?"

"She's walking out of the house," I reply. "She's talking to someone we can't see. She's stopped on the stairs and is looking to the back of the property."

"We'll be there in ten minutes."

She hangs up, and I've never felt so fucking useless in my life. "I don't know what to do."

"We'll flank her," Rhys says, standing to the other side of Mallory. "And we'll keep her as physically safe as possible."

"But it's a metaphysical fight," Gabby whispers, watching with wide eyes. "Thank God the kids aren't here."

Mallory walks down the sidewalk to where Gabby had the old slave quarter buildings moved so guests can see them and learn about the history of our plantation, and others in this area.

"Mallory, I'm right here," I say, but there's no response. "You're safe, baby."

"How can she not hear you?" Rhys asks in frustration. He's very much like me, a protector. And when someone we care about is struggling, we *need* to help them.

"I don't know for sure," I reply, shaking my head. The wind has picked up.

"There was no storm in the forecast," Gabby says with a frown.

Mallory reaches out, as if to hug someone. Her mouth is moving with words, but no sound is coming out. Her red hair is a riot in the wind, and her eyes are hauntingly black.

"We're here!" Lena exclaims as she and an older woman I'm assuming is her grandmother run to us.

"What's happening to her?" I demand.

"She's speaking with the dead," Lena says. "This is my grandmother, Sophia."

"Where were you when it started?" the older woman asks.

"We were eating dinner inside."

Suddenly, Mallory whips her gaze back to the house and shakes her head *no.*

"We have to go in," Sophia says to Lena. "You and I must hold hands while we hold hers to ground each other. You chant what I do, just follow my lead."

"If this isn't safe—" I begin, but Sophia cuts me off.

"She'll die," she says fiercely. "He's here to kill her."

"Who?" I step back, stunned and panicked at once. "Who the fuck is trying to kill her?"

"The same madman that killed her grandmother," Lena says. "She's fighting for her life, Beau. We have to hold her hands, but *you* ground her the best. I want you to touch her shoulders, and stand beside her so she can fall back onto you if need be."

"Now," Sophia says, and the three join hands, and their pupils also go black.

"Jesus," Rhys mutters and rubs his hand over his mouth. "I'll stand on this side to steady them."

I nod and move behind Mallory, placing my hands on her shoulders. Every muscle in her body is tight. The wind is still swirling around us, and the three women are talking, almost chanting in unison, but they're not making any noise.

"I've never seen anything like this," Gabby says and slips her hand into Rhys's. "I think they're waging a war."

I nod, my eyes never leaving Mallory. Suddenly, Lena and Sophia blink their eyes and wake up, looking at each other. They both sag in exhaustion, and Rhys steps up to let them lean on him.

"Where is she?" I demand when Mallory doesn't blink and come back to me right away.

"She's saying goodbye," Lena says sadly. "But we

killed that horrible piece of shit."

"Where?" Gabby asks, looking around. "There's no one else here."

"Not physically," Sophia says and wipes her forehead on her sleeve. "But he was here."

A tear slips down Mallory's cheek.

"Who is she saying goodbye to?" I ask.

"Her grandmamma," Lena says.

Finally, Mallory blinks and takes a gasping breath, falling back against me.

"Mal? Baby, are you with me?"

"I'm here," she says, searching frantically for her phone. "I have to call Lieutenant Williams. Where's my damn phone?"

"Who?" I pass the phone to her, and she thumbs through until she finds the number she wants.

"The sick shit who kidnapped, raped, and starved little girls just died, and I know where they are."

"Holy fuck," Rhys says in shock.

"This is Mallory Adams. I know the location of the missing girls."

***

"Are you okay, Beau?" Mama asks a few hours later. She brought the kids home to the plantation, helped get them settled, and chatted with all of us for a bit before I took an exhausted Mallory out to my old place in the former carriage house.

"I don't know what I am," I reply honestly.

"How's Mal?"

"She's asleep out in the carriage house."

"And why aren't you with her?"

I shrug and lean on the kitchen counter, crossing my arms over my chest. "I have never felt so helpless as I did this evening."

"And you're the fixer," she says with a nod. "Not everything in this world is fixable, Beau."

"It's my job to protect my family, and I brought a medium right into their house and it scared the shit out of all of us."

"So it's Mallory's fault?"

"I didn't say that," I reply in frustration. "But she didn't tell me what was happening with the psycho who had targeted her. She didn't tell me how her grandmother died. Those are some pretty big things to forget to mention."

"Perhaps she just wanted to be a woman enjoying a man, and not a psychic."

"She's both," I reply with a frown.

"Does it make you love her less?"

"It scares me," I reply, evading the question. "What if it happens again? Or, what if it's even worse and it puts the family at risk? I don't know if I can continue with this if—"

I can't finish the thought, but Mama nods, understanding.

"You've always protected us, Beau. Before your daddy died, and even more so after."

"It's my job."

"No, my dear boy, it's not your job."

"I'm the eldest, and Papa's gone. Of course it's my job to see after all of you."

"But what about *you*?" she asks and slams her fist on the countertop, pissed off. "You're a man. You're a successful, intelligent, handsome man who deserves to love a woman, and have children, and everything else that goes with that. And rather than pursue a family of your own, you've spent your entire adulthood taking care of the rest of us. It's okay for you to take care of yourself for a change, Beau. We can take care of ourselves."

"I'm no martyr," I reply, just as pissed. "I'm just doing the right thing. And I don't know if bringing Mallory into our family is the right thing."

"Yes, you do," she replies, more softly now. "But I think you're scared of a woman, for the first time in your life. Not because of her unusual gifts, but because you love her."

"I do love her," I murmur. "I'm crazy about her."

"A mother knows these things," she says with a smile. "What could possibly be wrong with bringing the woman you love into your family?"

"She shut me out," I reply immediately. "She was in danger, and she didn't tell me. That's no way to go into a partnership."

"It always circles back to trust, doesn't it?"

I nod and pinch the bridge of my nose. "Always. The ironic thing is, Mal and I have talked about the importance of honesty and trust from the beginning of our relationship."

"And tonight you feel betrayed."

"I should have been prepared," I reply and push away from the counter to pace the kitchen. "I should have known what was happening so I could help her."

"You *did* help her."

"But I couldn't defend her against the guy trying to kill her."

"I didn't need you to."

Both of our heads whip around to the open back door

where Mallory stands, watching us with tired eyes, her hands firmly propped on her hips.

"It was not your fight," she says.

"I'm going to head out," Mama says with a smile. She walks to Mallory and kisses her cheek, then pulls her in for a hug. "I'm so relieved that you're safe."

"Thank you."

Mama winks at me as she leaves us alone in the kitchen.

"I thought you'd sleep for a while."

She nods and steps inside, closing the door behind her. "I woke up and you weren't there."

"I'm sorry."

"No, you're not." She smiles sadly and sits at the breakfast bar.

"So, you can read my mind now?"

"No." She shakes her head. "But I can read body language and facial expressions as easily as the next person, and you're not sorry. And that's okay. You needed to be alone."

"How much did you hear?"

"Enough." She looks down at the countertop for a moment, as if gathering her thoughts, and when she looks back up at me, there is so much sadness in her violet eyes it makes me want to scoop her up and tell her that everything will be okay.

But I don't know if it's going to be okay.

"I scared you today."

"That could be the understatement of the year."

She nods.

"I need to tell you some things, but first I want to say this: if you want to part ways as friends after everything that's happened tonight, and what I'm about to tell you, I completely understand."

I'm not fucking parting ways with you.

I lean back against the countertop and nod. "Okay."

"Okay." She takes a deep breath and lets it out again. "I'd like to explain about what happened tonight. I didn't understand all of it until it actually happened, and the pieces have just started coming together in the past week or two.

"The night I did the séance here, I saw a darkness. That's the only way to explain it. It appeared fast, and it was gone just as fast because I slammed my mind's door on it. Nothing like that had ever happened before, and I brushed it off as being something here at the inn, like a spirit.

"Then, the day I went to the cemetery with Miss Sophia and Lena, it returned, but stronger. And Miss Sophia knew what it was because she'd seen it before. It was the man who killed my grandmother all those years ago.

"He had been released from the mental institution, and was back at abducting and torturing young girls. And he was a powerful psychic, who targeted me because he assumed that because of who my grandmother was, that I would step in and try to help law enforcement find him."

"Why didn't you?" I ask.

"Because that's not my gift. I can't see the living psychically like my grandmother could. That's how she helped find so many lost children. I can only see the dead. So, after the encounter at the cemetery, Miss Sophia gave me more details about my grandmother's death, and she was researching how we should move forward with what was happening currently. She had put a protective spell over me, and I'd been bathing in lots of disgusting tea as protection too."

"And you didn't think that I'd want to be in the loop so I could also keep you safe?"

"I don't know how you could have done that," she replies. "You would have worried, but the dude in New York wasn't a physical threat; he was in my head."

I shake my head and pace as she keeps talking.

"I understand if you don't want me to be around your family, but I can promise you that I will never put them in danger. I'm not normal, Beau, and I never will be. I've discovered that I can do a lot of good as a medium. I'm not saying that I'm going into business and seeking out a television show, but there will be moments when I have to turn my attention to someone you can't see so I can help them."

"That's not my issue—"

"Let me finish." She holds her hand up, and I stop talking, listening instead. "I'm not normal. But I love you so much I ache with it."

I want to hurry around this island and take her in my arms to reassure her, but I wait, giving her space to finish.

"I've wanted to tell you for a long time, but I was afraid. It's stupid," she says and impatiently brushes a tear off her cheek. "Life's too precious and short to not say what you mean, so I'm saying it. I didn't withhold information to spite you, or because I didn't trust you. I just—" She shrugs, as if she's trying to find the words. "I just didn't know *what* to tell you."

"Everything," I reply and finally cross to her. I tip her chin up so I can look in her eyes. "I want you to tell me *everything*. Especially if it hurts or scares you. I was so thrown off guard and afraid for you this evening; I thought I was going to lose you."

"And if it wasn't for my family, you might have."

The thought turns my stomach. "You are everything to me, Mallory. You're not *abnormal*. You can do things that others can't do."

"Do you believe me?" she whispers, making me frown.

"What do you mean?"

"I know that you're a no nonsense man, and that you've indulged me, especially in the beginning. But Beau, I need you to believe me."

"I don't love you *despite* your gifts, Mallory. I love you, period. In the end, isn't that what we all want? Someone to choose us, to love us, no matter the circumstances?"

She nods, letting the tears fall unchecked down her cheeks.

"You are a magical, beautiful, amazing woman, Mallory, and I love everything about you. I do trust you."

"I'm a handful," she says with a wet smile, making me smirk.

"I have two hands," I reply, finally pulling her in for a hug.

"And you have me," she says against my chest. "You're my home, Beau. After Grandmamma moved on, all I wanted to do was come home to you."

"Which leads me to what I wanted to talk to you about earlier this afternoon," I reply and pull back a bit so I can see her face. "When it's time for me to move into the new house, I'd like for you to move in with me."

Her face lights up. "I love your house."

"I'd like for it to be our house."

"Oh." She takes a deep, cleansing breath. "Are you sure?"

"Never been more sure. You're my home, too."

She swallows and nods. "I'd like that. But do I have to help in the garden?"

"No, baby, we want to eat the vegetables. Not kill them."

***

She slept like a baby all night, wrapped around me. I didn't sleep a wink; instead I held her, enjoying the warmth of her, the smell of her hair, and the sweet way she would drag her hand up and down my side.

I couldn't get the image of the look on her face as she stood behind the inn, fighting a force I couldn't see out of my head. I'm not comfortable with the thought of not being able to protect her from everything.

I love her.

But I'm used to handling, well, everything.

Not that a woman is something to be handled. My mama would have my hide if she heard me say something like that.

As soon as I see dawn break, I untangle myself from Mallory's grasp, pull on yesterday's clothes, and walk out to the cemetery.

I haven't been to this spot since my dad passed away. There was never a need.

But I could sure use his advice now.

"You died too soon," I murmur and sit on the bench directly across from his headstone. "Although, any time would have been too soon."

It's quiet today. The sky is clear and full of pink and purple with the rising sun.

"I don't know what to do about her."

And I'm not even entirely sure what I'm hung up

about. I've asked her to move in with me for Christ's sake. It's not like I want to break it off.

Absolutely not.

But I'm unsettled.

Am I such a control freak that being with a woman who doesn't need me all the time emasculates me?

I wouldn't think so. I love that she's strong and independent.

And what in the ever-loving hell am I doing at my father's grave? It's not like I can see the dead. That's Mallory's gig.

I wonder if she's seen him?

That's an unsettling thought.

I rub my hand over my face and stand to leave. There aren't any answers here.

"Hi," Mallory says with a smile, surprising me.

"Well, hi. Did I wake you?"

"No." She looks at the headstone, then at me. "I have someone with me who would love to talk with you."

I cock a brow and glance around, but there's no one else here.

"Who would that be?"

She looks to her left, just a few feet from where I am, and nods.

"Your father."

"That's impossible," I reply. "My father is dead."

She sighs and shakes her head, her eyes filled with sadness. "You don't believe, Beau. You don't believe at all."

"Mal—"

"Just hold your coin and think of your dad. Then come find me when you have your stuff all figured out."

She turns to leave and I want to follow her, but instead I push my hand into my pocket and find the coin I always carry. You would think that as often as I hold it, I would wear it down.

"You always were the most stubborn child of mine."

My head whips up at the sound of the voice I'll never forget. "Holy shit."

"Indeed."

Chapter Nineteen

~Beau~

"What's eating at you, son?" my father asks, and I have to take a deep breath, shake my head, and rub my fingers over the coin in my pocket, not entirely sure that I'm not drunk.

Or asleep.

"Are you not speaking to me?" he asks with a grin.

"I'm not sure that you're really here," I reply.

"I'm here," he says and sits on the ground at his headstone, leaning against it. He's wearing his favorite old jeans and Tulane University sweatshirt. And he's so real, I could reach out and touch him. "And I know you. You're pissed."

"I am not," I reply and sit on the bench across from him. "Why would I be pissed?"

"Because you've come across something that you can't fix or manipulate." He shrugs. "I understand. I was the same way. It was my job to make sure that your mother and you kids were safe, and to provide for you all."

"You always did that," I reply.

"There were moments that baffled me, Beau. I'm a man, as are you. You're a powerful man, with an infinite number of resources at your fingertips, but there will be moments that baffle you, too. Because you're a man."

"I'm supposed to be the head of our company, and our family."

"Which you're doing a damn good job of," he says, and I just go still. I'm dumbfounded, and not embarrassed to feel my eyes fill with tears. "Do you assume that I'd think differently?"

"No, I've just wondered, since you passed, if you could see what Van, Eli, and I were doing with the company, and if you would approve."

"I'm so damn proud of the three of you, Beau. Of all of my children. You're intelligent, happy, successful people. I don't go into the office often, I'll be honest. A man should enjoy his retirement."

I can't help but chuckle and shake my head. "My God, you're really *here*."

"I'm always around." He tilts his head to the side. "I like to stick close to your mama. Not because she needs me, but because she's my heart, and by her side is where I'm supposed to be. But I check in with all of you from time to time."

"Have you talked with Mallory?"

He smiles brightly now and nods. "She's a sweet girl, your Mallory."

"She is," I agree, thinking of her kind smile, her gentleness.

"And she concerns you," he adds.

"I don't know what I'm feeling," I reply and rub my hand over my face. "And this is new to me."

"Well, that's love for you, son," he says and slaps his knee with a laugh. "You're going on forty years old, and you're just now finding it."

"I'm only thirty-seven," I reply. "And finding love was never at the top of my priority list."

"That was my fault," he says. "I pushed the business too hard—"

"No, you didn't," I interrupt. "I loved it. I still do. I don't regret one minute that I spent with you in the office. You taught me more than I ever learned in college. I just wish that you were still here so I could still call you with questions." I swallow hard. "I miss you, Dad."

"I know," he says. "I miss all of you, too. I can see you, but I can't always speak with you, and that hurts. But I'm here, Beau. I'll be here for quite some time yet."

"Mallory could help you, if you wanted to move on."

To my surprise, he just shakes his head, but then smiles widely. "You *do* believe her."

"Well, she's not crazy. Of course I believe her. But, I'm a black and white kind of man. I don't live in the grey area of life, and if I can't see it with my own eyes, well, I find it hard to buy into."

"And yet, here I am."

"Thanks to her," I finish for him and shove my fingers through my hair.

"Stop overthinking it," he says. "You're the most analytical of my kids. You overthink everything, and on top of it all, you're a control freak. That's great with business, but not with love. She's not a job, she's a woman. You're going to fuck up now and then, I can promise you that. She'll get mad and maybe even hurt. But let me tell you something, Beau, loving her will be the best thing you ever do in your life. Regardless of all of my accomplishments while I was here, being married to your mother was the best part of me."

"We knew it," I reply gruffly. "And she knew it."

"That's how it should be. So, I'm going to remind you of something that I always told you kids—you can't control the wind, but you can adjust your sails. That applies more in relationships than any other part of life, my boy. And while you didn't exactly fall in love with a sailor, the metaphor still applies."

We laugh together, and it feels so fucking good, I don't want to let go of it. Not yet.

"She's definitely not a sailor." I smile, watching the man that I love so much and miss more than words can say. "Are you okay, Papa?"

"What do you mean?"

"Where you are. Are you safe? Are you happy?"

His hazel eyes soften. "You know, your Mallory asked her grandmother the same question when she saw her. You two are more alike than you think. I'm perfectly safe, and I'm happy for now. You mentioned that Mallory could help me move on, but I'm not ready. I'll wait for my sweetie. And I hope she's here with you for a very long time."

"Me too," I reply with a nod. "Will this be the last time I see you?"

He takes a deep breath and glances around at the tall oak trees, the early morning blue sky, and then back to me. "No, I'll be around. But you don't need to come to the cemetery to talk to me. It's rather depressing, don't you think?"

I laugh, a full belly laugh. "I guess it is. I wonder why people do that? Maybe it has something to do with seeing your name, and knowing you're buried here."

"But I'm not," he says with a wink. "I'm not six feet under. I'm watching over my family."

"Can I touch you?"

He holds his hand out. "Help an old man up off the ground."

I take his hand, and it feels just as it did when he was living. Strong. I pull him up, and am immediately engulfed in his arms. My father was always a hugger, and I didn't realize until just now how much I missed that.

"I've needed this," I murmur as he pulls away.

"I know," he says and pats my shoulder. "Now, go find your girl and make things right with her. I love you, Beau."

"I love you too, Dad."

***

I head back for the carriage house, hoping to find Mallory.

I'm not disappointed. I find her in the kitchen, arranging a bouquet of forget-me-nots in a vase.

"Hi," I say.

"Hello," she replies and smiles stiffly. "How was your chat?"

I shake my head. "I don't think I have the words to describe it yet."

She nods and sets the vase of flowers on the table. "I'll take these up to Gabby before we leave so she and the guests can enjoy them."

"It was nice of you to pick them."

"I had to get some aggression out, and it turns out that ripping flowers from the earth is a pretty good way to do that."

I prop my hands on my hips and watch as she turns to me, raises her chin, and squares her shoulders as if she's getting ready to take a blow.

That's my fault.

"I owe you an apology, Mallory."

"I'd say you do," she says with a nod. "So let's hear it."

I want to pull her into my arms and kiss her breathless, but instead I lean on the counter, bracing my hands at my hips, and start talking.

"It's not that I didn't believe you, Mal. How could I *not* believe you? Especially after last night. At first, I believed that *you* believed it. And that was good enough for me. You see, I'm an analytical man. I live in a world with absolutes. It's either black or white; there is very little room for a grey area.

"And on top of that, I am a problem solver. Your gifts exhaust you, and sometimes they scare and *hurt* you, and there's nothing I can do to help you. I'm not comfortable with that."

"You do help me," she says. "There's a reason that I can't read you, Beau. You ground me, and you are my safe place. I felt you with me last night when I was fighting the darkness, and it was *you* that pulled me back. I needed you. I don't have to guard myself when I'm with you. I'm just a woman, not a psychic woman, when I'm with you. That is what you bring to my life, and that's what you *should* be for me."

"I'm learning that," I reply. I can't keep my hands off of her any more. I slowly cross to her and drag my knuckle down her cheek. "I'm sorry that I've been an idiot. I can't promise that I'll never be an idiot again, but I'll never intentionally hurt you again."

She grins, turns her lips to my palm, and kisses it.

"Apology accepted. And I apologize too."

"For what?"

"For making you feel like you were out of the loop. I didn't mean to do that."

"I know."

"You do?" She's watching my lips now, and the mood has shifted from apprehensive to longing.

I want her.

I glide the pad of my thumb over her lower lip, then replace it with my own lips, sweeping back and forth, soaking in the taste of her. She anchors her hands at my sides, fisting my shirt as I devour her mouth.

"I can't keep my hands off of you."

"Good," she mutters as I cup her ass and lift her to me. She wraps her legs around my waist and buries her face in my neck, kissing and biting. My semi-hard is a semi no more. I spin and set her on the countertop, spread her wide, and grind myself against her through my pants and her jeans.

"Need you." My voice is gruff. She manages to shimmy out of her jeans and reaches for my pants as well. "I'll never get enough of you."

"That's convenient," she replies as her hands slide down my bare ass. "Have I mentioned that you have a great ass?"

"Not today."

She bites her lower lip. "Great ass."

"You have a phenomenal ass," I reply as I nestle myself between her legs and just let my cock slip between her wet folds. "Gorgeous tits." I suckle on one, and then the other. Her head falls back with a sigh of pleasure. "The softest skin I've ever seen."

"Jojoba and melaleuca oils," she mutters, making me

grin.

"They work."

"I know." She gasps when I reach between us and lightly rub the tip of my cock over her clit. "You're really talented with that."

"It's a multipurpose tool," I reply and slip inside her. "Fucking hell, you're wet, sugar."

"Your fault," she says with a gasp, arching her back. "You're sexy."

Her hand roams from her breast to her pussy, pressing on her clit and then on the base of my cock.

She clenches around me, and it's almost more than I can take.

"Not so fast," I pant and pull her hand up to kiss her fingers. "I'm not ready to come yet."

"No?"

"No." I pick her up and carry her, still inside her, to the bedroom and lower us both to the bed. I don't want to fuck her senseless, I want to make love to her. I brace my elbows beside her head and she cradles my pelvis between her thighs, and we just stay like this for a moment, staring into each others eyes. "I love you so much, Mallory."

Her brow furrows in surprise, and tears pool in her gorgeous blue eyes.

"Don't cry."

"I've seen the love," she says. "I've seen it in your eyes, and I've felt it when you hold me, but it's an entirely different thing to hear it."

"I said it last night," I remind her.

"Yes, and then it felt like things had shifted overnight, like you had a chance to really think about what I am, and were having second thoughts."

"Not second thoughts," I reply and brush my fingers

through her hair. "I was just confused, and I'm an overthinker. Dad told me to cut that shit out and enjoy you."

"I love your dad," she says with a grin.

"I love you," I whisper against her lips. "You'll get used to hearing it because I plan to say it every day, just to remind you."

"That's lovely," she says. I move my hips slowly, pulling out and then pushing back inside, and she sighs.

"Is this lovely?"

"No, it's fucking amazing," she says. "It's like you were made just for me."

"Because I was, sugar."

Chapter Twenty

-Mallory-

Three Months Later

"You should go on home," I say to Shelly after she bags a customer's purchase and reshelves some items that another customer decided to pass on. "It's Christmas Eve. Go spend it with your family."

"Are you sure?" She frowns and glances about the shop. "It seems to be slowing down, but it could get busy again. People have a whole year to plan for Christmas, and yet it seems everyone waits for Christmas Eve so they can panic."

"Well, I won't complain too much because it was a lucrative day." I grin and reach for the envelope I already addressed to my assistant and pass it to her. "Merry Christmas."

She opens the envelope and looks up at me in shock. "This is too much."

"You deserve a bonus," I reply and pull her in for a hug. I'm much less worried about being touched these days. Even though Grandmamma was right and my walls are permanently down now, I'm learning to cope with this new way of life.

Part of me wishes I'd done it long ago. It's much less stressful.

"Thank you," Shelly says. "I brought you a little something."

She disappears into the office, then returns with a small red gift bag.

"Thank you." I'm ridiculously touched by her gift, and I haven't even opened it yet. I sincerely like Shelly, and I'm so happy that I have her on my team.

"Open it," she says with a grin.

"Okay." I toss out the gold tissue and find a beautiful sprig of mistletoe. "Oh, this is beautiful."

"I know it's tradition at Christmas, but I've also learned that it's for good luck, and a love talisman. I thought it would be perfect for your new home."

"It's absolutely perfect," I agree and hug her once more. "Thank you. I know just where we will hang it."

Shelly grins and reaches for her handbag. "You're not staying late, are you?"

"No, I'm going to close up in a minute. I'm ready to go home, too."

She nods and waves as she leaves. "Merry Christmas!"

"Same to you!"

I return the mistletoe to its bag, then set about the routine of closing up, counting the money drawer, closing out the credit cards, and taking out the trash.

We are supposed to go to Beau's mom's house both this evening and tomorrow to celebrate with the family, and I'm nervous. It's our first Christmas together. But they were kind enough to also invite Lena and Miss Sophia so we could all be together, and it made me fall in love with Beau and his family even more deeply.

And I didn't know that was possible.

I lock the front door and turn around to find a bottle of lavender oil suspended in the air, and then it's thrown and broken against the wall.

"Miss Louisa!" I prop my hands on my hips in frustration. "You've been throwing a tantrum for a month now. What's wrong?"

She never shows herself to me, but she sure lets me know that she's here. This isn't the first time she's thrown something, and she's become famous for talking in my ear, startling the hell out of me.

"If you want to tell me why you're angry, just come talk to me. I'm right here."

I stand still, listening. Everything is silent again, but I can still feel her here.

Suddenly, she walks out of my office, as if she works here and she's coming out to help me with a customer.

"Hello," I say, watching her carefully. "You're a beautiful woman. And a sad one."

She nods and looks around the shop, concern written all over her lovely face.

"Have I done something wrong?"

"I don't know why you're here," she says, surprising me. Her voice is soft and feminine. She's wearing a long blue dress with an apron, and her blonde hair is twisted up on the back of her head.

"I own this shop," I reply.

"I've been trying to make you leave," she says. "I don't want a ghost in my place. And you keep moving things."

I step back, completely stunned. Does she not know that she's dead? I'm tempted to shut her out and ignore her, the way I always did before three months ago when everything happened out at the inn.

But I'm learning that ignoring something doesn't change it. And Miss Louisa obviously needs me.

"I'm sorry, I didn't mean to be in your way."

"I can't bake my breads and sweets with you in the way."

"No, I imagine you can't." I blink and quickly try to decide how I'm going to handle this. "Miss Louisa, do you know what year this is?"

"Why, it's 1915, of course."

Holy shit.

"I'm so sorry, Miss Louisa. I should have talked to you sooner, to try to help you."

"I don't understand what's happening," she replies with tears in her eyes.

"I know that now, and I can help you. Do you remember *not* being here? I mean, do you remember the last time you went home for the evening?"

"No," she says, shaking her head. "I'm just always here. Sometimes I go up in the attic, but there are strange people up there too."

"I don't want you to be afraid. You're not in danger. But I have to tell you that you've passed away, Miss Louisa. And you're stuck here."

"No, that can't be true. My husband will be here any minute to pick me up."

"He won't be here," I reply softly. "But I can help you move on so you can be with him."

"You can?" she asks, her whole face lit up with hope. "I miss him. I haven't seen him in a very long time."

"That must be horrible," I reply and take a deep breath, close my eyes, and feel a swirl of warm air. When I open my eyes, the light is behind her. "There you go. Just turn around."

She looks behind her and her face lights up in delight. "Teddy! He's finally here for me. Oh, thank you!"

And with that, she walks through the light, and then it's gone, the same way it was with Grandmamma.

There's no lingering sense of her here. The store, and the upstairs loft, are completely quiet and, aside from me, empty.

Merry Christmas.

I walk back to gather my things and hurry home. It's cooler today, although we certainly won't be having a white Christmas. The city is bustling with people hurrying to spend time with their loved ones, so my drive home takes a little longer than usual, but I don't mind.

When I walk into our house, I'm welcomed with the warmth from the fireplace and the love of a very special man. The house is completely furnished now, and we are all moved in and unpacked. It seemed to take forever, but now it feels like we've always lived here. I can't believe how perfect it is for us.

"Merry Christmas, sugar," Beau says as I walk into the kitchen and find him plating our dinner.

"Merry Christmas," I reply as I take my jacket off, hang it on a barstool, and take in the scene before me. "I thought we were going to your mom's for dinner?"

"Well, that was the plan, but I decided that I'd rather spend this evening by ourselves. Is that okay with you?"

"Sure, but Lena—"

"And Miss Sophia are still going to my mom's," he replies with a smile.

"Well, then yes, this works for me."

He seems...*nervous.* Which is very unusual for my

Beau. He's the most self-assured man I know.

"Are you okay?" I ask as he passes me a wine glass and I take a sip.

"I've never been better," he replies. "Can you grab my glass and I'll take our plates to the table?"

"Of course." I follow him to the dining room, where he's thrown a black tablecloth over our farm table, and added candles and forget-me-nots, along with some fine china that I've never seen before. "This is fancy."

"It's Christmas," he replies with a shrug. "And I wanted it to be pretty for you."

"You've succeeded," I reply. "I feel quite spoiled."

"You're not spoiled," he says and tucks my hair behind my ear. "You should be indulged often."

"I won't disagree," I say with a laugh. "What did you make for us?"

"Lasagna with bread and salad."

"That sounds *amazing*. I'm starving." I set my napkin in my lap and take a bite of salad. "These tomatoes are fantastic. They're from the garden, right?"

"They are."

I smile and continue to munch away, not oblivious to his shifting in his seat, and eating little of his dinner. But if he wants to share what's on his mind, he will do so in his own time. That's something I've learned about Beau. He needs to stew over something for a bit, and then he will talk to me about it.

So I just continue to enjoy our Christmas Eve meal and the beautiful table he set for us.

"Business was good today. We were busy all day long. Shelly brought us a sprig of mistletoe for our house," I say and take a sip of wine. "It's for luck and love. I think I'll hang it in the bedroom."

"That was nice of her," he replies and then suddenly sets his glass down and takes my free hand in his.

Here we go.

"I was going to wait to do this until after dinner, but it seems this is one situation where my patience skills are non-existent." He smiles and pushes his dinner away from him, and I do the same, eager to hear what he has to talk about.

"What's up?"

"I know we haven't known each other for long, Mallory. But I also know that I adore you. My only regret about us living together is that we didn't do it sooner. I said once that you shifted everything else in my life out of focus, but now I realize that everything is clearer than it's ever been.

"You are an incredible woman. I love you so fiercely that it scares me at times. If I were to ever lose you, well…" He shakes his head as if the mere thought of it is mortifying. "I can't even entertain the thought that I could ever lose you.

"You make every day the best day of my life."

He reaches into his pocket and pulls out a gorgeous diamond solitaire.

"Wow," I murmur.

"Marry me, Mallory. Let me love you, every day, for the rest of our lives and through whatever may come after we're gone. Be my partner, my lover, and my best friend."

He reaches over to wipe a tear from my cheek. I can't speak. I'm so surprised that all I can do is stare into his eyes.

"What are you thinking, love?"

"That I'm going to be really pissed off if this is a dream."

He smiles and kisses my cheek, then my lips, and pulls back so he can put the ring on my finger.

"Is that a yes?"

"Oh my God, yes!" I jump into his arms and hug him tightly. "I've never wanted anything more."

He kisses the crown of my head. "I don't want a long engagement. It seems I'm not quite as patient as I thought I was."

I lean back to kiss him squarely on the mouth, and then admire the round diamond on my finger. "This is beautiful."

"It was my grandmother's," he replies and holds it up to the light. "It's just under three karats, and you can have it reset any way you like."

"I love it just the way it is," I say and kiss him again. "I can feel the love that was shared because of this ring. I don't want to change a thing."

EPILOGUE

~Benjamin Preston~

"Are you ready for this?" Eli asks Beau with a pat on the shoulder. We're standing at the altar in Beau's backyard, waiting for the girls to walk down the aisle. "You have time to back out."

"I'm not going to fucking back out," Beau says with a roll of his eyes. "The engagement was long enough as it is."

"You were engaged for a month," Declan reminds him. "And you're lucky that it's warm enough out here today to do this. You couldn't wait until spring?"

"No," Beau says and sends his brothers a glare. "I couldn't."

I just grin and stay silent, the way I usually do. I'm waiting for the girls to walk down the aisle as well, because I'll get a glimpse of the woman I've been in love with for as long as I can remember.

The music starts, and first comes Mallory's best friend, Lena. She's in her pink bridesmaid dress, smiling happily. She's pretty enough, but she's not my type.

There's only one woman that's my type.

And she's looking directly at me right now.

Savannah Boudreaux keeps her eyes on mine as she

walks slowly in her pretty pink dress, holding a bouquet of flowers. I'll never remember what she wore today, but I'll never forget the way she looks.

She's beautiful.

She's so fucking smart and sweet as can be.

And she will never be mine.

Blush For Me

A Fusion Novel
By Kristen Proby
Available Now!

Chapter One

-Kat-

"So, it was just a kiss," Riley, my best friend, says from the driver's seat next to me. "And it wasn't a particularly good one at that."

"Dump him now," I reply with a gusty breath, wringing my hands in my lap. "If he's a shitty kisser, it only goes downhill from there. Trust me on this."

"But the conversation was good . . ."

Sweet Jesus.

"Seriously. If there's no spark, move on. The spark is out there somewhere."

"You're right." She sighs and takes the exit off the freeway, following the signs to PDX. "How are you doing?" She glances at me and frowns. "You're sweaty."

"Am not," I reply. Yes, I am. So damn sweaty.

"When was the last time you flew?" Riley asks.

"I've never flown," I reply, and squirm in my seat. Why doesn't it take longer to get to the damn airport?

"Seriously?" She changes lanes, and there it is. The airport. Straight ahead. "I know you hate it, but I had no idea that you've *never* flown."

Fucking hell.

"I've told you, I don't fly."

"It's only a two-hour flight, at the most, down there."

"Two hours too long," I mutter, and take a deep breath. Shit, I'm going to pass out. I can't see. I can't hear anything.

"Open your eyes," Riley says with a laugh. "I've never seen you like this."

"I'll be okay." It's only the five millionth time I've said that this morning. "I don't really have to go to this conference, do I? I mean, I have plenty of friends who will be there and they can tell me all about it when it's done."

"You need to go, Kat," Riley says. "You'll learn a lot, and meet new people, and get to tour vineyards and drink wine that you love."

"I can do that in Washington, and drive there."

"You're not a wimp," Riley says as she pulls up to the departures. "You've got this. You have plenty of time to stop by a bar once you're through security to have a drink to calm your nerves."

"You're not coming with me?" I stare at Riley in shock.

"You know I'm not coming to Napa Valley with you."

"No, to the gate."

Riley laughs and I want to smack her in the head with my handbag.

"No, Kat. We haven't been allowed to do that since 9/11."

"See? One more reason that I shouldn't go."

"Get out of my car." Riley climbs out of the car to retrieve my suitcase for me.

"I've never known you to be this mean."

"You're going to have a great time." She hugs me

close. "There are lots of signs and people to ask if you get lost in there, but it's not a big airport, so you should be fine. Call me when you get there."

"*If* I get there," I say, and sigh deeply. "Why do I feel like I'm never going to see you again?"

"Because you're being dramatic," she replies, and smiles brightly. "Have fun!"

And with that, she waves and drives away and I'm left alone to figure out this airport hell.

But Riley was right. Checking in and retrieve my luggage. Finding security is easy.

Getting frisked by the TSA guy would have been more fun if he'd looked like Charlie Hunnam, but then again, everything would be more fun with Charlie.

I follow the signs, find my gate, and am pleasantly surprised to find a bar directly across from it.

There is a God.

But once at the bar, I'm just too nervous to drink.

That's a first.

Who in the hell gets too nervous to drink? This girl, apparently.

So I wander back to the gate and pace, dragging my small black hard-sided suitcase with red cherries on it behind me. People glance my way, but I ignore them. I'm used to it. You don't dress the way I do, covered in sleeve tattoos, and not get looks.

Finally, my flight is called and they begin boarding. Before I know it, I'm sitting on the plane, three rows from the front—if I'm going to die, it's going to be in first class—in the aisle seat.

"Hello," the man next to me says. I glance his way, taking in his light brown hair and green eyes, and if we were anywhere but here, I would totally flirt with him.

But we're on a motherfucking airplane.

"Hi," I reply, and swallow hard. The flight attendant asks us if we'd like anything to drink before we take off, but I shake my head no and stare at the pilot sitting in the cockpit. "Don't they close that door?"

"Right before we take off," my travel companion says. I'm surprised that I spoke aloud. "Hey, are you okay?"

"Fine."

He's silent for a moment and I keep staring at the pilot. I want to march up there and tell him to make sure that we get there in once piece. What are his credentials, anyway? I want to see his license, and a few letters of recommendation wouldn't hurt either.

"I'm Mac." I slide my eyes to him and nod, then whip my gaze back to the front.

"Kat."

"Have you flown before, Kat?"

"No." I swallow hard and tighten my hands into fists.

"Okay, take a deep breath," he says. He's not touching me, which is good because I'd have to break his nose, and this is already stressful enough. But his voice is soothing. "Good. Take another one. Miss, can we get a bottle of water, please?"

I just keep breathing. The flight attendant returns with a little baby bottle of water, which Mac uncaps and holds out for me.

"Take a drink of this. Just a small sip." I comply, the cold water feeling good in my throat. I feel ridiculous. This flight is full of people who are not having panic attacks.

"I'm sorry," I whisper. "This is my biggest fear."

"I can tell," he says gently, and I raise my gaze to meet his. He's a handsome guy, his short hair styled nicely, his jaw firm, eyes direct. He's tall, with long arms and legs and a lean body. "How are you feeling?"

"Better," I reply, surprised to find it true. "The water helped. Thank you."

"No problem. Are you going to Napa Valley on vacation?"

"Work," I reply, shaking my head. "I'm attending a conference."

"So you're a wine enthusiast, then?"

"You could say that," I reply with a smile. "I own a wine bar in Portland."

His eyes narrow for just a moment. "Really? Which one?"

"The one inside Seduction."

"I've heard great things about that place."

I smile widely now, intensely proud of the restaurant that my four friends and I have built from the ground up. Seduction is our baby, our pride and joy.

"That's nice to hear," I reply. "You've never been?"

"Not yet, but I'll make a point to go the next time I'm in the area."

So he doesn't live in Portland.

Bummer. Mac is one guy I wouldn't mind running into again.

But before I can give this much more thought, the door of the plane is locked and they're announcing the flight time and showing me how to use my seat belt—really, is not knowing how to fasten a seat belt a thing?—and use the oxygen mask if I should need it.

Please, God, don't let me need it.

The door between me and the pilot is closed, and the plane pulls away from the gate.

And I think I'm going to throw up.

"If you need to get sick," Mac says, seemingly reading my mind, "there's a bag here."

"I'm not going to get sick."

I hope.

"I like your tattoos," he says.

"Thanks."

The plane drives for what feels like forever, passing other planes and gates.

"Are we driving there? I had no idea this was a road trip. I would have brought some chips." I sigh deeply and rub my forehead, which is disgustingly sticky with sweat.

"We're taxiing to the runway," Mac says. "If you need to grab my hand, I don't mind."

"Are you *hitting* on me?" I ask, turning to him now, and finding him smiling widely at me, his green eyes lit with humor.

"No. I'm offering my hand if you're afraid."

"But you're *not* hitting on me."

Damn.

"Not unless you want me to." His lips twitch as his eyes lower to my lips, and I wish with all my might that we were in my bar rather than in this plane so I could flirt back and enjoy him a bit.

"I don't want to die," I whisper, and lick my lips.

"You're not going to die, Kat." His eyes grow serious now. He blinks once, his jaw firms, and he takes my hand. "You're not going to die."

"Okay."

I nod and sit back in my chair, but then suddenly the plane turns a corner and picks up speed, racing down the runway.

Oh. My. God.

It lifts up off the ground, and we're soaring in the air,

and I'm going to pass out.

"Deep breaths." Mac's voice is in my ear. I comply, taking a deep breath, letting it out, then taking another one. "No passing out on me."

"Are you psychic?" I ask breathlessly.

"No, you're turning blue." I can hear the smile in his voice, but I'm not brave enough to open my eyes to look at him. "If you could let up just a bit on my hand, I'd appreciate it."

I immediately let go of his hand and open my eyes. He's shaking his hand, as if I'd just almost taken it off, and I shake my head. "I'm sorry. I didn't even realize I was holding it so tightly."

"I think I'll have blood flow back in my fingers by next week," he replies with a smile. He sees me glance to the window and immediately closes it so I can't see the ground moving farther away. "If you don't look outside, it just feels like we're on a train."

"No, this doesn't feel like a train."

"Tell me about your tattoos."

"Why?"

"Because I'm trying to distract you from being scared," he says, and shifts in his seat. A bell dings, catching my attention. "That's just how the pilot communicates with the flight attendants."

"Like Morse code?"

"Something like that," he replies. "So tell me about your tattoos."

"No."

I shake my head and clench my hands in my lap.

"Why not?"

"Tattoos are personal, and I don't know you."

"You held my hand," he says, and then laughs when I

toss him a glare. "Okay, no personal stuff. What are we supposed to talk about, then?"

"I don't think we're supposed to talk."

"Sweetheart, I think that if we *don't* talk, you'll make yourself crazy with reliving every *Lost* episode you ever saw."

"I wasn't even thinking about that until now!"

"Where did you go to high school?"

"I was homeschooled," I reply. "Graduated at sixteen, then went to college. Now I run a bar. That's pretty much it."

"I think there's probably more to you than that, but okay."

"Why is the flight attendant walking around? Shouldn't she have her seat belt on?"

"She's going to serve us refreshments," he says. "She's used to this. Trust me."

I don't know why I trust him, but I do. He's nice. I also don't know why I'm on this freaking plane. This was a very bad idea.

"Damn them for dangling a sexcation in my face."

"Excuse me?" Mac grins, but I just shake my head.

"Nothing."

"What can I get you to drink?" the flight attendant asks, and sets a napkin on the armrest between Mac and me.

"More water, please," I reply, proud of myself for having enough wits about me to answer her question. She delivers the water, and a snack, and I sit back, relieved to find that Mac's right: it really does feel like a loud train ride.

"You're doing great," he says a few minutes later as he munches on a bag of chips. "How do you feel?"

"Better," I reply. "I don't love it, but I think I'm going to survive it."

"Good."

Just as I'm beginning to think that I'm a pro at this flying gig, the plane starts to shake and dip. The pilot comes over the speakers and tells us all to buckle up and the flight attendants to return to their seats.

And I look at Mac in blind panic.

"It's just rough air," he says gently.

"Seriously? We have to fly through rough air on my *first flight*?"

"I'm quite sure it's a conspiracy," Mac replies, his face dead sober. "We should write a letter to our congressman."

"Shut up," I snap, and wince when the plane shakes some more. The flight attendants hurry to stow their carts and get in their belts, and for the rest of the remaining hour to California, we are restricted to our seats while the plane takes us on the ride of terror.

"I'm sweating again," I mutter, and wipe my forehead with the back of my hand.

"Here," Mac says, and passes me the napkin from under his drink. "It's cold."

"Thanks." It feels good on my head. I shudder to think what my makeup must look like, but then again, I don't give a shit. If we die in this tin can, it won't matter what my makeup looks like.

"We're not going to die," Mac says.

"Stop reading my mind," I reply.

"You said it out loud," he says with a laugh. "I'm sorry this flight is so bumpy. It isn't usually this bad."

"I need to get on the ground." I turn to him and grip his hand tightly. "I can't do this anymore. I need to be on the ground."

"Okay, sweetheart, take another deep breath."

I do, and turn away, but he pulls me back to look him in the eyes. "No, you stay with me. Deep breaths. Listen to my voice."

"You have a good voice."

"Thank you."

"Are you a doctor?"

"No." He grins and drags his knuckle down my cheek. If I wasn't so terrified, I'd climb him.

"What do you do?"

"I own a business," he says. "Has anyone ever told you you have gorgeous eyes?"

"I don't know." And I don't. I can barely remember my name right now. Between being scared and looking at the sexiest man I think I've ever seen, I'm a mess.

"Well, you do."

"Thank you."

"Ladies and gentlemen, we are beginning our descent into Santa Rosa. We should be on the ground in about fifteen minutes, but it's going to be bumpy. Seems we have a lot of wind coming in off the ocean. Hang tight, we'll have you on the ground in just a few minutes."

"Oh God."

"You're doing so great," Mac says, and I can't help but laugh. "You really are. We're almost there."

I nod and hold his hand tightly as we descend. I hate the way it makes my stomach roll. I've never been good at amusement park rides or long road trips.

Motion sickness is a real thing.

Finally—*finally*—we're on the ground. I've never been so happy in my life.

"You did it. You survived your first plane ride." Mac

smiles proudly, and I smile back.

"I did it."

I'm going to throw up.

We're soon parked at the gate, and the doors open. I stand, grab my suitcase, and make a run for the Jetway. I need a bathroom.

Now.

I'm sweaty. My heart is pounding. Of course, leave it to me to have a panic attack after the fact.

Thankfully, there's a bathroom near the gate. I rush inside, find a stall, and heave until my body aches and I'm drenched in more sweat.

Sweet baby Jesus, I need to get to the hotel.

But I survived, and that's all that matters.

[no ornament]

It's amazing what a hot shower, a thirty-minute nap, and room service can do.

A few hours later, I'm feeling much better. Which is good because I have to go down to the welcome party and socialize.

I have made some friends in the wine business, most of which has been online or over the phone. I'm excited to meet them in person and put some faces with the voices.

I lean in to apply my lipstick, then grin at my reflection.

"I rocked that flight." I snort. "Okay, I survived it, and that's kind of the same thing." I shrug and take stock of myself. It's a vast improvement to when I arrived. I can't even imagine what poor Mac must have thought of me as I rushed off without even thanking him. I was afraid that if I opened my mouth, I'd just throw up all over him, and that would have been horrific.

But now my hair is back in place, with big curls and

cute pink bunny pins holding it off my face. I'm in a black dress, military style, with chunky pink heels, and I brought my awesome pink patent-leather handbag to match.

I'm ready to mingle, drink some wine, and meet new people.

The ballroom is already mostly full of people. This week-long conference is comprehensive and big. There will be tours through most of the wineries in the area, workshops, dinners.

I'm most excited to tour the vineyards. It's my favorite thing to do.

I walk to the bar, order a glass of a local Pinot that I don't know well, and turn to take in the room.

"Are you Kat Myers?"

I turn and grin. "I am."

"Sally Franks," the pretty redhead says, and holds her hand out. "We've talked a few times."

"Yes! Hi, Sally." I shake her hand. "How are things in Denver?"

"Great," she replies. "But it's nice to get away. How was your flight?"

"Bumpy." I smile, but I immediately want to change the subject, not wanting to relive the terror from this morning. Someone walks up behind me. Sally's eyes go wide.

"You look like you're feeling better."

Mac. That's Mac's voice in my ear. A shiver runs through me as I turn around and look up, way up, into his green eyes.

"I am," I reply, and take a sip of my wine. Was he that good-looking on the plane? "I didn't realize you were attending this conference."

"You had other things on your mind earlier," he says smoothly, and motions for the bartender. "I'll have what she's having, and another for her as well."

"What if you don't like Pinot?" I ask and tilt my head to the side.

"I like it all," he says with a wink.

Oh my.

"Do you know many people here?" he asks, nodding toward Sally, who has moved on to chat with another group of people.

"A few. I've not met most of them in person, unless they were up in Washington or Oregon. How about you?"

"Same," he says with a grin. "This is my first conference down in Napa Valley. And it's off to a great start."

"Right." I laugh and shake my head. "Dealing with a crazy chick on the plane is exactly the best way to start your trip."

"It is," he says, and looks me dead in the eye. "She wasn't that crazy. She was scared. There's a difference."

"Well, she's fine now."

"I'm glad." His lips tip up into a smile and my stomach clenches. He has a dimple in his left cheek.

I want to lick it.

I take a sip of my fresh glass of wine and smirk to myself. Perhaps Mac fits the sexcation bill.

"What just went through that gorgeous head of yours?"

"I'm not drunk enough to tell you yet," I reply honestly. Mac's eyes widen briefly, and then he simply smiles at me.

"There's a lot of wine in this place."

"Thank God for that."

A few hours later, after chatting with many people, new and those I already know, including Mac, he escorts me up to my room.

Sexcation.

But when we reach my door, he leans in and kisses my cheek. Just the cheek. I frown up at him.

"This is supposed to be a sexcation, not a fucking dating game." It's a grumble, but I'm shocked to hear the words actually leave my lips, rather than stay in my head where they're supposed to be.

"A what?" Mac asks.

"Nothing." I shake my head and pull my key card out of my handbag. "Good night."

"Kat?"

"Yeah." I look back at him and sigh a little at the sexy dimple in his cheek and the way his shirt pulls against his shoulders as he leans on the doorframe.

"I'll see you in the morning."

"It's already morning," I remind him.

"It won't be too long, then." He kisses my cheek again and walks away, and I let myself into the room, set my bag down, and plop onto the bed.

"Dumb sexcation isn't working out the way it's supposed to." I pout, but before I know it, I'm drifting to sleep, dreaming of a sexy green-eyed man with a dimple in his cheek.

About Kristen Proby

New York Times and USA Today Bestselling Author Kristen Proby is the author of the popular With Me in Seattle series. She has a passion for a good love story and strong characters who love humor and have a strong sense of loyalty and family. Her men are the alpha type—fiercely protective and a bit bossy—and her ladies are fun, strong, and not afraid to stand up for themselves. Kristen spends her days with her muse in the Pacific Northwest. She enjoys coffee, chocolate, and sunshine. And naps. Visit her at KristenProby.com.

Other Books by Kristen Proby

The Boudreaux Series:
Easy Love and on audio
Easy Charm and on audio
Easy Melody and on audio
Easy For Keeps

The With Me In Seattle Series:
Come Away With Me and on audio
Under the Mistletoe With Me and on audio
Fight With Me and on audio
Play With Me and on audio
Rock With Me and on audio
Safe With Me and on audio
Tied With Me and on audio
Breathe With Me and on audio
Forever With Me and on audio
Easy With You and on audio

The Fusion Series
Listen To Me and on audio
Close To Me
Blush For Me (preorder)

The Love Under the Big Sky Series, available through Pocket Books:
Loving Cara and on audio
Seducing Lauren and on audio

Falling for Jillian and on audio

Baby, It's Cold Outside and on audio
An Anthology with Jennifer Probst, Emma Chase, Kristen Proby, Melody Anne and Kate Meader